CAPTAINS
of the
RENOWN

TWEEN SEA AND SHORE SERIES
Book II

Cover design by D.E. Stockman

Interior design by Jacqueline J. Cook

Edited by Faith Hunter

ISBN: 978-1-7353545-8-3 (Paperback)
ISBN: 978-1-7353545-9-0 (e-book)

BISAC Subject Headings:
FIC002000 FICTION / Action & Adventure
FIC014000 FICTION / Historical / General
FIC047000 FICTION / Sea Stories

Address all correspondence to:
Fireship Press, LLC
P.O. Box 68412
Tucson, AZ 85737

Visit our website at:
www.fireshippress.com

Visit the author's website at:
www.stockmanbooks.com

This book is dedicated to my children,
Robert, Lorien, and Krista with deepest love.

"Hell is truth seen too late"
—John Adams

A Note to the Reader

This is the second of the *Tween Sea & Shore Series* of historical nautical novels that follow the lives of fictional and historical characters in the mid-1700s. French names are included in the *List of Selected Characters* to help facilitate pronunciation for the reader.

Go to www.stockmanbooks.com for a free booklet containing nautical terms and other information to make reading nautical books more enjoyable. Please refer to these sections for ease of reading.

Please note that this story begins two years before the end of the first book in the series, *The Ship's Carpenter*.

List of Selected Characters

This story is historical fiction, however, the actions of some characters follow closely the actual time, locations, and actions taken from historical and nautical references. Fictional license was taken for character development, dialog, continuity, and dramatic effect.

Burston, British ship lieutenant on the *Lark* (FICTIONAL)

Caffieri [kah-fehr-yee´], French master sculptor at the Brest shipyard and designer of ship decorations

Bompar, Maxim [bahm • pahr´ • mahk-zeem´], admiral, French naval officer in the West Indies fleet (1759)

de Conflans, Marquis [deh • kohn-flons´ • mahr´-kee], French naval officer, governor of Saint-Domingue, and admiral at the Battle of Quiberon Bay (1759)

de Kersaint, Guy [deh • kehr-sahn´ • ghee´], French naval officer

de Saint-Alouarn, François [deh • san´ • tah-lew-arn´ • fran-swah´], French naval officer

de Saint-Alouarn, Louis [deh • san´ • tah-lew-arn´ • lew-ee´], son of François, French naval officer, husband to Marie

de Saint--Alouarn, Madame [deh • san´ • tah-lew-arn´], wife of François, mother of Louis

de Saint-Alouarn, René [deh • san´ • tah-lew-arn´ • ruh-nay´], knight, French naval officer, brother of François

Drouallen, Marie [drwehl´-lehn • mah-ree´], wife of Louis

Façonneur, André [fah-seh-nyehr´ • ahn´-dree], ship pilot in Brest, brother of Yvette (FICTIONAL)

Façonneur, Anton [fah-seh-nyehr´ • ahn´-tohn], carpenter in Brest, father of Yvette and André (FICTIONAL)

Façonneur, Gaëlle [fah-seh-nyehr´ • gah-el´], wife of André (FICTIONAL)

Façonneur, Louise [fah-seh-nyehr´ • lew-eez´], wife of Anton, mother of Yvette (FICTIONAL)

George, II, King of Great Britain (1727–1760), born 1683

George, III, King of Great Britain (1760–1820), born 1738

Goubert [goo-bayr'], Madame, unmarried Breton in London, friend of Yvette (FICTIONAL)

Hastings, Selina (nee Shirley), Countess, wife of the Earl of Huntingdon

Louis XV [lew-ee'], King of France (1715–1774), born 1710

Mackenzie, George, British naval officer

Maitland, Frederick Lewis, British naval officer

Moore, John, commodore of the British fleet in the West Indies (1759)

Shelly, British naval officer under Captain Mackenzie (FICTIONAL)

Pitt, William, The Elder, British statesman (1746–1768), born 1708

Pocock, George, commodore of the British fleet at Havana (1762)

Robinson, Abraham, English shipwright (FICTIONAL)

Robinson, Michelle, adopted daughter of Abraham and Yvette (FICTIONAL)

Robinson, Yvette (nee: Façonneur), daughter of Anton and Louise, sister to André, wife of Abraham (FICTIONAL)

Shirley, Anne (nee: Elliott), daughter of John Elliott, Esquire, wife of Washington

Shirley, Laurence, 4th Earl Ferrers, Washington's brother

Shirley, Mary (nee: Meredith), granddaughter of Sir William Meredith, Countess, former wife of Laurence, 4th Earl Ferrers

Shirley, Washington, British naval officer, 5th Earl Ferrers

Young Pretender, Bonnie Prince Charles Stuart, Jacobite Rebellion leader (1755–1756)

CAPTAINS
of the
RENOWN

TWEEN SEA AND SHORE SERIES
Book II

D. E. STOCKMAN

FIRESHIP
PRESS

The French Prize

They stripped the *Renown* in 1752, tied her to a cable, and left her afloat on the shallow River Thames near Deptford. The navy removed her masts, guns, sails, and rigging and stored them ashore. While the small crew who manned the frigate protected her from sinking, they did little to maintain her beauty. Worms and algae fouled her hull, while rain and fog rusted her iron. During the previous war, she glided across waves as the fastest ship on the seas—a racehorse, sleek and a marvel to sailors' eyes. However, being the captured *la Renommée* and French-built, she did not conform to the British Admiralty's Establishment. Her lightweight timbers, low profile, and gun weight made her an exception to their construction regulations; they disapproved of exceptions.

Decommissioned and in Ordinance, for five years she lay bobbing in the ripples of passing ships, unneeded and deprived of deep blue water and sea foam. When the new war with France ignited, demands for more frigates called for her great repair and a recommission in 1757.

"Robinson, you're to patch up a frigate in Ordinance." The supervisor had switched him from building hulls, to the boring task of repairing worn vessels. "She's an old Frenchie, the *Renown.*" He smirked.

"Sir, the *Renown?*" Abraham's eyes widened.

"That's right. You're familiar with her?"

"Yes, sir. I framed her in France at the Brest yard." His face glowed with pride as he spoke. "I remember every beam and plank."

The man squinted at the mention of working for the enemy. "You worked for the Frogs, huh?"

"Yes, sir. At their Brest shipyard before the last war. Then I returned to England and shipped out as a carpenter in our navy. I went back after the war, and they dismissed me again when this war started." Abraham had grown used to telling bosses how he came to work for the French.

"Well then, you can fix her for towing better. Now get a move on," he said with a snort, waving him away.

"With pleasure, sir," Abraham replied with a grin as he grabbed his leather bag and tools, leaving the other shipwrights still waiting for assignments.

When he reached the crowded berth, the sight of the *Renown* stole his cheer. She looked in terrible shape with rotted hull and deck planks, split railings, and a cracked main mast. Even the glorious figurehead of the Goddess of Fame showed neglect.

The gang chief on the frigate, an older man, motioned him over as soon as he stepped onboard. "You Robinson?"

"Yes, sir." Abraham smiled and answered, still eyeing the worn and beat-up ship.

"We're to tow her to Portsmouth for repairs and need her seaworthy." He pointed to the bow. "Inspect and fix any damages to the catheads, foremast footings, and bitts. She came from France so they're bound to be poor."

"Not so much this one." Abraham chuckled. "She's the fastest frigate on the sea."

His boss grunted and shook his head. "Fast or not, she doesn't measure up to our standards. Her frames looked scanty, same as most French builds."

"You're right. They gave up bulk for speed." Abraham explained his history with the ship to the chief and spent the rest of the day making her secure for tow cables.

A week later they finished the bow section and Abraham stood back to examine the ship. His expert gaze picked out the damages they'd need to patch in Portsmouth and then settled on the figurehead. Rot had eaten away the top half of one wing. The flaw spoiled the frigate's distinct form more than any other. Abraham looked for his supervisor.

"Do you mind if I repair the figurehead?" He asked and waited, expecting a refusal.

The man eyed him and pointed at the bow. "Didn't you say you were a carver on her in Brest?"

"The master sculptor, Caffieri, did the figurehead." Abraham shook his head. "I mounted it, the panels, and decorations to the hull."

The crew chief thought a moment and agreed. "A fine figurehead defines a warship. Without, one ship resembles any other, like all rowboats look the same. That half-wing spoils her. She doesn't leave for another week, and I'd rather see you do it than those wood butchers in Portsmouth—go ahead. We'll send a proper goddess to them."

Thrilled to restore Caffieri's masterpiece, Abraham tried to create a mirror image of the good side. After three days, he had twinned the original, and given the entire statue a fresh coat of yellow paint to resemble gold.

"Now that returns the frigate to her rightful status as a respectable warship," said his boss, standing beside Abraham and admiring the overall effect. "Well done, Robinson."

The chance to work on the *Renown* again had flooded him the whole time with pleasant pre-war memories of Brest. When Abraham arrived home that night, he greeted his wife, Yvette, with a perky, "My darling! Good day?" He had a lilt in his voice and hoped her day equaled his.

"*Trés bon!* I visited my friend, Madame Goubert, in the afternoon while looking for work. She wants me to attend another Calvinist meeting next week with her." Yvette stopped sewing and rose to hug him. "Lady Huntingdon will speak. I haven't seen the countess since we returned from France."

"The countess always fancied you and will be glad to see you." He expected she might even help Yvette find a position. "I thought she was a Methodist?"

"She converted, and so did Madame Goubert. I've never met a more giving and charitable person than the countess." She smiled.

He added, chuckling. "And she's nobility, too."

"That's not why I like her. Besides, I've known other nobles if you recall." Her gaze dropped suddenly.

Abraham said nothing as he recalled the other noble she knew. He loathed the rascal René, a French nobleman and naval officer, who stole her away from him once. She still held lingering emotional attachments, even after so many years. To recall it bothered them both.

Within minutes, old memories slipped her into the letdown of not working and being thirty-five and still childless after nine years of marriage.

Abraham sensed her mood swing and suggested they stroll to a nearby chocolate house, the Cocoa-Tree. The rich, hot beverage had found a place in her heart; she couldn't resist. The French also believed the popular and expensive hot drink enhanced fertility. A minute later, they left their flat for the short walk through crooked alleys to her favorite destination.

After settling into a booth, they watched a crowd of patrons playing at the dice table, and others drinking their beverages or eating. Musicians played a viol and violin for the audience.

As Abraham finished his second ale, an old fellow of at least sixty entered, tugging behind him a young girl who looked seven or eight. The raggedy man stood her on a table and spoke to the two minstrels. Then she sang the lyrics to a popular tune they played as her guardian wandered between tables with his hat out.

Abraham's attempt to direct Yvette's thoughts away from children had failed. She sat watching the girl sing a maudlin ballad about a lost love with gestures that enhanced the performance. Yvette's eyes glazed as a tear dropped from one. Her most purposeful desire could not be escaped.

∞

During the previous year 1756, Captain Washington Shirley enjoyed his *Monmouth's* size when the late fall winds kicked up higher seas off Martinique. She rode the peaks and troughs better than his previous ship, the *Mermaid,* a smaller frigate. He had requested command of the sixty-eight-gun newly-launched warship within days of returning to England from the American colonies. The Admiralty seldom denied Washington's appeals, being a Shirley and brother of an earl and member of the House of Lords. His family's support of the crown, together with their estates, titles, and ancient political status, made them the favorites of the king and the royal navy.

He and another captain discussed their experiences in the *Monmouth's* cabin.

"Duty in the West Indies is a blessing for me. The American colonies taxed my conscience." Washington scowled and tapped his head.

"Did the savagery in frontier skirmishes vex you?" asked Captain Byron of the *Vanguard,* noticing Washington's frown.

Washington leaned back in his chair and grimaced. "No. Butchery exists everywhere, not just in the wilderness. The Acadian deportations from Nova Scotia weigh on me. They stain our British principles. Although most Acadians speak French, they remain British citizens and should be regarded so."

"Yes, but our American colonists regard them as an enemy. They cause harm to our commerce, threatening our colonies. Privateers and pirates prey on our ships and slip back into Louisbourg. Natives led by priests and Acadian rebels attack innocent English farmers. They support the French not the British." Captain Byron repeated what most held as the situation, his finger held upward.

Washington turned away from Byron and sighed. "No doubt a few Acadians and French who live there favor our foes and rebel. Though, most appeared loyal and still our troops herded them onto transports and shipped them to different colonies." He looked down. "It broke my heart to see mothers crying for their children and husbands waving farewell to their families."

Captain Byron believed in eliminating the French from Nova Scotia, Cape Breton, and all of Canada in favor of an English North America. It paralleled the empirical aims of Pitt, the head of the British cabinet and Parliament. "Did you take part in the relocations?"

"Not the civilians. I transported French troops after they surrendered their forts in Nova Scotia," explained Washington still looking away.

"Since they're gone, no doubt we'll manage and farm Nova Scotia easier without their problems," Byron asserted with a wave of his hand. "So, we've erased a worry. Is there peace now on Nova Scotia?"

"No more than before. The Mi'kmaqs, who lived in harmony with the Acadians, attack the settlers who try to take over the Acadians' farms and more of their land. If anything, it's worse." Washington's jaw tightened.

"We'll be taking Louisbourg as in the last war." Byron added, with a mocking smile. "When we command the entirety of Cape Breton and Nova Scotia, we'll force the natives and remaining Acadians to obey. They won't have the French supplying them or priests to incite them anymore."

"You're right. Without the Fortress of Louisbourg controlling the Gulf of Saint Lawrence, the enemy's influence will lessen. But what happens to the Acadians determines the righteousness of our actions." Knowing the deportations would continue, Washington rose from his chair shaking his head and the two captains left to go on deck.

Days later while patrolling in their ships off Barbados, they spotted a sail far to the southeast, heading north.

"Looks like a merchantman, maybe a snow!" Washington yelled through his speaking trumpet to Byron across the waves.

"Aye! Probably French coming up from the Spanish colonies. She might be headed for Guadeloupe or Martinique. Care to race?" Byron shouted with a grin.

"Aye, and a pound wager for the winner!" Washington laughed. He hurried to go against the eastward wind that forced the *Vanguard* onto his lee side, his sails stealing the breeze from the trailing warship. Byron hauled to port to catch up as Washington pulled ahead.

Their prey also headed east to escape and then south. Washington, to the starboard of Byron and in a better position to intercept her, sped across the waves with his huge spread of canvas. Having turned northward, Byron fell behind as the *Monmouth* raced to close first on the merchantman.

An hour passed, and the *Monmouth* approached within a quarter-league of the fleeing vessel. "Send her a warning shot, Lieutenant." Washington's first lieutenant fired a bow chase gun at the target.

With little chance of escaping the larger ship, and their ten cannons no contest against sixty-eight guns, the snow turned to shoot one cannon in defensive honor. Then she hauled down her French flag.

Washington surveyed his prize. "Well, well, their captain chose wisely, Lieutenant. Prepare a boarding party but post marines along our midship rail in case he tries something."

The lieutenant sped off to gather men and marines, and lowered boats to row to their capture. With enough sailors boarded to handle her, the lieutenant brought back the captain of the surrendered snow. The *Vanguard* arrived and lay to on the other side of their captive.

Washington asked the ship's commander in French, now seated in his cabin, "What is your name, sir, and from what port did you embark?"

"I am François Le Brun, master of the *Nannon,* monsieur. We were sailing to Martinique with a shipment of Dutch cargo from Cayenne." He frowned with crossed arms.

"Ah, so not French but Dutch cargo? I see," Washington snickered. "I have yet to seize an enemy merchant who does not claim the cargo is a neutral country's. Then you have papers to vouch for what you say, no?" Le Brun's eyes looked away, shifting around in his chair. "I'll know in a short while what you're hauling and where it was going when my lieutenant finishes his inspection of your hold, Monsieur Le Brun."

Later the lieutenant returned to report the ship's lading and smiled, rubbing his hands together in glee. "Sir, she's a rich one. *Nannon's* hold contains cotton, coffee, indigo, sugar, and cocoa, headed for France.

And a couple of surprises."

"Oh? Tell me, Lieutenant." Washington expected some of the various goods that might be onboard after coming from Cayenne on the South American coast, but wondered about the surprises.

"There are cases of birds, sir. Dead and stuffed with cotton. Damnedest thing I've seen. And two statues, bronze, I believe." The officer's eyes widened, accenting the strangeness.

"Birds and statues?" asked Washington, perplexed. "Go ask Master Le Brun what they intended to do with them or check the papers and let me know."

In minutes, the lieutenant reported. "The statues, sir, were for the Catholic church in Martinique and the birds belonged to a French naturalist and bound for France."

Washington sat for a second and thought. "Have them haul the cases and statues on our ship. They'd be of no value as prizes."

As the three ships headed northward, Washington stopped off at Antigua.

"Why did you want to anchor here? We could have gone further before getting water." Byron said to him on shore at Saint John's, the island's port capital, and largest town.

"We have business at the church." Washington smiled.

Byron chuckled. "Church? If we're praying for our souls, it is far too late for me."

"You'll see." Washington winked at the other captain.

Later in the afternoon, the crew hoisted the two bronze statues onto boats, rowed them ashore, and hauled them to the church.

That night, the entire town celebrated Washington and Byron. Food, wine, and rum flowed for not only the two captains, but for their crews. The Anglican church's priest thanked them before the crowd for the donation of the two life-sized statues, one of Saint John the Divine and one of Saint John the Baptist.

When they departed, the citizens lined the beach and cheered and clapped as they wished good voyage to the ships. "Sir, they'll name a park after you," laughed Washington's first lieutenant.

"I couldn't think of another place more appropriate for statues of two Saint Johns than the Cathedral of Saint John in Saint John. It seemed their destiny." Washington joined in the laughter.

"And the cases of dead birds, sir? Do you know of a cemetery on Bird Isle for them?" joked the lieutenant.

"No, but someone would have buried them at sea if we didn't keep them. I enjoy the sciences and I'll examine them during our return to England. A naturalist there may want to research them."

Upon docking in Plymouth months later at the end of 1756, the *Nannon* prize went up for auction, along with its cargo. Washington and his crew profited handsomely. An English naturalist, a Mason like Washington, took the exotic bird carcasses for study.

Pardons, a Prize,
and Politics

In early May 1758, Captain George Mackenzie, a Scot, took command of the repaired *Renown* as her cutwater plied the sea to war once more. A brilliant day glowed with cloudless skies and a good wind, perfect to challenge the frigate's reputed speed on her first voyage out of Portsmouth. He put the wind two points off *Renown's* beam and watched billowing canvas strain against the spars. To his disappointment, regardless of sail configurations, the great repair had slowed her by two knots. The swift French *la Renommée* sailed no more; the shipwrights had reworked her into a thoroughly British *Renown,* still fast, but little more so than other Royal Navy frigates.

Returning to port, he searched out Captain Washington Shirley, who had taken *la Renommée,* and became her first British commander in 1747. He wanted to compare her handling characteristics to before her rebuild. Years earlier he had sailed on patrol with Washington in the West Indies where he grew to despise the man.

Washington Shirley's family had positions in all levels of the government. Mackenzie didn't like English noble families in particular. They expected and demanded more than titled Scotsmen. And in most instances, they got it. He and Washington met in a tavern.

"What ship do you command now, Captain Shirley?"

"The *Duc d'Aquitaine,* a sixty-four-gun."

"I'm not familiar with her." Mackenzie sensed a presumptive behavior in just the way Washington spoke the sentence.

Washington nodded. "And with good reason the name is strange to you, we captured the French East India merchantman only last year."

Mackenzie assumed Washington had requested the new warship, and of course, the Admiralty obliged him. He was a Shirley after all. "I took command of the *Renown* a few months back after her repair. I wonder if she handles the same as when you had her?"

"I expect the rebuild has slowed her somewhat. How did she run in gale winds?" Washington, who liked Mackenzie, smiled as he asked.

"Soon out of port we had the chance when a gale hit off Ushant. I'd heard she made fifteen knots when the French sailed her in the last war. But stunsails, staysails, and topgallants made naught a difference. Thirteen knots in gale winds topped her speed." Mackenzie raised a brow. "Did she handle that way for you?"

"No. She made fifteen for me also, with just foresail, mainsail, and topsails when I had her. It is a pity the repairs slowed her so. The bigger cannons and thicker timbers and masts must weigh her down so she draws more draft." Washington smiled remembering. "The *Renown* became the envy of frigate captains, and many a smuggler in the Caribbean learned to fear her."

Mackenzie considered Washington pompous and was only telling him things he already knew. "Aye, I first heard of *la Renommée* when she sailed under de Kersaint off Louisbourg. How did she handle before they put the nine-pounders on her?"

Washington sat back and laughed. "She dove into the sea when running with the wind or sailing full and by, flooding the decks. Though suffering, the water cost us little compared to her merits. She seldom rolled and in fair winds kept her bow down, even-keeled, to catch more wind but needed much trimming."

"As I noticed. She may be wet but still an improvement over most of our ships, although she went slow in wearing and close-hauled. I saw the same when I commanded the captured *Amazon* for a short while in '46. The French, however, know how to build frigates for speed."

Washington's eyes widened. "So, you captained the *Amazon?* You know, she's the sister ship of the *Renown* and launched earlier in Brest. The day before I captured *la Renommée*, she had gotten into a fray with the *Amazon,* losing her fore topmast. Had she not caught on fire, she might have taken *la Renommée.* This happened the year after you commanded her."

"You were lucky she damaged *la Renommée,* it helped you catch up to her." Mackenzie imagined if he had still been in command of the *Amazon,* it might have been he who caught the noted French frigate.

"True, their fight spoiled her greatest asset, her speed. But she defended herself well that day, no less." Washington frowned. "Had it not been for my carpenter's help, I may not have taken her even though I out-gunned her by seven cannons a broadside."

Mackenzie jerked his head back. "A carpenter helping capture a ship is rare."

"Now that's a story." Washington grinned. "His name was Abraham and the damn best carpenter I ever saw. He had built the *Renommée* for the French. When the war came, France expelled him. Then our navy pressed him and he ended up on my ship. The day of our encounter with the frigate, he recognized her and told me how sparse her scantlings were. I directed my fire to the waterline and nearly sank her. Her captain, de Saint-Alouarn, struck after three hours."

Mackenzie, wide-eyed, had heard of the gallant de Saint-Alouarn duo from Brest, as had most British captains on the Channel fleet. If Washington had bested one, then at least he could fight well, he conceded to himself. "One of the de Saint-Alouarns? They've made a name for themselves. Which surrendered her?"

"François captained, his brother René acted as second in command. They were transporting Count de Conflans to Saint-Domingue to become the new governor general. Because France booted out a carpenter, they never made it." Washington chuckled.

"Then this is to the carpenter Abraham, who constructed the *Renommée* for the French," Mackenzie raised his glass of wine, "and captured her to become the *Renown* for the British."

Smiling, Washington drank to his old carpenter's health. "I'd give a guinea to know where he is right now, probably in a shipyard pounding away on a hull."

For two years, Louis de Saint-Alouarn and his uncle, René, had remained prisoners in Leicester, England after the British captured their *l'Esperance*. As officers, they received privileges with relative freedom in the town as long as they returned to their quarters at night. When the British finally granted them pardons in 1757, the de Saint-Alouarns rode east to Norfolk in a canvas-covered wagon with another captive.

"Your choice to sail on *l'Esperance* instead of with your father for training turned into quite an odyssey." René, elated to return to France, wondered if his nephew regretted the decision to sail with him.

"One that taught me a lot, Uncle. Yet, looking over the last two years as a prisoner, I must admit I enjoyed most of it. The people in Leicester treated us well and few held us in contempt. I also improved my English." Louis's gaze returned from the passing fall-colored woods of browns and golds to his uncle.

"Meeting the Countess Ferrers became a nice diversion for you, too." René held in a laugh at his nephew's feckless infatuation with the young married noblewoman from the nearby estate of Staunton Harold.

"You had to remind me of that. Yes, I found her charming. I suppose Mary suffered after the earl found out about us and banned her from Leicester. Pity her life with such an ass." His attachment to the young countess ended with an effortless sword-duel victory against the unskilled Earl Ferrers and it still embarrassed him.

"We can hope he'll change for her sake, yet that seldom happens.

His bitter acts will pile like stones weighted upon his back. He'll pay for his abuses someday." René reflected on his own guilt over his infidelity to his long-lost beloved, Yvette.

Memories of the Countess Ferrers bothering him, Louis changed the conversation. "Will you seek another commission when we return? I need to go to sea right away. We've been gone for years."

"Yes, as soon as we're in port. We took no vow of neutrality and there's nothing to stop us from rejoining the fleets, but certainly you will want to visit your family first." René hoped Louis's fixation to sail with him had ended.

"Of course, if Father is in Brest when we arrive, I'll ask him for permission to go on his ship."

The coach horses clopped mile after mile and after two days the Frenchmen boarded a ship to Dunkirk. By mid-November, they landed in Brittany. René prepared for his next assignment while Louis continued on to the de Saint-Alouarn country manor.

"My darling!" cried Madame de Saint-Alouarn, Louis's mother, as she embraced him in the foyer. "Are you well? When did you arrive in France? Tell me everything."

His sisters came running from throughout the house, and he took his mother's hand and led her to the salon. Everyone found seats after embraces and kisses to listen to his great adventure.

Louis started with the trip to Canada on the *l'Esperance* and how he and Uncle René had fooled British patrols by going north around Newfoundland to get to Louisbourg in Cape Breton. The entire way they confronted British patrols, icebergs, dense fogs, and ice floes. Then he recounted the battle with the *Orford* in the Bay of Biscay on the return to France where he took a head wound, and finished with the terrifying capture and sinking of his ship.

"Show us your scar!" begged his oldest sister.

"It's hard to see it now." Louis bent his head low and removed his wig to show the four inch red line where a musket ball had grazed his scalp. "It bled like a river but healed fast."

Madame de Saint-Alouarn winced and turned her head away, imagining what might have been if the ball had been just a fraction of an inch lower.

"And father? Does he hold it against me for taking my training with Uncle René instead of him?" Louis's face reddened, and he turned away.

"Louis," Madame de Saint-Alouarn told him with a gentle smile, "you hurt your father's pride. Since you were a child, he dreamed of the day when the two of you would sail together. Papa has so much he wants to show and teach you. It upset him. Then, when you became a wounded prisoner of war… he tried not to show it, but it devastated him."

"I realize how much hurt I caused you both. Uncle René tried to persuade me to sail with Father, but I chose to go with him. My selfishness embarrasses me. Please forgive me. I swear I'll try to be more considerate of your desires."

Madame de Saint-Alouarn smiled. She didn't tell him of the deep fears she had for his safety and that she wanted him never to sail again. Instead she said, "Now that King Louis himself made you an *enseigne de vaisseau* for your bravery, you need not train with anyone. And Papa is at sea anyway. So, this is no longer a quarrelsome topic. Will you be leaving soon on another ship or staying ashore?"

"I expect an assignment to a new warship soon after I get back to Brest."

Louis stayed on leave with his family, traveling to Brest every week for news on an assignment to a new ship. Because of his family's prestige, within two months the navy gave him an honored position, an order to board *le Défenseur*, the admiral's flagship. A week later Louis climbed up the ladder onto the seventy-four-gun.

At the end of November 1758, his ship commander and head of the fleet, Admiral Maxim Bompar, called a meeting of the officers aboard *le Défenseur*.

"Gentlemen, we have a critical task before us." His posture, straight as a topmast, did not show the sixty-year-old body beneath the dark blue uniform. "The enemy's amphibious assaults, raids on Fort Duquesne, taking of Fort Frontenac in America, and losing Louisbourg, all signal the intent of British aggression. France's foe is not content with destroying our agricultural and trading centers, now they aim to conquer them and set up footholds in our territories. Our possessions around the world face jeopardy. We learned of an attack to come against our colonies in the Antilles a short time ago. This fleet departs to either prevent their capture or destruction, or if they've fallen, to recapture them. We will proceed to Martinique to assess the situation."

Louis listened, his mouth pinched, disgusted over the enemy's incursions upon French soil. He recalled the antagonistic actions off Labrador during his cruise there, and his father's descriptions of how adversarially the British behaved, even during peace times.

The admiral, stern-faced, continued, "Our commerce on these isles has become of great importance to France and our king. The islands create the richest source of revenue in the Western World, and if they fall under enemy rule, it seriously undermines our economy. With the loss of Louisbourg, a critical port for ships returning to our country has vanished. The harbors in the West Indies must now act in its stead as supply havens for ships from the Far East, Caribbean, and South America.

"Our fleet will search for the British in force. I am confident that if engaging them, we shall vanquish them. The orders you will receive after the meeting lists the battle line of order. Above all, we must remember that our actions on this venture will affect every Frenchman at home. The enemy *must not succeed.*"

The admiral thanked them and an attendant gave out the signal codes and ship battle positions. As officers debarked, Louis leaned over the railing midship gazing at the clear sky and sea expanse, wondering if the fleet could stop their foe's domineering strategy.

"Lieutenant de Saint-Alouarn," Bompar approached and spoke to him for the first time.

Louis turned, his body jolted and stood rod-straight when he saw the admiral come, expecting an order.

"It's good to have your kind of blood aboard. Your father is as great a sailor as he is a fighter; I hope you are following in his lead. Few receive the honors from the king and secretary of the navy as he has. Take pride in his accomplishments, my boy, and seek to emulate them." With that, the admiral left him.

Louis could only get out, "Y-yes, sir! I shall." He had never considered his father a noteworthy captain. François had been always just Papa. For Bompar to laud any captain underscored the uncommon contribution François had made to the navy. It remained a moment in Louis's life that he remembered forever.

∽

In 1758, June's warm breezes found Mackenzie's frigate back in the Portsmouth harbor after a fast voyage to Jamaica. The navy assigned him to Admiral Howe's fleet assembling nearby at the Isle of Wight for a dramatic offensive against the French. British politicians had reverted to the old strategy of "descents," amphibious invasions of France's ports. These aimed to capture, destroy, or damage the enemy's major anchorages and divert troops from French positions inland.

As the *Renown* drew near the new fleet, Mackenzie stood beside his first lieutenant on the quarterdeck.

"There, Lieutenant Shelly, gathers over a hundred storeships, transports, and warships." Mackenzie slid his hands across the railing, proudly eyeing the still untested fleet.

Lieutenant Shelly, not yet twenty-two years old, smiled as his captain did. "How many troops will complement the invasion, sir?" The young man followed his father's vocation, always eager to learn.

"There will be nearly sixteen battalions of infantry, artillery, and cavalry. The financial costs are enormous; its goals audacious, but victory is assured. Our opening assault will be at Saint-Malo."

The lieutenant swallowed, fidgeting with his neckcloth, and responded so quietly that the captain had a hard time hearing him. "Sir, this descent is my first."

"No cause for anxiety, Lieutenant Shelly, it's not mine." The words rolled out with confidence from a captain who had long overcome pre-battle jitters or skepticism. "I commanded in the fall of '46 during the storming of l'Orient and again off Louisbourg. Our venture will be a success."

On June 1st, the winds blessed them and the expedition departed eastward toward the French coast for the two-day crossing. That night the weather turned harsh and cresting seas slowed them and then forced the ships to a stop.

At dawn, they proceeded onward and sighted the continental shoreline. The enemy had seen the distant sails approaching and sent riders racing from the ports to raise the alarm.

As nightfall came, again the swells loomed. Signal flags ordered the fleet to anchor, storm-bound in the rough waves near the island of Alderney while the gale rampaged throughout the night.

Aboard the *Renown,* through darkness and sheets of rain, Lieutenant Shelly caught sight of the squadron lights drifting away. He hurried to the captain's cabin and roused him from sleep.

"Sir, the fleet is dispersing in the storm." Once back on deck, he pointed to the distant receding glimmer of ship lanterns.

"It does appear as though they are moving…" Mackenzie agreed after watching, then rushed to the bow with the boatswain and each grabbed an anchor's hawser. Both felt vibrations on the tense cables.

"The other ships aren't moving, we are! It's a foul bottom and we're dragging anchor across the seabed. Short haul and back the anchor with another before we run upon the island astern." The gale wind pushed the ship leeward toward the rocky shore in the dark.

Curtains of falling water obscuring his vision, Mackenzie couldn't tell how far his frigate had drifted from being dashed upon the shoals at their rear. Men on the capstan struggled to shorten the first heavy cable attached to the anchor to lash another anchor to it. But if the heavy iron became freed from the sea's bottom, the winds would push the ship faster into the reefs.

"It's at short haul! Make fast the hawser to the other anchor and be quick!" the lieutenant shouted to crewmen above the wind's howls.

Mackenzie stared aft into the blackness, afraid he might see the outline of the island approach. "Drop when you can, Lieutenant!" He relied on the lieutenant to know when to drop the anchors again. Every day, the young man showed more worth.

The shout "Cast!" at the bow relieved him as the frigate jerked on the taut hawser. The great heavy flukes of the anchors had bitten deep into the bottom and held there. With the ship now secured and no leeward movement, Mackenzie returned to his cabin for a nerve-settling glass of port.

"Join me Lieutenant Shelly. We need to splice the main brace."

It was the first time the old saying had been used with the lieutenant by a captain, and he felt honored. They sat in his cabin, cold and dripping wet, each with a glass in his hand, but relieved the ship no longer drifted.

"Do you have family near Portsmouth, Lieutenant?" Mackenzie smiled, relaxed.

"Not too far, sir. My mother and wife live near Hastings. I had hoped to see them this year, but our tours have kept me from them so far." With effort, he smiled; a puddle of rainwater had formed around him on the floor.

"After this mission, if time permits, you'll have a chance." Mackenzie winked, rewarding the man with an unspoken promise. "You worked the anchors well tonight. We were in danger of running aground or smashing into the reefs. Your noticing that the distant lantern lights had changed saved the ship, young man." He understood the officer had only done his duty, but the lieutenant's attentiveness possibly saved everyone's life. They sat for an hour talking and then both retired for the remainder of the night.

At first light, Mackenzie raced up to the quarterdeck to see how close they had come to the island's rocky shore. He shook his head and crossed his arms, leaning on the taffrail in wonder. The *Renown* had stopped a mere fifty yards from the water's edge. The fleet had awakened to discover they had lost no ships. Then Admiral Howe signaled to sail onward again in the high seas.

Near the island of Sark around noon, a transport carrying troops struck a reef, with the men making it off just before she foundered.

The delays stripped everyone's hopes of surprising the enemy. Late in the morning two days later, the fleet laid a scant two leagues east of Saint-Malo. They lowered flat-bottomed boats, and the infantry disembarked to the shore with minor resistance from one lonely battery.

The British first marched to Cancale, a coastal settlement outside of Saint-Malo, and routed the few defenders. After the French regulars fled, a brave old miller manned an abandoned cannon near his windmill. He thwarted their advance and continued firing volleys until captured. Throughout the day, the soldiers sacked the town, burned the small seaside homes, raped women, and committed many atrocities. Only after executing three of the culprits did the officers regain control of their rampageous men.

As word spread of the invasion and misdeeds in Cancale, the citizens from the neighboring towns and villages fled inside the protective walls of Saint-Malo. The fortified port lay on an island connected to the mainland by a long narrow causeway.

On his ship, Mackenzie viewed the smoke rising from Cancale. "There's the first village put to the torch." He stood beside Lieutenant Shelly, wondering if the lieutenant fathomed what that meant: the loss of innocent lives and destruction or pillaging of anything of value.

"They'll burn everything on their way to Saint-Malo, I imagine, sir." The lieutenant watched through his spyglass, his face grim.

"If the people flee and don't pay the tributes to our army, they will. At least that's part of the usual rules of engagement. Although, holding men back from destroying the villages, regardless of regulations, becomes a challenging task for officers." Mackenzie had long since stopped questioning the barbarity of war. He had seen horrible deeds over the years that raised hairs on his neck at the memory. Yet, he understood the need for a quick resolution in an attack, and ferocity and savagery aided victory.

As they stood watching, the sound of sporadic cannon discharges onshore marked the advance of the army. More boats carried supplies landward at the same time. Through their spyglasses, they could see their pioneer troops and cavalry units moving forward. By evening, the British had advanced next to Saint-Servan, a village near Saint-Malo, where they set up artillery and a camp.

Spying heavy smoke drifting skyward that evening, Lieutenant Shelly reported, "Sir, the troops must be burning ships in Saint-Malo's harbor." The lieutenant motioned excitedly with his hands as he relayed the new action to the captain in his cabin.

Mackenzie hurried up to the quarterdeck to watch the distant spectacle in the darkened western sky. Vessels at anchor were in flames that lit up the scene, clouds of smoke and embers billowed upward as sounds of the fight rumbled to them. Not long after, loud explosions rocked the air as the magazines in the blazing warships ignited. Close to the tall walls of Saint-Malo, supply warehouses and naval stores burned along the harbor docks. Fortress guns fired with an incessant roar that reverberated to the *Renown*. The battle lasted for hours until the night grew silent except for the occasional blast of exploding ammunition as the British withdrew from the port in the darkness.

By the afternoon of the next day, the same troops burned Saint-Servan and Solidor. At sunset, heavy rains fell, but they were too late to save the smoldering villages, reduced to blackened beams and heaps of ash.

With Saint-Malo's many guns too formidable to attack and news of a large French army approaching, the Duke of Marlborough and Admiral Howe ordered their troops to return to their ships.

The duke and admiral, pleased with the destruction of the ships and villages, and the burning of the supply warehouses, set out to descend upon other ports. A week later, the squadron arrived at Cherbourg to try another amphibious landing.

"Most of the enemy ships stood out for sea or are hugging the defensive redoubts along the shore." Mackenzie pointed to the far sails.

"It'll be unlikely we see action then." Lieutenant Shelly sulked as he anticipated the descents might provide more action for his ship. To date, the *Renown* played a sedate role, giving the youthful officer no opportunity to show his courage or skills.

"Oh, the day is young." Mackenzie saw how the young man wanted to prove his worth. "If there's no action today, we will be taking part in a bombardment, no doubt."

As they glided on, a fresh gale began to blow once again, and one French corvette dashed from the harbor to escape the British fleet.

"How many guns?" the captain called upward upon hearing the

sighting.

"Twenty-six, ah, no, twenty-two, sir!"

"Lieutenant Shelly, set to pursue. To quarters—man the guns. Helmsman, bring her two points port!" Mackenzie instructed and watched as topmen scurried up the ratlines and gun crews made the cannons ready. Others ran to fill and place fire buckets and spread sand.

"She'll not outrun the *Renown,* Lieutenant. We'll have her before the sun sets this day." He smiled, knowing the lieutenant would get his chance in a fight.

Their warship sped across the rough waves as the storm intensified. Mackenzie, near the helm, watched as his frigate gained. To the stern, he saw the *Rochester,* a bigger fifty-gun wearing to join in the chase.

"The Frenchman is heading north, out to open sea in the Channel. We can outsail her with this wind." His frigate could overtake the twenty-two-gun, and Mackenzie's position in the fleet was the only warship close enough to give immediate chase. The *Rochester,* lurching to turn in the rough seas, would take a long time to catch up to them if he engaged the enemy.

After twenty minutes, the fleeing corvette headed westward toward the Guernsey island of Alderney, ten miles off the coast. Both British warships followed.

Almost an hour later the *Renown* shot a warning that flew over the French warship. The threat ignored, the vessel continued its flight. Just as Mackenzie had expected, he neared close enough within minutes to turn starboard and offer her a taste of his guns.

Iron landed skillfully on her starboard waist and left jagged holes in her freeboard. The smaller warship responded in kind and did little damage other than punch tears in sails. Turning into the wind north-by-northwest, the French captain hoped the *Renown* might struggle. Mackenzie's ship plowed the waves and slowed. The sea poured over her bow, swamping the deck. Yet, she kept pace with the corvette.

Then the enemy turned westward once again. Now in good range, Mackenzie laid into her with a rolling broadside that split her fore topgallant yard. Moments later, the enemy's return volley successfully damaged his jibboom. "Lieutenant, see if our carpenter can make fast a fish to the boom. We can't lose our jibs or we'll lose our Frenchman."

Lieutenant Shelly ran to the carpenter. Given the power to affect the repairs, he took over, commanding the man and his helpers to hurry the fix. When they completed it, he returned to the quarterdeck.

"She'll hold until we return to Portsmouth, sir." He ended the announcement with a confident nod.

"Well, done," Mackenzie said. Parceling out praise in small bits to a new officer was more effective than none at all or too much all the time. He'd trained many a lieutenant and midshipman in his day and had learned how to draw the best from them and either change or ignore their weaknesses. Lieutenant Shelly had become the best first officer he'd ever overwatched, and he liked his quick analysis of threats, treatment of the men, and grasp of tactics.

For over an hour, both ships followed the circular tactic to find the best firing position while exchanging cannonballs at any opportunity.

Mackenzie sensed the time had come to take their prize. "Lieutenant, we'll close on the next turn to steal her wind and board her if we can." The *Renown* now closed on her prey's starboard quarter and drew nearer. As the French warship turned, Mackenzie caught the breeze and came around within musket range, both ships exchanging iron for iron in a dreadful scene of falling lines and men. Marines threw grappling hooks, but the enemy cut the lines or dislodged them. The ships now ran parallel and blasted away at each other in a firestorm of flashing cannon throats and dense smoke. The deafening cacophony of their thunder hid the shrieks and pleas of fallen men.

As the damages grew on both warships, Mackenzie saw the *Rochester,* its massive hull drawing nearer on the far side of their opponent. One fusillade of the fifty-gun had more than twice the weight of iron to throw than the corvette. Two chase cannons on the two-decker blasted at the small vessel. The French captain, now exposed on both sides to ships out-gunning him at a four-to-one disadvantage, saw the pointlessness in continuing and struck his flag.

The *Renown,* closer and more maneuverable, moved in to claim its reward. Mackenzie sent over marines and Lieutenant Shelly to take control of the battered warship. The *Rochester* took aboard the French captain and officers as more men from the *Renown* boarded their capture, the *Guirlande.*

Aboard his own ship, Mackenzie assessed the damages. It had taken nearly as severe a beating as the *Guirlande,* with lines and wood shards covering her deck. Below, little damage had been inflicted and the carpenter reported no leaks in the hull. The captain set sail with his trophy to return to the fleet.

After rejoining the squadron, they learned Cherbourg garrisoned over 7,000 infantry, too strong for a short assault the fleet's dwindling supplies demanded. The weather had become blowy once again and the cavalry horses had taken no fodder for days and were near starvation. Worse, disease had sprung up among the troops onboard.

These obstacles forced a withdrawal and the next day the admiral led the ships back to the Isle of Wight and Portsmouth.

The *Renown* put into Portsmouth for battle repairs days later and the crew transferred to an accommodation ship for the month or more it would take. Mackenzie took leave of the frigate and left for Scotland.

⚬⚭⚬

At home near Inverness by July 1758, Mackenzie had settled into a routine by the third day. He rose late, ate, read, and spent the afternoons looking over the family finances or talking with his wife. His son, only five, often interrupted this schedule with youthful questions.

"Father, when you were little, did you live on a ship?" Thomas stood in the doorway between the study and hallway and twined his hair with his finger.

"Why would you ask such a question, Tommy?" asked Mackenzie, eyebrows raised. "I lived in a house as a lad. Where did you get that idea?"

"You're away all the time and never at home."

"Now, I'm sure Mother has explained why I must be gone. If I lived here, enemies might attack and destroy everything. I protect the isle while at sea."

"Hmm, you have to fight them. Will they come here?"

"Nae, lad, they'll not. Our warships are many and the enemies are far away. You need never fear that," he explained with a wide-faced smile at the boyish logic. "And someday I shall take you on one of my ships and show you."

Tommy's forehead wrinkled. "Tomorrow?"

"Not until you are older. When you study aboard as a midshipman and learn from me. I have much to teach you about the seas, ships, and winds. There are ten thousand skills to learn and you will then become a captain as I did."

"And I'll fight the enemies."

"Aye, if you must. Who knows, in the future you may become an admiral."

"Like Admiral Anson?"

"Better than that treasure hunter." Mackenzie frowned. "You'll sail to save Great Britain from its foes, not for glory, power, and wealth, but for our flag."

Mackenzie chaffed at the thought of young Thomas someday resembling the First Lord of the Admiralty Anson, the vainglorious gold-seeker whose deeds the public glorified. He may have enriched the treasury with captured Spanish gold, he thought, but Anson squandered the blood of hundreds of British crewmen to do it. Mackenzie closed the ledger he studied, disturbed by the knavery.

"In time, my laddie, I shall instruct you on right and wrong and the naval codes of law. Without them, we'd be but savages and pirates." He rose and picked up a golf club from the table.

"Do you want to see me hit a golf ball in the garden? Come on, it's time for your first lesson in our great Scottish sport."

He took Tommy onto the lawn near the gorse and bluebells and dropped a few balls on the grass, showing him how to swing. When he had finished tutoring the boy on the particulars of golf, Mackenzie found Alana, his wife, writing in the drawing room. He had nicknamed her the old Celtic name *Alana,* or *beautiful,* during their courtship, replacing her real name, Ann.

"Alana, our son has a natural talent for golf. You should see the bonnie lad with a club."

"Aye, but you'll not be taking him to play the silly game. He's much too young, and you'd be carrying him after ten minutes." Her eyes were still on the paper as her lips restrained a smile.

"Nae, not until he's older. I'm just delighted with his skill at so young an age."

"You must be around more if you want him to master it. A lesson once a year or so won't hold." She shook her head. "It's sad that you'll be missing his youth while you're away."

Alana had missed her husband, as she had every time he set out. His naval career aboard ship, like a sea merchant's or fisherman's, bore the bitter fruit of an incomplete family life. She watched their lives together slip though time, his absence tallied each hour by the clock chimes.

"True, but there's naught to be done for it. If the war ends I might get a posting closer and return more often. There's no telling where I'll be next. Yet, I know I'll still be on the *Renown*. She has a fine reputation and is a hardy sailor, and the *Guirlande* capture proved it." Mackenzie sat across from her, hoping that his accomplishment might bring about a stationing in the Channel.

He added, "At least some benefit came from the expedition for me. Word of my seizing the corvette has gotten around and will merit my naval service. And the prize share should augment my earnings well."

Alana had listened without speaking or interrupting and put the book in her lap. The military strategies meant little to her. "Everyone is tired of the fighting, dear, and wants it ended. Although I appreciate the celebrity and money, it doesn't lessen the emptiness Tommy and I endure when you are at sea. We shall not be content until peace returns with you near home. Not a lull in battling between wars, but a permanent accord."

"Aye, this victory must be conclusive. Britain must dominate and give nothing back at the treaty signing or it will begin again. The descents will put the pressure on them to end the war without us having to concede anything." Mackenzie, like most, saw the futility in truces if they did not settle the causes.

Alana smirked. "An agreement may be further off. Remember how long it took for the accord in '48." Alana felt the present circumstances paralleled the previous war's. "France still has large fleets in the Mediterranean and Atlantic. Other than the descents, they have lost little for all our efforts."

"Back then they captured Madras, and we took Louisbourg, and they exchanged them during the negotiations." Mackenzie defended his position. "Now France has nothing. We've captured Louisbourg again and they are losing this war. We can manage their fleets. Like a cat outside a mouse hole, we have them sitting afraid in their ports. If they dare take to sea, we await them with claws ready."

Alana, feigning agreement to his logic and smiling at his overblown description, nodded. She was accustomed to Mackenzie's pride in his navy and belief that Britain's fleets performed superior to other countries'. Perhaps he knew better, but she simply wanted the fighting to end.

Not an hour later, a knock upon the door brought a messenger with a sealed letter in his hand for Mackenzie.

"Lord Fortrose has requested we attend a private dinner at Brahan Castle tomorrow." Mackenzie's head tilted. "Why would the clan chief ask us to dine? He's never before had us visit."

"I have no idea." The invitation likewise puzzled Alana. "But send a reply right away. It must be for a good reason and it's an honor." Her mind raced… a supper with the lord, and in a castle, no less!

"A privilege I find intriguing. What on earth prompted him to invite me; and why has he returned from London?" Mackenzie paused. "This dinner is peculiar to me." The request flattered, yet bothered, both of them the rest of the day.

Late the next afternoon, they took their carriage northward from Inverness for the two-and-a-half-hour trip to the castle. Mackenzie wore his best captain's uniform and Alana dressed in a lavender gown. As they approached the manor's stone bridge, Mackenzie turned to her, grinning with one raised eyebrow.

"I believe I have a thought on why he invited us. It may have to do with the descents along the French coast. We shall see."

Upon arrival at the wide castle entrance, an elderly man dressed in a worn footman's uniform greeted them. "The lord is awaiting you, Captain and Mistress Mackenzie."

The servant showed them inside and they passed through two long halls. Each foreboding hall held but a single flickering candle. Neither had seen the manor house before and followed their slow guide, unable to enjoy the paintings and tapestries in the dim passages.

Entering a better-lit room, they found to one side a small dining table that held gold-rimmed china, crystal stemware, silverplate utensils, and a bottle of wine. There were four place settings. The old attendant motioned for them to sit and pulled out the chair for Alana across from Mackenzie.

"The lord will be with you soon, sir, madame. Would you prefer I pour?" He picked up the wine. They refused, and he walked back into the dark hallway, fading into the shadows.

Mackenzie raised his eyebrows looking around at the shaded paintings on the walls, and turned to his wife. She shrugged and squinted at the darkened portraits. After two minutes in silence, the servant's footfalls having diminished, Alana cleared her throat.

"We may as well have the wine since we'll be here for a while, I assume." She reached for the half-full carafe and filled a goblet for each.

"Strange we should have to wait alone." He widened his eyes as he whispered. "These accommodations are not the most joyous we've beheld."

"This table spread is nice. But, the walk from the entrance seemed…" Alana twirled her hand in the air before her looking for the right word.

"Frightful or dismal?" Mackenzie finished her sentence in a hushed tone.

"Both." She put a finger on her lip and laughed.

"If such be the luxury of nobles, they can keep their manors and castles. Our little home is far more appealing." He joined her in a quiet laugh.

They sat for five more minutes sipping the wine when they heard the slow steps of people approaching.

"Good evening, Captain and Mistress Mackenzie. I do apologize for not meeting you in the foyer." Lord Fortrose appeared in the doorway. He looked in his forties, a few years older than Mackenzie and Alana. His dark blue vest and frock made him blend into the unlit doorway, ghostly, as if his head floated free of a body.

Mackenzie shot up and with a slight bow, put out his hand. Alana nodded and kept her gaze down in a respectful gesture to the clan chieftain.

Lord Fortrose shook Mackenzie's hand and sat at the head of the table. "I'm sure you are curious why I've asked you to dine with me. The reason, although serious, will come later as we eat. Since my wife died these many years ago, I dread eating without conversation. So, why not resolve both, nae? My son Kenneth will sup with us, too."

A young teen's face peeked around the corner. The youth, not much older than sixteen, looking nothing like his father, grinned at them both, and sat in his chair.

Moments later the old servant entered the room carrying a platter of steaming food. He went straight to the lord's end and began serving roast fowl, potatoes, and greens before doing the same for the rest. Before leaving, he placed a large silver basket of bread in the middle of the table.

"Our fare here at the castle is not as appointed as what I serve to visitors in London. I hope you can forgive this meager supper." Lord Fortrose smiled at them.

"Oh, it looks very appetizing, I have not had this bird in over a year! As you know, sir, my dinners at sea can be quite a challenge to stock, cook, and eat. Caged hens are as close as I can get to capercaillie." He smiled broadly as he cut a piece of the Scottish fowl.

They dined and chatted about Inverness society. Lord Fortrose, spending most of his time in London, appeared eager to hear the latest gossip. After they had finished their meal, he changed the topic.

"Your recent naval service brings me to the reason for requesting your presence tonight." The lord placed his fork on his plate and sipped his wine, his eyes distant. "As you are well aware, I am the Member of Parliament representing Ross-Shire. Since I needed to return to the Highlands for personal business, I thought I'd get your opinion on the actions along the coast of France. I've been told you were present at the descents on Saint-Malo and Cherbourg. There's been much talk by other members of Parliament on their effectiveness."

Mackenzie prided himself on guessing the reason for their attendance, glancing at Alana knowingly. He smiled and answered, "The confusion in Parliament over our mission has been rumored among naval officers. What is it you desire me to tell you, your lordship?"

"As a nautical man, you can best understand the government's situation if I describe it as one of varying winds. There are those whose aims do not jibe to my views. And to add more seaman's parlance, frankly, they wish to sink members who are my mates." Lord Fortrose chuckled at his description. "To counter the threats, I need to discover the actions in particular of the Duke of Marlborough, Admiral Howe, and Lord Sackville."

"Ah, more attacks against Pitt and the Patriot Whigs." Mackenzie shook his head. "The descents are unpopular among his critics. Compelled then by my own affinity to the secretary of state and his leanings, I shall give you as true a recounting as I may." Mackenzie favored the imperial political strategies the bellicose William Pitt followed, chiefly: a strong navy, financial support for military allies, and expanding profitable colonies, in essence, to create an empire. Both also believed that England's superiority at sea and in the colonies would determine the war's victor, not the traditional battlefields on the continent.

Mackenzie straightened in his chair. "If those in opposition feel that the duke, lord, and admiral lacked in martial spirit to achieve our intents, I can avow they performed from the arriving moment with the greatest audacity. The first day, the Duke of Marlborough and Admiral Howe took a small cutter to reconnoiter the coast at Cancale and came under fire but continued on for almost eight hours to complete their survey." Mackenzie's brows dipped slightly. "Whereupon the admiral then switched his broad pennant to a frigate to lead a bombardment on a French battery blocking the landing of our troops. After disembarking, Lord Sackville and the duke boldly led a column to Saint-Malo, where under a barrage from the guns of Saint-Malo, they accomplished the destruction of all the ships anchored in the harbor."

Lord Fortrose held up his hand and shook his head. "These exploits do reveal an intrepid character, but the most pressing issue is why we did not capture Saint-Malo."

"Sir, the duke and Lord Sackville made every plan to lay siege to the port. And the admiral repositioned our warships to blockade and bombard the defenses. However, the very narrow causeway with massive emplacements protects the fortress so well it might resist any but a long-standing assault of weeks, if not months." Mackenzie's voice took a stern tenor. "Taking Saint-Malo would have been a travesty."

"So, we left with our tails tucked." The lord summed up, unimpressed.

To which Mackenzie countered with his jaw jutting while he nodded, "A well-executed withdrawal proved wise upon learning of a ten-thousand-man enemy army advancing upon us. Better, my lord, a strategic and honorable retreat than losing our troops in foolish obstinacy to a superior force."

The lord raised his head higher. "And Le Havre and Cherbourg?"

"Nature delivers the ultimate orders to sailors, your lordship. Storms and high seas prevented any possibility of landing troops or executing plans for a siege, unusual for the bright month of June. Worsening weather limited Admiral Howe and the Duke of Marlborough's options with each dawn." Mackenzie shrugged. "In the end, our lack of supplies, illness within the transports, and the wisdom of our leaders determined a return to English shores our only course."

Lord Fortrose leaned in toward Mackenzie, pointing his finger at him. "Who made the final decision, the duke or the admiral—who?!"

Mackenzie's mouth turned downward, speculating. "Well, sir, I suspect the duke's seniority in age and military experience had superseded the admiral's."

"As my opponents will press, the duke's decisions prevailed. This will play against Pitt as a promoter of the duke, in addition to Pitt's insistence on the descent strategy," replied the lord, frowning.

Mackenzie appealed to consider the descent's successes. "Regardless of not taking the ports, sir, we certainly harmed the enemy's sense of security. Not to make light the damages they incurred by the sinking of over one hundred ships, the burning of their villages, and the loss of supplies in warehouses. Plus, my *Renown* captured a French corvette!"

"Yes, Captain Mackenzie, I'm aware. But the corvette returned to our shores *the only* material gain from the entire month-long expedition." Lord Fortrose wagged his finger at the captain. "Many in Parliament find the exorbitant expense and size of the endeavor misspent for the rewards. The Treasury is near emptied from war costs and descents. As much as we are both in agreement with Pitt, his foes may catch the public's ear by declaring it a folly."

Mackenzie tapped his fingers on the table in thought. "Perhaps if the public became aware of the political advantages first before it explodes into an emotional matter. We destroyed many of their privateer ships that will prove advantageous to the safety of our shipping commerce." He added with a steady gaze. "And the battalions that must be diverted from the battle fronts now to protect their ports will have a beneficial effect on British army and ally strategies in the field to end the war."

Their host laughed. "When has the public ever thought logically about cause and effect? It's always emotional with the rabble. The farthest they can see is the price of a pig this afternoon for supper tonight." Shaking his head, he proposed a solution. "Pitt will have to depend on the recent taking of Louisbourg to help him jump this sharny brook. At least, however, I have your insights, and from one who distinguished himself there. I shall use it in debate."

"Thank you for the compliment, my lord. I hope my candid description and opinions will be of service to our cause." Mackenzie bowed his head slightly and the lord nodded.

"There is one additional thing I have to ask of you, Captain Mackenzie. It will prove to our mutual benefit if at times you apprise me on your missions, relative to how it might impact Pitt and our aims." Lord Fortrose smiled. "An occasional report should suffice."

"Whatever I can do to help you in Parliament, I consider not only my duty but a privilege, my Laird." The captain bowed.

"The descents are a clever strategy. If you find yourself on another such endeavor, I'd find it most advantageous to learn of its effectiveness before my opposition in London." Lord Fortrose turned to his son.

"Kenny, have you anything to say to our guests?"

The young man spoke with the high-pitched voice of youth. "Captain Mackenzie, did you stand with the Jacobites in '46?"

Lord Fortrose, abashed at his son's brazen question, barked at him. "Son, you should not ask such questions these days of Scots! It's all in the past."

"Sorry Father. I wanted to know if the captain had suffered oppression for his political stance." His face reddened.

Mackenzie grinned at the boy's naivete and explained his position during the uprising. "Nae, laddie, I supported the crown and the united governments during the rebellion. It'd become a hard time for us Scots. The fork in a long road of persecution and advancement forced us to choose one side or the other. I looked to the future and what Britain might be, some saw the past in what Scotland was. Neither side stood wrong in the choosing, only wrong for the consequences."

"Well said, Captain Mackenzie. My only son has much to learn to become the Mackenzie Laird when I pass on. It is well known that my dear wife, bless her, chose to help the rebels. But I, like you, sided with the commonwealth whilst my father favored the Jacobites in the first Jacobite rebellion in 1716, losing his title and his power." He shook his head but then he grinned. "I hope someday to reclaim a title for us if King George would only begin to create them again. Aye, he's a tight-fisted king."

"People say he promises titles to sway Parliament to his liking and then as quickly forgets the commitments." Mackenzie frowned.

"His father wasn't as parsimonious with titles. Yet, by helping Pitt, whom the king now again favors, I may gain influence for my hopes. If not for me, then perhaps someday for my son."

"If I can help in any way to serve you to that end, then just ask it of me, Laird of the Mackenzies." He proffered his allegiance, while hoping a just reward for it in turn.

"I already have." Lord Fortrose smiled with a steady gaze.

When later they left in their carriage, Mackenzie asked with a brow raised, "Did I sound too brash in my thoughts, my dear? It could benefit us to have a patron in London."

"No." She smiled back, and touched his hand. "You made your stance clear without bluster or boasting. Both of you being in support of Pitt, this evening should affect no ill consequences to your career. This may elevate it."

Mackenzie returned to the repaired *Renown* a few weeks after his supper with Lord Fortrose. He still remained in Admiral Howe's fleet for Channel patrol and had attended a meeting of captains on the admiral's flagship. As the gathering concluded, the admiral called him to remain.

"Captain Mackenzie, Portsmouth informed me they finished the survey of the *Guirlande,* that little French corvette you took off Alderney." His stern face held piercing eyes. "They estimated her value at two pounds per ton and are commissioning her into the fleet as the *Cygnet.*"

"Admiral, its worth will delight my crew when I tell them." Mackenzie smiled, though, he had also wanted to discover how much she'd fetch.

The admiral continued, but his face now glowered. "Yes indeed, our adventure off Cherbourg will profit you well. We had hesitated in besieging Cherbourg, but my counsel with the Duke of Marlborough convinced him to go. It is most rewarding that I had *some* influence in the expedition, and that you gained from it financially. Perhaps my decisions, subordinate to the duke's as you feel, were beneficial after all." He turned around scowling, and without a word more, walked away.

Mackenzie's mouth dropped open. The admiral had learned of his discussion with Lord Fortrose and took exception to being seen as subservient to the duke. Perhaps Lord Fortrose during a debate had exaggerated what he had said, Mackenzie wondered, and even more, would Howe do anything because of it?

Before the month ended, Mackenzie got his answer. He received orders for the *Renown* to be transferred out of Howe's fleet to Admiral Boscawen, the Admiral of the Blue Fleet. Mackenzie expected a posting in the American waters, far from his dear Alana and son.

Soon after, they learned the *Renown's* next station was, once again, in Jamaica. At the close of November 1758, Alana and Tommy journeyed nearly the length of the isle to Portsmouth to be with Mackenzie for a little while before he departed.

"Halifax or even the Mediterranean but why the West Indies?" Mackenzie stomped on the bare wood floor. The small parlor rumbled in the house he rented in Portsmouth.

"George, you're acting like a child over this. At least you're familiar with Port Royal. Admiral Howe could have stationed you in India. We might have not seen you for years." Alana tried to soothe his disappointment. "Your placement before in Jamaica lasted only for five months. Perhaps this one will be as short."

"I abhor that station. No sane captain stays there for more than a month. There's nothing but heat, hurricanes, and disease. We lost four crewmen last week to desertion when they found out the destination." He frowned. "They'd rather suffer flogging or worse than serve there."

"We'll pray it is a short stay in the islands." Her concerns centered on enemy patrols, not illness. He had always avoided diseases. Alana's lips smiled. "Are you departing alone?"

"The *Renown* is joining a squadron for the crossing. How big of one I have yet to learn." He straightened his back and lifted his chin. "As much as I dread the West Indies, though, it is my duty. Too often I forget the navy's needs outweigh my petty dispositions. Although missing you and Tommy does hang on me."

"A squadron of warships eases my fears somewhat." She knitted her brows. "Will Admiral Howe force other difficulties upon you?"

He brushed off the worry with a wave of his hand. "No. I am under command of Admiral Boscawen now. The transfer punished me for trespassing on Howe's vanity and I don't expect more."

A week later, Mackenzie attended matters in Portsmouth and prepared to sail. In one office, he noticed a familiar captain. Washington approached and Mackenzie quickly turned away, pretending to take interest in a posted notice on the wall. He found the man irritating.

"Good day there, Captain Mackenzie." Shirley's face spread a broad smile as he approached Mackenzie.

"Captain Shirley, fare you well?" Mackenzie forced a grin.

"Indeed, sir. How is our French frigate now that you've had her on the descents?"

"Well enough to snare a corvette a few months ago off the Guernseys. I'm bound for the West Indies again. Are you part of the fleet?" Mackenzie pointed in the direction of the harbor, expressionless, hoping Washington wasn't part of the expedition.

"Not your fleet. I'm on the *Temple* with Admiral Hawke on the Channel." Washington's eyes widened. "Tell me, was that corvette you took a fast one, too? Are they selling her off or commissioning her?"

Mackenzie puffed his chest. "The French *Guirlande* becomes our *Cygnet* in a few months."

"Then let me give you some advice. When they calculate the price per ton be sure to fight it. The Admiralty, of late, undervalues every capture and you'd be cheating yourself and crew out of your rightful prize shares if you don't." Shirley winked.

Annoyed with Washington lecturing him, Mackenzie spit out a quick answer. "Admiral Howe informed me she's gone for two per ton. It seems fair. So the prize share will be well over three thousand pounds with the head count. She crewed over two hundred men."

"Did you damage her much? Was she hogged or old?" His brow rose.

Mackenzie shook his head. "Nae, she launched only two years ago; and we put just superficial wounds on her."

Washington pouted his lips. "A clean take?"

"The *Rochester* assisted at the last moment with a couple of cannon shots." Mackenzie understood Washington's point of sharing with the other ship.

"So, a fifty-gun shoots off a few warnings. You do most of the fighting but have to share the capture with their bigger crew." Washington wagged his head back and forth. "You will get but a fraction of what you should. I believe the *Guirlande* could be worth more than two per ton, perhaps two-and-a-half to three pounds per ton if she's anything like the *Renown*. They offered me four per ton for the *Renown* and I fought and got five."

"Aye, the corvette is a speedy one and new. When I return after this cruise, I'll discuss it with them." Mackenzie had no intention of doing so. He didn't want to bring negative attention to himself in a prize share haggle against the Admiralty. He turned his head away from Washington and rolled his eyes.

Washington smiled again and said, "Well, I must be on my way. Fair seas in the West Indies, Captain Mackenzie." Washington patted him on the shoulder and departed.

As he walked away, Mackenzie let out a sigh of relief. Perhaps, he mulled, those English nobles with influence could fight the Admiralty on ship values, but he couldn't. Mackenzie had little respect for privileged captains like Washington, believing the standard practices of the peerage cleared a golden road for men of higher social rank. As he'd seen in so many officers, their sort seldom felt regulations applied to them. This inequity soiled the esteem Mackenzie held for the brotherhood of naval commanders.

As the days passed and his fleet assembled, the number of ships and men sailing impressed him. He hadn't expected to be part of such a large squadron and realized they had picked the *Renown* for an important role.

When Mackenzie set out to sea, the orders read Barbados as the next port, not Jamaica as he had anticipated. He didn't know the purpose of so huge a fleet, however, he anticipated it would likely be an invasion, and somewhere noteworthy.

꘎

Abraham took a boat to the Blackwall shipyard by Deptford, looking for work. As he approached the gates, another drew near.

"Abraham?" he called.

"Well, well, ah… Samuel, it's been a long time. Do you work here?" Abraham hadn't seen the shipwright since he left the Woolwich yard over a decade earlier.

"I do. What ship are you working on?" Samuel asked, grinning.

"None yet, I don't work here. But maybe they have an opening."

Abraham replied.

The man looked down at Abraham's left hand that had fingertips missing. "I see your hand healed well."

"It did, but I had a devil of a time finding work after I could use it again. I crossed to France and worked at the Brest yards until the war started."

"Oh, too bad you didn't stay in England. They were begging for workers just before the fighting but filled up in a few months."

"Yes, just about the time I arrived back in England. Do you know if they are hiring now?" His eyes opened wide.

"No, I don't believe they are. But, if you go to slip two, ask for Mister Jackson. Tell him you used to work at Woolwich and he may find you something. Mention my name if you want." Samuel smiled. "Good to see you again and good luck."

After the two walked through the gate, Samuel continued on to his shop while Abraham headed for the slip. When he found Mister Jackson, he related his experience, and the man told Abraham he had a place for him for the next few months on a two-decker under construction.

For Yvette, the morning wasn't as fortunate. The owners of every bookstore she entered frowned and shook their heads at her requests for employment. Even though she had a letter of reference from her old boss, her heavy French accent and being a woman played against her. Discouraged, she walked to her friend's house.

Yvette spent the rest of the afternoon at Madame Goubert's in a wealthy neighborhood with wide avenues and paved sidewalks. It contrasted the crowded, dingy, and filth-strewn alleys near her own run-down flat house. It soothed her and relaxed the stresses after earlier feeling inadequate for employment. At least, Yvette often reminded herself, she had married a loving and patient man; although Madame Goubert lived in a luxurious home, her spinster life remained empty.

Yvette wrinkled her nose. "You've met no one at the Calvinist meetings that suits you?" She and Madame Goubert had discussed potential matches for almost an hour.

"No, most have wives or are too, too common. A year ago, I caught the eye of a naval purser, but he sailed to India." Madame Goubert took a sip of tea and sighed. "I may never see him again."

"Hmm, I wonder if Abraham is still familiar with any former officers who would fit your needs. As a ship's carpenter when he served, he met lots of navy gentlemen." Yvette squinched her mouth to the side, wondering how to solve her friend's dilemma.

"When I inherited the estate from my late uncle, a Huguenot, and moved to London, I assumed I'd meet people he had known and get married. I wasn't aware he lived as a recluse. I gained from it financially, but lost my friends in Brittany. I'd move back to France if not for the war."

Yvette's eyes lit up. "Might you talk to the Countess Huntingdon about your problem? She has always been so helpful to me."

"Selina? She's a religious leader and speaker, not a matchmaker. Besides, she'd match me with a Calvinist and I'm still Catholic at heart. The French men I've met in the area are all married." Her hands knotted in her lap, and her eyes drooped.

"Oh, I think the countess may have Catholic friends. She helped me in '45 during the Catholic expulsions from London when the Jacobites attacked England." Yvette nodded and grinned.

"Ah, I remember. You stayed at Donnington Hall a few weeks, didn't you?" Madame Goubert added, her head cocked.

"She'd help and doesn't forget repaying favors, either."

Madame Goubert tilted her head. "What do you mean about repaying favors, Yvette?"

"I suppose I never mentioned to you what occurred at Donnington Hall." Yvette smiled, remembering the incident. "The countess asked to keep it secret, but it happened so long ago, she won't mind if I tell you."

"The countess owes you for a good deed?" Her brows rose.

Yvette gazed off for a moment and then recounted the story. "Yes, in a way. At least she thinks she does. As you may recall, when Bonnie Prince Charles marched with the Jacobites from Scotland, Parliament feared he'd march on London, and kicked the Catholics out of the city. When I asked her for help, she invited me to stay at her estate near Leicester. One morning after a few days, we heard a ruckus in her foyer. The countess ran down the steps from the nursery where we were playing with her children. Soon, shouting alerted me that something was amiss, and I raced to the entrance. There, standing before the doors, were the countess, her butler, and three uniformed soldiers, one with a wounded leg."

"Military? Had they come to quarter troops in the hall?"

"No, they spoke French, not English, and carried weapons. The countess tried to explain to them no doctor lived near there. But they couldn't understand her." She laughed, "So, I interpreted for her."

"Oh, my. They came from the Jacobite army?" Madame Goubert sensed the danger everyone faced.

"Yes, but they didn't act hostile. The injured officer bled from a shot wound in his calf. The countess couldn't decide what to do. If she helped them, she'd be a traitor. If she didn't, she'd be unchristian. Her choice of actions became either a crime or a sin." Yvette pointed her finger one way and then the other. "I told her and the butler to go and I handled the situation.

"I told the three men to follow me to the gardener's pot shed and hid them. Then I got bandages and salves from the butler and fixed up the soldier's wound."

"Have you trained as a nurse?" she asked, eyes open wide.

Yvette nodded. "I used to volunteer at the hospital in Brest and dressed all kinds of wounds, many a good deal worse than the French officer's little hole. A farmer had shot him with a fowling musket. Lucky for the soldier, the small ball had passed clear through the muscle. It was easy to clean and bandage.

"Then I returned to the hall and asked the butler to give me some food and blankets for the poor devils. I showed them the road north to their army and told them they'd best go before sunrise the next day. Later, I learned the Jacobites had advanced to within ten miles of the estate before they retreated into Scotland."

Madame Goubert knitted her brows. "I wonder what became of the Frenchmen?"

"We shall never know. My hunch is they made their way back to

France after the Battle of Culloden. At least, I allow myself to imagine that happened. I still recall how scared the wounded one acted, not knowing what fate held for him. He looked no older than I." Yvette's eyes looked downward, as she imagined the destruction of the Scottish army at Culloden. "Since then, the countess has always felt indebted to me. In truth, I only tried to help my countrymen."

"When will these wars end? So much bloodshed," Madame Goubert replied, shaking her head.

"Year after year, war after war. As a species, we're dumber than worms," Yvette surmised.

When Yvette returned to the flat later that afternoon, Abraham was sitting at the kitchen table reading a book, unusual for that time of day.

"I didn't expect to see you home so early," she said, head cocked.

"Excellent news. The Blackwall Yard is hiring me and I begin tomorrow." His grin widened. "It should last for some time. They have a backlog of work."

"The drought is over, thank goodness." Yvette clapped her hands. "Will they let you join the guild?"

Abraham's smile fled and his shoulders slouched, "No, not yet. They only allow you to join if they hire you for permanent work at the yard. My position is still temporary. It strikes me as peculiar that after so much experience that the master shipwrights don't take me on for anything but short-term work. When I belonged to the guild in Woolwich before the wars, it seemed easier to get in than now that I have better skills."

"Hmm, that seems strange." She frowned. "You're more qualified than others but they don't choose you for lasting jobs. What are the reasons they do that for others? Perhaps we can figure out why."

"Some men have criminal records for theft or bad references. Men often try to steal wood or metals. I have neither. My navy record is clean of anything bad when I sailed as a master ship's carpenter." He sat with his hand on his chin and elbow on the table, his cheek bunched to one side.

"Are you sure a previous shipyard didn't give you a poor reference? Perhaps you made an enemy at one of the shipyards."

"No. Most times, they say they want to take me on for good if they can. I've always gotten along well with my fellow carpenters." He frowned with his hands curled into fists. "I can't understand why it's so difficult for me."

Yvette shrugged and grinned. "Well, at least we can start to pay back Madame Goubert when you get paid."

Abraham hated thinking about their financial shortages. Yvette had told him she borrowed from Madame Goubert while he had been out of work for a long time. The amount wasn't huge. It totaled around eight pounds, but it was eight pounds they didn't have.

"When do you think Madame Goubert will want her loan back?" Abraham frowned. His gut clenched. She had never had to ask help before from friends for his shortcomings.

"She didn't set a time limit. But I suspect that now you have work, she'll assume we'll repay her right away." Yvette's face sagged.

He shook his head. "She'll have to wait until we save enough for it."

"She would have told me if she needed it." Yvette forced a smile. "So, don't worry. We'll pay her back a little at a time."

The embarrassment over the debt weighed heavily upon her. Yvette didn't want him to stew over the matter, and she wanted to resolve the issue herself. She decided that instead of looking just for bookstore work, she'd take the first thing that came along.

A few days later, she haunted the bookstores near St. Paul's Cathedral and then wandered eastward into Spitalfields, looking for the few shops it held. As she passed by the crowded flat-houses and weavers' factories, she stopped an old woman to ask for directions.

"Pardon me, madam, could you direct me to a nearby bookseller?" Yvette asked, slouching and tired from walking.

"Je ne comprends pas l'anglais," she replied, expressionless.

In French, Yvette continued, "Oh, I'm from France, too. I wonder if you know if there is a bookseller store nearby."

The old Frenchwoman smiled, "You're from Brittany, aren't you, my dear?"

"Yes, and I'm trying to find work at a bookstore. Are any around here?" Yvette smiled, thrilled and slightly surprised by the comment.

She too could tell by her accent that the woman came from Normandy.

"Not here. You'll have to go nearer the river. What work do you do for booksellers?" she asked, squinting her wrinkled eyes.

"I was a book-buyer and clerk many years ago at one. But I've had difficulty in finding a store owner to hire me." Yvette held her palms up.

"Ah. Times are terrible for jobs. You may be in luck if you don't mind using other skills. I need a sewer at my flat. Do you sew well?" Her forehead creased.

"I do." Yvette replied, smiling. "In France, I embroidered and did needle tatting." After over a year of frustration in finding work, perhaps the time had come to try something new, she thought.

"I'm Madame Donnet. This way, let me show you what you must do." The stranger curled her finger to follow. "My home is only a block away."

They climbed two sets of stairs to a small flat. In the larger room, a young girl not much older than twelve sat in a chair stitching together a silk purse.

"Lucie, show this lady what you have there." The old woman pointed to the purse. "Then show her a finished one."

Lucie held up the small cloth purse and grabbed a completed one, holding both for comparison.

"Lovely work, Lucie, tight and close stitches." Yvette complimented the child and turned to the old woman. "Is this what you'd like me to do?"

"No, Lucie finishes the purses. You'd stitch the linen liner inside the purse." She answered with a grin.

"Ah, I see." She eyed the purses' quality. "How much do you pay for sewing the linings, might I ask?"

"Halfpence each. It's more than others give. You can start today if you're a good sewer." The woman squinted again at Yvette, her eyesight for making purses herself had weakened many years earlier. "Take a seat here and show me." She handed her an open piece of linen and a needle with thread.

Yvette's shoulder drooped as she sat and wove the thread in and out of the material. Her debt to Madam Goubert had now forced her into menial cottage work, the lowest of any. When she finished, she showed it to her new boss.

"Yes, that's good enough. I pay at the end of each month and expect you to finish at least twenty-five a day. Lucie will inspect them." The woman reached behind her. "Here's a bolt of fabric. Cut pieces to shape first until you have as many as you'll need today. Then start sewing."

Yvette introduced herself to them and told them where she lived, not far from Spitalfields. Wanting to impress, she worked fast and accurately. The three chatted as they worked and Madame Donnet often dozed off.

As the sun set, Lucie told her to stop and gathered the purses they had finished, put them in a basket, and wrote a count in a ledger. Yvette left for home, feeling that regardless of the humble work, she had started to pay off her debt.

"Where were you? It's not often I get home first." Abraham laughed when she entered their kitchen.

"Working." Yvette smiled proudly.

His eyes popped. "You've found a position with a bookseller?"

"No. I'm sewing purses in Spitalfields." She winced.

"Spitalfields? When did this happen?" He frowned. "You know how I feel about Spitalfields."

She shook her head. "Don't worry. It's not in a bad area and near a main road. A Huguenot offered me the job and I took it. I was tired of looking for booksellers."

"What's the pay?" He tipped his head, expecting poor compensation for her labor.

"A shilling a day. That sounds awful, I know, but the work is easy, although I suppose my fingers and eyes will hurt after a full day." She smirked and added, "I'll be able to pay Madame Goubert back in five or six months."

For the next month, Yvette got to know Lucie and Madame Donnet better. Both were Huguenots, although the old lady had been born in France and fled the persecutions decades earlier. Lucie had been born in London but her mother had died giving birth to her. Every night, her father, Jacques, came to escort the child through the somewhat seedy neighborhoods to their home not far from Yvette's.

When they learned that Yvette was Catholic, none held it against her. In certain areas of Spitalfields, Huguenots beat Catholics they found. Such was the animosity they still held for being tyrannized, hunted, and brutalized in France earlier, and still ongoing there. Lucie's father, however, also held no old grudges. He appeared a somewhat stern man, although good-looking and the same age as Yvette.

One evening as they left their workplace, Yvette, Lucie, and Jacques noticed a small mob in the street not far away. The shouting and jeering showed them to be anti-French rioters who in a fit of patriotic zeal, had come into Spitalfields to terrorize the French living there.

"We'll have to take side streets over to Bishopsgate. There are more constables and we can get home that way." Lucie's father pointed to a narrow alley that led away from the Spitalfields Market area where the brutes had gathered.

As he said this, four of the ruffians spotted them turning down the alley and came trailing. Yvette and Lucie ran ahead while Jacques followed to protect them if the men should overtake them.

"Hurry! Faster! They're gaining," Jacques cried, his eyes steady on the chasers. "Down this street!" They made a quick turn onto another cobblestone lane that went toward Bishopsgate Road.

"There! There!" shouted one of their pursuers, stalking them down the new route.

They stayed ahead and zigzagged their way until they exited the maze between flat-houses and found themselves on the broad, heavily-used Bishopsgate Road. The three turned southwest and slowed.

"Get them—over here!" the shout echoed. One of the pursuers had spotted them again.

"Run!" shouted Yvette, her heart throbbing and pulling Lucie along as they threaded their escape around passersby, looking for a constable as they ran.

It dawned on Yvette that they were not far from Madame Goubert's house and she led the others off Bishopsgate Road and down a posh boulevard. Certainly no ruffians would dare follow, she thought.

As they approached her friend's house, Yvette looked back and spied the four men standing far away, afraid to chase them further into a wealthy neighborhood.

"It is best if we stop at my friend's home where we're sure to be safe." Yvette smiled encouragement to them.

The three, sweating and out of breath, climbed the steps and Yvette knocked on the door. In minutes, the group found themselves in the parlor describing their adventure to Madame Goubert.

"Dreadful! What can we French do to stop such madness?" Madame Goubert's eyes rolled. They spoke in French the entire time and drank tea.

Lucie had never been in such a richly appointed home and her glances darted around the room from the fancy brass candleholders to the beautiful upholstered furniture and paintings. The threat of the chase had already left her mind.

"Lucie, would you like a pastry?" Madame Goubert winked at the young girl's father, pretending she didn't know the answer.

"Yes, thank you," Lucie answered with a wide smile. "You have a beautiful home, Madame Goubert."

"One that needs a child like you to help fill it, I'm afraid," she answered, shaking her head. She motioned for the maid and told her in English to bring sweet rolls.

Jacques, who had remained mostly silent until then, spoke. "I'm very curious, madam, how long have you lived in England?" His smile could warm anyone's heart and he leaned toward the hostess.

"I arrived not long before the previous war, back in '38. My uncle, a clock maker, had done well for himself here. He died and left everything to me. At just eighteen at the time, I moved from Quimper in Brittany into this house." She smiled broadly, candid with the handsome man. "Were you born here?"

"I'm French, also, from near Rennes. My father was a designer who brought us here in '35. We're Huguenots." He grinned and shrugged. "We had to leave."

Madame Goubert's brows rose up as she smiled. "A designer? What do you do, Jacques?"

"I've carried on the tradition, I suppose. I paint designs on bellows. Sometimes, though, I emboss patterns onto the leather."

Then Yvette noticed the way they stared at one another. Their eyes sparkled when they addressed each other and glanced often at the other's physique. She decided to simply sit back and let it happen. God knows, she thought, my poor friend has waited long enough for someone!

That evening at home, she explained what had transpired, expecting Abraham to be upset over the rogues who had chased them.

"Those mobs can appear anywhere, so it'd be unfair for me to chide you on working in Spitalfields. I'm relieved Jacques helped get you out of the trouble. Perhaps, though, you should accompany Jacques and his daughter to and from work each day." His serious face then turned into a smiling one and he added, "Well, I believe your debt may result in something more than just a financial repayment. Perhaps Madame Goubert will pocket something far better than just your eight pounds in a few months." They both grinned.

Shipmates and Stalemates

The *Renown* had put out in the vanguard of the fleet as one of eight frigates of the squadron of ships of the line, bomb ketches, and transports. Mackenzie kept an eye on the horizon, his frigate leagues in front of the others, often returning to them to report sails or land ahead.

After a crossing of seven weeks to the Windward Islands, the fleet dropped anchor in the clear blue British waters of Carlisle Bay off Barbados on January 3, 1759. Commodore Moore gathered the captains together and announced Martinique, after resupplying, as their first descent target. The French colony provided major profits for France, exporting the white gold—sugar—and even coffee and indigo back to its motherland. Other islands in the West Indies also presented excellent targets for Pitt's plans for colonial expansion and to cripple France's economy.

Soon after, many of the 800 marines and 3,600 infantry on the ships under the command of Major-Generals Hopson and Barrington began to suffer from diseases: yellow jack, scurvy, typhus, and even smallpox.

Mackenzie told his boatswain and ship's surgeon, "Send ashore those ill men to recuperate and to prevent spreading the disease on board. They're wretched and need fresher airs than the hold's putrefaction. Just their moaning takes the heart out of the healthy."

"I fear, sir, that half the marines on board have taken to chills and fevers. Some can barely stand." The surgeon wiped his sweaty brow after coming up from the hold's heat. "They'll have a better chance to survive in hospital than on these noxious vessels."

Crewmen lowered longboats and the first fifteen of the sickest men debarked for the port's hospital. Mackenzie and the surgeon went with them to make arrangements and direct their care.

As the sick men trudged from the dock in the stifling hot sun, Commodore Moore approached from the opposite direction along the quayside road.

"Captain Mackenzie," the commodore growled, "what leave of senses strikes you to send these men on liberty?"

"Sir? These are the infirmed from my ship. They'll need care in port to serve us later for the descents." Mackenzie pointed to the obviously fevered, sickly sailors.

"Infirmed? They are walking, Captain Mackenzie. They look not afflicted to a great degree. Get them back to their ship. A seaman who can walk is a seaman who can work." The commodore continued on his way to his ship without a moment's pause.

"Sir, if that is not the stupidest order I've ever heard," the surgeon whispered to Mackenzie after the commodore left.

"Aye, and one that will kill half of the poor buggers. It may also kill my healthy crew as well." Mackenzie stood thinking, then smirked, and added. "Perhaps we can comply but yet prevail. We shall return to the ship."

The gang of ailing marines and sailors turned around and hobbled their way back to the boats.

Once the men climbed onto the *Renown,* Mackenzie addressed them. "Men, you heard the commodore. Only those who cannot walk may go ashore to the hospital. Who among you cannot this moment do so?" He raised his eyebrow, grinning.

The men looked at one another, the cleverest getting the gist. "Aye, sir. Of sudden, I cannot," said a sailor. Then each repeated the phrase until every man agreed he felt too unwell to put one foot in front of the other.

"Surgeon, pick seamen to carry these *infirmed* men on stretchers to the hospital." Mackenzie chortled. He believed in total obedience to a superior's commands—when rational.

A daily litter-carrying party transferred the newly bedridden men to the hospital as the sickness spread. Within a week the ship's epidemic tapered off until none came down with the chills. At that time, some of the sick crew, nursed with fresh meats, fish, fruits, clean water, and care, began to arrive back to the ship on the mend or cured of their maladies.

On every ship of the fleet, men returned to duty, although they lost almost ten percent of their marines to the pestilence. The commodore, now with a sound complement of seamen to begin the first descent, sailed January 13 for Martinique.

At dawn two days later, the squadron made for Port Royal and late that afternoon entered the bay. *Le Florissant,* a large French ship of the line carrying seventy-four cannons, and the frigate *la Bellona* had anchored beneath the port's citadel. Safe under the longer-range guns, they commenced discharging their weapons as the British closed.

"Not much of a reception for us, Lieutenant Shelly. I expected more ships in harbor. Although there may be more hidden land gun positions that haven't begun firing at us yet." Mackenzie peered through his glass at the coast. He glimpsed down at the lieutenant's hands holding the railing. The knuckles were whitened from the tight grasp.

He needed to soothe the young man's fears. "Most of their fire will target our larger warships that are positioned closer. Quite likely, we'll see little damage and no losses of men in this one."

The lieutenant's shoulders immediately eased and his hands went to his sides. "Aye, Captain, the citadel's blasts can't reach us this far out. But if we try to make a landing, the marines will be in peril." The lieutenant frowned.

Mackenzie remembered how every battle had frightened him when he began as a new officer, too. He'd have to occupy the lieutenant's mind with something besides fear.

"It's too late for an assault with troops today. The commodore will wait until the morrow." He placed his spyglass to his eye again as a signal flag raised. "He's signaling us to begin the bombardment on the port. Order the gun captains to open up on the citadel when we get closer. I want you to direct the starboard guns' fire on the lowest level of battlements. Hop to it, Lieutenant!"

The *Renown* drew within range and a volley thundered as her nine-pounders belched shot. Soon the bay filled with powder smoke as the ships returned volleys of cannonballs at the gun defenses on the shore, and the clamor of the battle grew.

As night's darkness crept across the sky, the cannonades slacked off and then stopped. Minimal damage had ensued to either side with few lives lost. The citadel, high upon a hill, domineered over the harborage and suffered minor battering. Without indications of silencing any of the shore batteries, Commodore Moore elected to move the fleet up the coast to Point Negro, three miles away at the beginning of the bay.

At daybreak the *Renown* joined two large warships in an assault on a small fort upon a hill. In the thick growth down near the shore, another gun emplacement brought metal upon the vessels with four cannons.

"We'll never get in close enough to assault the fort until we destroy those guns on the shore." Mackenzie nodded toward the smoke floating on the breeze from the half-hidden guns. All three ships targeted the mounded earthworks with over sixty cannons in total. The ground absorbed most of the iron until one hit their magazine. It exploded in one violent upheaval of earth and the redoubt fell silent.

"Now concentrate our aim along the tree line with grapeshot to push back any infantry that could repulse the landing, Lieutenant Shelly. It's where the marines will need to beach to attack Fort Negro."

Every order the captain gave instilled more confidence in the inexperienced officer, an attitude he'd need to captain his own ship some day. To Mackenzie, it likened to the slow process of polishing a stone into a gem. With such a fine lad, he enjoyed every minute.

Two hours later, the invasion force in long boats moved steadily landward with seamen dipping oars in unison behind the huge *Cambridge,* an eighty-gun flying the commodore's flagship pennant, leading the way. All the ships now focused their fire on Fort Negro, overlooking and shelling the slow-moving craft.

Only a few hundred yards from the shore, the *Renown* showered iron on the fort's defensive timber walls. The larger ships' pelting tore down parts of its stockade with their heavier cannonballs.

"Sir, the troops are ashore to the right! See?" The lieutenant pointing, called his attention to the first to land on the island. Mackenzie smiled, tickled by the young officer's enthusiasm.

Mackenzie's eyes widened, wondering. "It looks as though there are no French troops to stop them from debarking. Curious. Have we caught them asleep?" Soon, however, the cracking discharges of muskets came from the dense woods.

As more boats made it to the shoreline, flashes in the trees attested to hidden enemy infantry opposing them. Within two hours, the entire mass of troops had leapt onto the sand and moved up into the green hills toward Fort Negro, pushing back the French defenders.

The marines and infantry climbed up and attacked the fort, and reaching it, found it abandoned, and burned it. Their brigades reformed and the 4,800 men now marched into the jungle southward toward Fort Royal. As night fell, they formed a square and set up camp between two ravines.

"Looks as this may be an easy descent, Captain." The lieutenant grinned. "So little has challenged their progress."

"Perhaps, but it will be the first. We paid a dear toll at the villages on our way to Saint-Malo. They may have withdrawn their men to St. Pierre and Fort Royal. I'm sure the commodore would agree we must be very cautious in thinking the rest will fall as swiftly. Enemy troops might be behind every tree the closer we get to the port. The citadel is well fortified and anyone can guess the number of French regulars there." Moist from sweat in the warm evening air, his furrowed brow informed the lieutenant of Mackenzie's concern.

Commodore Moore proposed to land heavy guns ashore on the point beneath the Fort Negro ruins and haul them overland to attack Fort Royal, a mere four miles. However, General Hopson informed him of the impossibility of moving the cannons through the thick vegetation and steep terrain. That night, pestering raids by French colonists and soldiers disrupted the sleep of the British troops and wounded many.

As the sun's rays broke above the horizon, General Hopson called for another council of war on the *St. George*. He suggested taking artillery ashore nearer the citadel and that the commodore begin a bombardment at the same time. But the winds and currents moved against such a tactic. The commodore and generals agreed to cease the advance and instead to proceed downwind to a larger town.

"Lieutenant Shelly, we'll strike at St. Pierre next instead of Port Royal. The elements play against us." Mackenzie shuffled across the deck, already worn out by the muggy heat of the morning. "The commodore has ordered the troops back to the ships. Why the infantry doesn't attack the citadel in force is beyond me, even without a barrage. They secured a good position but must now withdraw. With over 4,000, we surely outnumber the French if we assaulted them. The citadel sits so high that a ship bombardment couldn't destroy it in either case."

Mackenzie took issue with the logic of a withdrawal after losing a hundred men already to take just Fort Negro, an insignificant achievement. The real goal centered on taking the capital or St. Pierre, and he expected huge losses.

The marines marched back to Point Negro and re-embarked onto the ships by late afternoon.

No gunfire disturbed that night's stillness. "Tomorrow should determine our chances. If St. Pierre falls, then so will Port Royal." Lieutenant Shelly leaned against the deck rail peering off toward the flickering lights of the ship lanterns.

"Indeed. We have yet to see their real strength. By mid-day we shall know if St. Pierre is well defended." Mackenzie remembered his younger self every time Lieutenant Shelly's comments showed progress in martial strategies. The lieutenant's father sank with his ship years before, and Mackenzie noticed more than once the impressionable officer's eyes hinted at adulation of his captain.

With the first sunbeams, a lee shore wind guided the fleet to the bay near St. Pierre. The *Rippon*, a sixty-gun, moved close in to still a small redoubt, accompanied by two bomb ketches, firing upon the town. Forty merchant ships sat before the town under the port's protective guns of four additional cannon emplacements scattered along the shore and hills. The artillery and muskets targeted the *Rippon*, unable to move away because of the shoreward breeze.

Half a league from the harbor, the *Renown* had dropped anchor with the rest of the fleet. "The *Rippon* is in danger, Lieutenant. She has no leeway and can't withdraw. She's taking hits from shore."

"What can her captain do, sir? His options are few." Lieutenant Shelly watched as the enemy shots fell upon the vessel, unable to sail away.

"The commodore will either have us raise anchors and attack in force or send help to her to tow her away," replied Mackenzie.

Soon after they spoke they spied boats lowered and rowing toward the *Rippon*. Within an hour they hauled the ship back out of harm's way.

"Sir, the commodore's signal requests you for another gathering." The lieutenant had spent the entire day on deck in command and summoned Mackenzie from his cabin.

"Ah, now perhaps we'll have a go again at Fort Royal... finally!" Mackenzie grabbed his hat and boarded his little gig for a row to the *Cambridge*.

The officers at the meeting stood about in the commodore's great cabin as the generals discussed the difficulties they'd encountered during the descents. Commodore Moore recapped the defenses the enemy possessed and ended by offering to hear the captains.

The commodore looked up from his maps to the assembly. "What do you gentlemen contend to be our best move?"

A few suggested attacking St. Pierre again, although most advocated the situation warranted another landing and assault on Port

Royal. Commodore Moore listened attentively and fell silent for a few moments.

"Men, we have made a brave and costly incursion on the French positions here in Martinique. We hold the power to continue more descents and cannonades to take either St. Pierre or Port Royal. Now, however, we must weigh a success here against additional losses from battle and persistent diseases, and losing the main objective of our expedition. Every day we dally in Martinique allows Guadeloupe, the greater goal, to better fortify itself as our crews and troops grow weaker. I have decided that we will depart for Guadeloupe without delay." The commodore then gave the fleet formation orders and dismissed the officers.

Mackenzie agreed with the commodore's strategy and reasoning, yet he recalled his discussions with Lord Fortrose over coming away empty-handed. France valued Martinique's commercial exports, though not as much as Guadeloupe's. Still, if the next descent failed, what criticism might befall Pitt in Parliament, as occurred after the descents at Saint-Malo and Cherbourg? A second failure could end his political standing.

The next morning, January 20, the ships sailed for Guadeloupe with the commodore, generals, captains, crews, and troops glum over not taking Martinique. Each hoped the enemy could not repeat at the next island the stiff resistance they had encountered at the last.

The geography of Guadeloupe, unlike others in the Lesser Antilles, comprises three main islands. The slightly larger one, Guadeloupe to the southwest, joins to Grande Terre, the second largest island, by a small spit of land. Marie Galante, a much smaller isle, lies off to the southeast from the others by about three leagues. The British eighty-five-ship squadron passed north of Dominica on January 21, 1759, and approached Guadeloupe the next day.

Two days after departing Martinique, Mackenzie sat in his cabin studying the chart of the islands with Lieutenant Shelly. "This descent is crucial to the entire expedition." Mackenzie's finger tapped his chin. "I assume the commodore intends to make an amphibious assault on the citadel at Basse Terre on Guadeloupe first while we still have the troop strength. That is the French's strongest position. Then we can move on to the isles of Grande Terre and Marie Galante.

"It's quite a shame that Martinique has slipped away from our control." Mackenzie rapped the chart with his knuckles and the lieutenant nodded. "I feel we should have made more effort there. Let's hope the commodore is more in the mood for a good, stiff fight at Guadeloupe."

Later, Mackenzie sat at his desk and penned a report to Lord Fortrose on the actions at Martinique.

> *My Most Esteemed and Honorable Lord Fortrose, Member of Parliament, Laird of Clan Mackenzie: Our descent on Martinique in January of this year was not cause for the jubilation we envisioned at outset. However, as my account will show, we accomplished much. The French, in great numbers, had fortified the island with many forts and redoubts to prepare for our arrival that hindered the advancement of our marines and infantry. Our first incursion, Point Negro, lay at one end of the bay overlooked by a small fort. We landed successfully, advanced, and took the fort. The thick jungle between this victory and the main citadel prohibited further progress. General Hopson re-boarded the troops, and we sailed to St. Pierre, making an assault upon the settlement. The winds being contrary to our intent and fevers afflicting our men, Commodore Moore abandoned further attacks at Martinique. The attacks on Fort Royal and St. Pierre, however, resulted in great destruction to their buildings, fortifications, and croplands with few casualties to our squadron or troops. And as at Saint-Malo, our efforts will greatly confound the enemy king. It is not for me to judge if more aggressive tactics should have been used to secure the island in its entirety, although many commanders in the fleet question the aforesaid disengagement. Commodore Moore will defend his decisions, as be his wont, with substantial reasons for withdrawing to sea in pursuit of a descent on Guadeloupe. I*

shall again report to you after the next campaign.

Your Most Humble and Obedient Servant, Capt. George Mackenzie, on the Renown, January 22, 1759.

At six o'clock that evening, the commodore held a meeting aboard the *Cambridge* to reveal his plans.

"Our spies have told us that they have added a few new cannons to the fortifications at Basse Terre. Still, only 47 citadel guns will face a total of 122 from our ships of the line bombarding it. We also will outgun the other four batteries ashore by over three to one. I shall pass out the ships of the line duty orders after the meeting." The commodore paced back and forth while delivering his assessment.

"Although illness still ravages our troops, an amphibious landing of healthy men should overwhelm the few French infantry stationed there. Ships of the line will take the front barrage position. Frigates will assist by relaying signals and providing shore barrages for our descents that will take place when Basse Terre is defenseless. Transports and stores ships will anchor abaft the squadron. We have every reason to expect a victorious outcome." Commodore Moore, resolute to prove his ability, discussed the order of disembarking the troops and the landing order. Few questions arose among the captains and the assembly ended within an hour.

When Mackenzie returned to the *Renown,* he envisaged this venture, unlike the previous, to be a triumph. "First, we'll bombard next to the *Woolwich* and then assist the amphibious landing on Basse Terre. The shoreline shouldn't be as difficult as Martinique's, allowing the troops access for a frontal advance on the citadel. Finally, Lieutenant, it appears we may take an island." Both he and Lieutenant Shelly were in high spirits with success lying before the fleet.

"The sooner we take Guadeloupe the more likely we shall head home. The devil take these islands, Lieutenant. Tell me, does your wife expect your return this year?" The same as the captain, the lieutenant dearly missed his young wife.

"Sir, I informed her that I would not return until next year at the soonest. It would be fortuitous if we returned before year's end." His eyebrows popped up at the thought of being home for the holiday.

Mackenzie also remembered how it took many missions before Alana had become used to his own absences. "Aye, and it may be so if we can readily force the governor to capitulate the colony. I cannot imagine a squadron this large lying idle for the whole of winter."

At half past seven the next morning, January 23, the commodore signaled the start of the mission. Within half an hour, the warships fully engaged shelling the town and Basse Terre's fortress. Likewise, the French artillery hotly responded. The citadel, on a high prominence above the settlement, directed its fire on the warships, like a treed fox snapping at a pack of hounds, with as little effectiveness overall.

"There, over there, Lieutenant Shelly!" Mackenzie pointed to four French artillerymen rolling a fieldpiece into a nearly hidden position on the shore to fire upon the *Woolwich.*

"All guns use grapeshot and barshot on that gun!" Lieutenant Shelly shouted to the gunners.

The shots from the *Renown* at once left the fieldpiece unmanned and seconds later the barshot destroyed the carriage and wheels, the muzzle now useless and pointing to the ground. Just then, the captain's attention focused on a new concern.

"Sails a point abaft the port beam!" The mainmast lookout had spotted white upon the horizon.

"Weigh anchor and signal the *Woolwich* we will reconnoiter the sails-up." Mackenzie worried that a French squadron might approach their unguarded rear.

After hoisting the anchor and setting sails, the breeze pushed the *Renown* seaward. She glided over the waves, speeding faster than any other in the fleet could. The vessels, four leagues distant, appeared small to Mackenzie in his spyglass.

"What comes?" Lieutenant Shelly called aloft while standing midship with the boatswain.

The lookouts eyed the sail configurations and path of the approaching ships. "Two squaresails, frigates maybe and two smaller!" And then another shouted. "British-rigged, sir!"

"Thank God." Mackenzie said to no one in particular near the quarterdeck rail. He looked down to his first officer below. "We'd have been in quite a spot if caught with our transports to the rear and our ships of the line leeward along the shore. Let's see who these fellows are, Shelly." A slight smile of relief lit Mackenzie's face.

An hour later and the four ships came closer to the *Renown*. Mackenzie identified one, still a league away, as his old *Amazon*. The other turned out to be a sloop, the *Spy*. Lagging behind trailed two small transports.

"Ahoy, Captain Norton!" Mackenzie shouted through his speaking trumpet across the water when they neared.

"Captain Mackenzie, we spied the smoke! Are you at Basse Terre?"

"Aye, the whole day, the towns afire!"

"We have more troops for you!" The *Amazon's* captain nodded to the vessels following.

"Good. Come join our spit-roast!" Mackenzie laughed and pointed to the rising columns of smoke from the burning port.

When they joined the fleet late in the afternoon, most of the shelling had just ended, and the small settlement lay in ruins. Scarcely a building remained upright and the rum and sugar in vats, barrels, and warehouses burned furiously. The cannonade of relentless shelling had lasted over five hours and stilled the enemy cannons except for those at the citadel. Two British ships, damaged severely, had withdrawn from their positions. The *Rippon* had grounded and took a dreadful bashing until two warships relieved her and destroyed the nearby fortification that had mauled her.

As the early evening of the tropics set on them, two bomb ketches continued their shelling of the citadel. The other ships' cannons went still for the night.

In the morning light, the town, once a gleaming settlement of white homes and workplaces, now scarred the shore with blackened, smoking timbers poking skyward. The walls of the citadel, although now silent, showed little signs of damage; it bothered Commodore Moore. General Hopson, too, feared the French waited for the British landing to unleash a fury of body-shredding grapeshot.

They paused until mid-afternoon and when neither gunfire nor any signs of life appeared, the commodore rose flags to begin the descent.

By five o'clock, thousands of troops landed just north of the town along a sandy beach near a destroyed battery. The infantry led the march along the beach toward Basse Terre with the marines flanking them nearest the jungle. Expecting fire from the heavy growth or citadel, they approached the devastated wreckage at a slow, cautious pace.

Entering the settlement, they discovered it abandoned and scaled the rocks toward the stronghold. The feared resistance never came. They found the citadel empty with its cannons spiked, and the Highlanders raised the British colors. An occasional shot rang out from the thick sugarcane fields as defenders tempted the British to enter. One squad of men, led by an overzealous sergeant, entered the thick stalks of sugarcane, only to be wiped out to the man.

Orders from General Hopson said to camp in the town, guard the citadel, and patrol along the shore. Even so, no enemy remained to surrender the port or Guadeloupe. The island's governor had retreated to a plantation far from the port, expecting relief from France to save his isle.

Days later, the general sent a delegation to propose surrender terms to the governor. But the senior official defied the offer, clinging to hope. Guadeloupe's French infantry had bivouacked inland with artillery on a high, unassailable precipice overlooking a river. French colonists staged hit-and-run attacks on patrols. The island, invaded but not yet taken, still posed stiff resistance.

Over the next few weeks, General Hopson played a waiting game, expanding their territory each day until a five-mile radius from the beach lay under his control. During this time, more men became ill with diseases. Nearly 1,500 names filled the sick list, almost a quarter of the troops and seamen. General Hopson sent 600 ailing men on transports to Antigua, not expecting many to survive either the voyage or the hospital.

"Sir, this is insane. We're rotting under the tropical sun and foul airs. Men are losing morale as well as their health. Without a purposeful plan of action, the attrition will defeat us, not the enemy!" Lieutenant Shelly expressed his point in a serious and untempered voice. "We must do something to save our crew." His face reddened with the impassioned plea.

"I'm aware of the situation." Mackenzie glowered. He hated over-cautious army generals as much as he detested cowardly naval commanders. "If General Hopson cannot attack from his current position, he should re-embark and land where his men can damage the enemy. However, he's the army, Lieutenant, we're the navy and have little say over what he should do. We must wait." The lieutenant's passion impressed Mackenzie. That quality instilled action in men and he saw the lieutenant as almost ready to be an outstanding commander. He held himself blessed to take part in training the young officer.

Guadeloupe had neither been conquered nor surrendered and the standoff took a toll on the British. Commodore Moore and General Barrington begged General Hopson to move against the French and clinch the success of their expedition. Yet General Hopson, now ill himself, refused to advance inland.

The frustrations triggered the commodore to create an alternative action of his own and called a meeting of his best captains to put forth an offensive strategy.

"Gentlemen, the army is making little progress in the colony's surrender and that requires *we* force the colonial governor into submission. I have drawn up plans to attack and descend on Grande Terre on the other side of Guadeloupe. You six captains, under the command of Captain Harman, will hasten to Fort Louis with tenders and two bomb ketches to attempt a landing and capture the port. Reports say it is lightly defended, although the enemy may have reinforced the position since our invasion. Take care. The entire expedition to the West Indies may well hinge on the success of the troops you carry if it impels the French into surrender." He then gave specific instructions and dismissed them.

Mackenzie walked straight to Lieutenant Shelly on the quarterdeck when he arrived back on the *Renown*. "Thank heavens, Lieutenant, we're at last venturing something. We'll be departing for Fort Louis on Grande Terre by the end of day. Ours will be the only frigate with the ships of the line, ketches, and tenders. We'll go ahead to scout the coast. Our prayers have done their work, prepare to get underway."

71

By evening the small squadron maneuvered windward southeast out to sea for the trip to Fort Louis, less than forty miles away. Both strong currents and winds fought their progress, and tropical flows pushed every ship leeward.

The morning after they arrived, the *Renown* ventured toward Fort Louis, sounding the bottom as she approached for those who followed on a lee wind. When half a league from the fort, the French sent shots her way as the trailing ships moved to within cannon distance and Captain Harman ordered the barrage to begin.

"Guns fire as you bear!" the lieutenant called to the gun captains. Lieutenant Shelly joined Mackenzie on the quarterdeck. An occasional iron from the fort punched a hole in their sails, but overall the attack progressed well and without great danger or harm to their ships.

Lieutenant Shelly stood ten feet away and pointed landward. "Sir, it appears that…"

Over the clamor of cannons and shouting men, Mackenzie detected a sudden whoosh and thud that interrupted the sentence. He let out a small gasp as Shelly's head burst into a pink cloud. Bloody tissue splattered behind, covering the deck and railing with a cannonball's grisly proof of a direct hit to the face. The headless body slowly crumpled upon the deck, blood pouring out and darkening the planks.

The captain, although long conditioned to the horror of battle, turned away, and placed his hand on the mizzen mast to steady himself. He had erred by allowing himself to become attached, and would now pay the price with months of sorrow.

The captain then straightened his back and composed himself. "Midshipman Thomas!" He called to the gun deck for the youth. "Fetch three men to remove the lieutenant's body from up here, and bring buckets and mops to wash down the deck!" His command, emotionless, offered no evidence of sympathy or sadness. A commander's rank demanded control at all times, his stoic bearing hiding his deep remorse for his first lieutenant.

After six hours, just as at Basse Terre, the cannonade had destroyed the village and silenced most of the fort's guns. Then the landings began and a large wave of marines and Highlander infantry rushed upon the beach toward the French entrenchments. Vastly outnumbered and hearing the Scottish Highlander war screams in a full, basket-hilted Claymore sword charge, the defenders ran from their positions and the fort into the jungle. Captain Harman stationed hundreds of men to hold the ground, claiming triumph.

Two weeks later, with no movement to retake Fort Louis, Captain Harman left troops there and sailed the warships and tenders back to Basse Terre to rejoin the squadron.

Still grieving his first officer's death, Mackenzie replaced him with a junior lieutenant and joined the officers' meeting on the commodore's ship two days after returning.

Commodore Moore stood stern-faced in his cabin, a dark shadow, back-lit by the gallery windows. "Our recent capture of Fort Louis has placed the French in a poor position. General Barrington is scouting the shore for additional places to land troops to burn villages and homes. We are destroying everything we can to force the governor to give up the island. Crops, livestock, homes and any means to produce commerce get the torch or sword."

Mackenzie watched as the commodore walked back and forth, laying out his plans. The occasional light rays striking the hairs of his wig from behind made the Commodore Moore appear with a halo, Archangel Michael cleaving the heathen.

"Another attack inland might put a stop to their obstinacy, although General Hopson still opposes any advances and contends we must wait for the French governor to counterattack our positions." The commodore shook his head vigorously. "General Barrington and I do not agree with that strategy. Attacks against our men from hidden locations are depleting our patrols. Illnesses also continue to plague the troops and we now have 1,800 either sick or dead at present, over a quarter of our men!

"The entire expedition rests on the shoulders of General Hopson at the moment. Naval officers should refrain from sending any sailors to shore, transfer the ill to hospital ships, and stand ready to strike the enemy if the general changes his mind."

The stalemate cleared two days later when General Hopson died of his fever. General Barrington took command of the army but could find few healthy troops. He dispersed the men to live in separate huts to stop the epidemic in the close-quartered tent camps.

Then, on March 1, he garrisoned troops in Fort Saint-Charles on Basse Terre and embarked his remaining troops onto the transports to sail back to Grande Terre.

The *Renown* joined the warships once more and lumbered days later to Fort Louis. General Barrington, upon arriving, received bad news from Commodore Moore; the French had anchored at Martinique with a large fleet under Admiral Bompar.

Mackenzie felt they wouldn't go out to meet the enemy. It wouldn't make sense to the commodore to lose more men and possibly his ships to meet the foe in battle. He reflected on the commodore's tepid approach to action at Martinique and failure to subdue it. Commodore Moore moved like a chess player at heart, not one to be bold for the sake of glory or gambling, he mused.

The next day a council of war disclosed exactly what the commodore planned. He withdrew the fleet to Dominica, just nine leagues south, between Guadeloupe and Martinique. General Barrington's troops pressed on with the invasion of Guadeloupe in hopes of a French surrender. The ships departed and anchored at Prince Rupert's Bay in Dominica.

Commodore Moore called Mackenzie into his cabin for special instructions three weeks later. "Captain, I am transferring you to the Jamaica station at once. The *Renown* is our fastest ship and you'll transport Colonel Haldane, the island's governor, back to Port Royal. This must be done tomorrow, winds permitting. The governor must quickly prepare Jamaica against Admiral Bompar's fleet. Our possessions in the West Indies are now in danger."

"Yes, sir, in good haste," Mackenzie replied. Inside, he fumed at the orders. It meant when the squadron returned to England at the end of the season, he'd stay in Jamaica with the disease and heat, far from his home.

The next morning, he shipped out with the currents and breezes to the west, carrying the governor.

The Loss and the Gain

Louis de Saint-Alouarn, as an *enseigne de vaisseau,* carried out the duties as *le Défenseur's* newest junior lieutenant with meticulous attention after leaving Brest. The admiral's lofty acclaim of his father François had obliged Louis to work harder. Until then, he regarded his actions as an independent measure of his own competency. But now, he couldn't disappoint the senior officers who compared him to his celebrated father.

His earlier baptism in combat aboard *l'Espérance* off the foggy and berg-filled North Atlantic was more than most cadets experienced on a first voyage. Nevertheless, with so much to learn of naval sea life, it made his quick promotion from cadet to lieutenant premature in his mind. Throughout the winter month of February 1759, Louis spent every waking moment struggling to glean knowledge. This intensified education and his superiors' expectations strained him to the point of illness. Many nights he tossed for hours trying to sleep as the ship pushed across rough swells in the dreary winter's Bay of Biscay.

As February passed into March, the westerly winds and fast currents off the Canary Islands pushed the fleet toward the West Indies on fair seas and good weather. Louis's stress lightened, and he enjoyed his watches in the clear skies and warm latitude. The daily sailors' songs relieved him of his tenseness. Light squalls on the balmy ocean provided everyone with a welcomed diversion, and fresh drinking and bathing water.

Almost two months after leaving Brest, with stunsails reaching outward to catch the breezes, the warships neared their goal: the British squadron that threatened their possessions in the Lesser Antilles. Louis had become friends with another junior lieutenant during the voyage, Pierre Jacques de Kerespèr. His new mate had graduated from the naval officer cadet school in Brest several years before Louis had entered.

Pierre and Louis stood on the forecastle peering through spyglasses at a distant green dot on the line splitting the sky from sea.

"The sail master said it's Saint-Lucia. He must have the eyes of a hawk to make out any details." Louis shook his head in disbelief.

Pierre took down the glass from his eye, chortling. "He's usually correct. God knows how he does it. Crewmen say he smells the difference. Once we were in the thickest fog I'd ever seen and he claimed Ushant was just off our starboard. It was." He twirled his finger in the air by his head. "This nautical lore must have your head swimming, though. But you'll get used to it." He had taken to Louis as his mentor.

"It keeps me in constant awe. Off Labrador I saw a berg that appeared out of a mist. It was enormous and had swirling ice crystals of light around it that mesmerized the entire crew." Louis turned to his new friend and smiled. "The sea is fascinating. Just observing the sunrises and sunsets are worth the storms and damp chills."

Pierre's eyebrow rose. "And battles?"

"Well, those are another unfortunate price we pay to our watery mistress." Louis's face had a drawn expression. "When I recall the action on l'Espérance, I always block out the dead men and the amputated parts I witnessed, and just try to remember the pleasant sights. Although I still dream about the gore… if anything keeps me from a life at sea, it will be the butchery and sounds of war." He rubbed his eyes as if it might erase the horrific memories.

"Yet, it must be. Or else, we'd fall under the enemy's sword." Pierre put away the spyglass and turned to walk aft.

Louis, frowning, joined him. "Let's hope the British fleet sank in a storm and never reached the islands."

"Too soon for the hurricanes, Louis." Pierre slowed his steps and looked directly at him. "Instead of dooming the British fleet, pray for the salvation of our own. Waves will come towering over the bow in a month when the season begins."

Below they heard orders shouted to the helmsmen to steer two points to port. *Le Défenseur* slowly curved away from the far island until it was further to the north of them with the fleet following her lead.

Louis speculated. "Looks as if Grenada, south of Saint-Lucia, will be our next port." His inexperience and superficial judgement surfaced once more.

"I don't think so. With so many sick men on board and being low on supplies, the admiral will probably head for Martinique. That port is big enough to handle all of our fleet's ships and men. The Grenada station is too small." Pierre's knowledge had provided Louis with a wealth of tutoring over the weeks. "Besides, Martinique is a bigger target for the enemy, not the smaller isles."

An hour later, the ships then bore further northward and away from both Saint-Lucia or Grenada, as a course for Martinique might require. Soon after, a Dutch merchant ship met up with them and detailed Commodore Moore's attempt to capture Martinique a month and a half earlier. He reported the enemy had bombarded both Port Royal and St. Pierre for two days, damaging many buildings and torching crops. Although outnumbered ten to one, the 300 French infantry and 100 colonists had defended the island against over 4,000 invaders. Six days after arriving, to the astonishment of civilians and military alike, the British had coasted away toward Guadeloupe.

Louis laughed when he heard, thinking the handful of Frenchmen had scared off the invasion force. He assumed the British to be cowardly, a much too simplistic conclusion.

"Don't gloat, my friend." Pierre cautioned. "If they left, they did it for a reason. Our foes have commanders who are just as intelligent as our own. More than likely the bravery of a few hundred defenders had nothing to do with why thousands did not prevail." Pierre's stern expression held Louis's attention. "Something far more urgent forced them, perhaps a shortage of supplies, or illness, or even hearing a false rumor. We shall never know."

With Pierre's every comment, reprimand, or discussion, Louis learned more about martial tactics and sea life. He held his learned friend in higher regard every day.

The next afternoon, March 8, Admiral Bompar's squadron of French warships and transports arrived at Fort Royal in Martinique. Seamen carried the sick to the hospital and slaves lugged barrels of foodstuffs and water onto the anchored ships. Louis, who'd never seen so many shackled men in one place before, wondered if slavers had transported an entire nation from Africa to the island. As he and Pierre walked the streets in the harbor town, he felt out of place among the many creole and dark-skinned laborers who bustled in their trades. Thousands of them repaired the cannon damage to the buildings and even more labored in the sugar cane fields checkering the landscape. The sweet smell of boiling cane, wafting from the sugar factories, saturated the port.

Most of the sugar shipped to other countries, including England, and the plantations provided tax revenue to France. Rum, the most lucrative of its exports, traded in the English colonies and Canada, although never in France. The king had outlawed importing rum, a competing liquor to French-produced brandy.

The bay they sheltered in was almost five miles wide at its greatest but mostly marshy. To the north lay Mount Pelee, Louis's first glimpse of a volcano that sparked a fear in him, despite being dormant for hundreds of years.

Admiral Bompar sent men into town to help restore its forts and earthworks. Most of his sailors, rested and fed nutritious foods, recovered from their diseases to rejoin their crews. Hundreds of old buccaneers, who had ravaged the foes of France decades earlier, arrived to volunteer to save Guadeloupe. Weeks passed without action against the enemy, then with everything ready and favorable winds, the fleet departed for Guadeloupe on April 23. After a day at sea, Admiral Bompar called a council of war among his captains upon his flagship.

"As we've seen," the admiral began, "Commodore Moore's fleet is engaged in destroying or interrupting our commercial trade here in the West Indies. He has gathered thirteen ships of the line, adding more to those that left England. Since we are but nine, it diminishes the chance of a sea victory." His concerned look conveyed the dire circumstances the squadron faced. "We must avoid an open confrontation with the British." With too few cannons, their mission had now changed from offensive to defensive.

"Before leaving France, I requested two more warships and an additional two since then. We embarked without them although the admiralty promised to send them later. Until more vessels come to balance this mismatch, our operations will be to land men and munitions on the islands to assist in their defense. If our fleet can find protected harbors under fort guns, we may help their defenses in providing a naval wall of protection if attacked."

The situation dredged up memories of Louis's voyage on *l'Espérance* and how the British fleet had outgunned them at every turn. Louis grunted when he heard of the admiral's remarks after the meeting.

"I find our lack of daring frustrating." Louis frowned and stood with his hands on his hips.

Pierre grinned. "Although I agree, what admiral dares put his ships and men at risk? On a patrol a captain can afford to be gallant and chance the dangers to secure prizes and fame. He has only his ship to account for and the crew benefits from their pluck and boldness, rewarded by shares of the prize. Admiral Bompar's mission was more pointed: to save Martinique, Guadeloupe, and the other colonies from British hands. If King Louis learned that he lost ships engaging Moore's fleet while at a disadvantage, the king would dismiss Admiral Bompar from his post. Versailles has demoted more than one admiral for less."

Louis stayed upset. "Yes, the political dangers are real, but I believe the strategic hazards for France are just as clear. The more the enemy keeps our navy impotent, the more we will lose in our colonies. It's a David and Goliath predicament and our commanders and admirals should commit to damaging the British wherever possible. We've won battles before when far greater odds were against us.

"Martinique stands as an example! The island's governor, seeing thousands more British troops invade than he had to defend, held out. They fought them off!" Louis's voice grew stronger. After years of British superiority at sea, he craved a great victory, or at the minimum, a sound repulsion of the invasions.

Pierre cocked an eyebrow and shrugged. "As I said before, Commodore Moore didn't know how many French protected the colony." To emphasize the point, Pierre rose his finger in objection. "The English generals may have feared more than what they saw. On the sea, it is obvious who has more guns and who has the wind and current advantages. There can be no ghost ships on open water to scare the enemy like the unseen number of snipers in the jungles on Martinique."

Louis smirked and clenched his fist. "So, shall we turn tail at every encounter with them?"

"No, of course not. But Bompar must execute precautions to put the mission goals first and not give in to a hasty decision that may doom them." He sided with Louis's aggravation and frustration, yet Pierre used logic and debate over bold hyperbole, passion, and assumptions.

His voice tempered, Louis let his thoughts move on to what all feared. "Last year they took the citadel at Louisbourg. The next step in their plan is Quebec, no doubt. Should we consider it lost already?"

"Quebec has sufficient troops garrisoned there. It will fall only at a substantial loss to the British if it does. We cannot supply them using our ships, however, and the lack of provisions may hinder their effectiveness." A concern Pierre often considered, and he pursed his lips.

"The same might occur now at Guadeloupe." Louis's thoughts compared the northern colonies to those in the Caribbean. "If British ships blockade the isle's ports, we won't be able to provide men and materials. It could fall."

Pierre frowned. "I'm afraid you're right. Let's hope we land on the islands before Moore takes them."

∞

A day and a half later, Admiral Bompar's squadron slipped north past the shores of Dominica on the little-used eastern seaboard and approached Guadeloupe. No warships blockaded the island, and the admiral remained confident they had arrived in time to save it.

Standing by the midship rail, Pierre grinned. "We're in luck, the enemy is nowhere in sight." He, like all onboard, relaxed.

"Perhaps the colony is still ours. Once our infantry and the buccaneers land, Moore will have a force to contend with," added Louis with a gleam.

Pierre smiled at the hopeful idea but added, "The only great threat might come if Moore's fleet intercepts us at sea. They could be on their way here right now...."

Louis peered out to see in his spyglass for the rest of the day for enemy warships. Everyone onboard thought the same, not knowing the British fleet faced opposing winds in Rupert Bay on the far west coast of Dominica and remained moored there.

The admiral feared that Commodore Moore's ships had harbored near Basse Terre on Guadeloupe. So, Bompar's fleet sailed to the other island, Grande Terre, and on April 27, dropped anchor not fifteen miles from Fort Louis by Sainte-Anne, a small fishing village. French marines, Swiss infantry, and Martinique buccaneers landed and marched to relieve Fort Louis.

"Lieutenant Saint-Alouarn and Lieutenant de Kerespèr, debark and join the troops as naval liaisons and take a code book to interpret our signal flags for the army." Louis's captain laughed. "And neither of you are to join in any ground assaults!"

The two arrived at the leading unit of army officers and general in charge of the column. It proceeded west on a dusty road toward Sainte-Anne. As they entered the town, a mounted French army officer met the group. He informed them that the governor had agreed to surrender Guadeloupe that very day. The officer rode to relay the terms to the settlements along the shore side.

Louis's head hung low. "Had Admiral Bompar not tarried in Martinique, we may have saved the island."

"Or if the admiral didn't wait for the other four ships of the line to arrive. Or if the winds were more to our favor in crossing. Or if after three months, Guadeloupe had held out for one more day." Pierre snickered. "You see, there were a thousand chances to avoid this outcome. We cannot now change any of them and this coincidence is just us noticing the intersecting time of events. Pay it no mind."

"So, what's to be done? Should the army march to recapture Fort Louis?" Louis's eyes opened wide. "I imagine that violates war protocol after proposing to surrender."

Pierre agreed as the troops marched into the village. The British had torched half of the houses and plundered the rest. Only a few residents had returned to their ruined homes from inland hideaways.

The general ordered the courier to make haste with a message for the governor to ask if he had signed any official capitulation documents yet or if he wanted them to attack. Two days later, a rider carried a response for the general. The governor refused to go back on his word to the British, nevertheless, he left the decision to attack up to the general.

A council met and decided the troops, buccaneers, and officers should return to the awaiting ships.

"This is a sad end to our expedition." Louis grimaced as Pierre joined him on deck.

"Yes, the king and ministers will have Bompar's head on a pike for it, I'm afraid." Pierre, like most, regretted the loss of Guadeloupe and shook his head. "Yet, we still must keep them from taking more colonies. They may return to Martinique. Saint-Domingue and Saint-Lucia may be next, or Grenada. I imagine the admiral will make for one of them."

Louis joined in the head shaking and then raised his eyes in thought. "Now that the rainy season is upon us and diseases are increasing, the British will also lose personnel. If they are experiencing the same rate of fevers, they're too under-manned to descend on any other islands."

Pierre liked it when Louis followed his thoughts further, using logic. It showed he could strategize instead of merely reacting. "Hmm, yes, I suppose. It's curious that they haven't one warship in the harbor near Fort Louis." Pierre paused at the oddity, and continued. "They know by now we've arrived in the islands. Why did Moore choose not to attack us? Does he fear getting caught up in a hurricane or us? We've been here days without seeing them."

Louis shrugged. "When we got back onboard, someone mentioned that one of their frigates spied us two days ago and bolted away, likely back to their fleet to reveal our whereabouts. Perhaps Moore's on his way right now." Almost by habit, Louis popped his spyglass to his eye and scanned the horizon.

The next day, Louis's fleet returned to Martinique, and for the following month, both the French and British squadrons eyed one another with frigates for movement but neither fleet stirred from its harbor. Then Admiral Bompar raised anchors and headed south to Grenada to deliver supplies, weapons, and men to prepare against any descents by Moore. At the end of June, he continued on to Saint-Domingue to do the same.

As the hurricane season grew in strength, one severe tropical storm sped across the Windward Islands and a hurricane hit the Gulf Stream with such ferocity it submerged the Dry Tortugas. One ship's captain dropped anchor during the storm. When the water receded, he discovered his anchor had lodged in the top of palm trees that had been below him. Both the French admiral and British commodore refrained from any aggression toward the other, fearful of the fast-changing weather.

By October 1759, Commodore Moore secured all of Guadeloupe and dispersed troops to other British colonies, much as Admiral Bompar had done. Their fleet then returned to England with Moore staying to monitor the French.

The encouraging report of the British fleet's departure for their homeland came also with distressing news: Quebec had fallen to the enemy. Louis's squadron was ordered home and sailed for Brest soon afterward.

ᘓᗢᗢᕽ

Mackenzie sat in his chair aboard the *Renown* at Port Royal, earnest in his desire to write a letter to Lord Fortrose, yet hesitated in committing to it. He twilled the quill pen between his fingers. The changing directions of the plume mimicked his predicament.

Commodore Moore took Guadeloupe, it was true. But he ignored many opportunities to assault the French at sea. Martinique ranked as a priority for descent and capture, but the commodore only tried halfheartedly to take it. Brigadier General Hopson held victory in his hand on Guadeloupe but failed to press against the enemy to attain surrender. These, he felt, made up the shameful truths he ought to write in his account.

On the other hand, if the population and Parliament exalted Moore as a hero, they'd see Mackenzie as a scandalmonger, and that might slight Pitt's efforts. To be honest in his opinions while unaware of the mood in England stayed his hand from penning a single word.

Procrastination was not a trait he presumed in himself. Mackenzie resolved, at times, inaction may be the best action. He laid the quill down and stepped topside.

The *Renown* stayed berthed in Port Royal for almost two months during the rainy season from October through November 1759. The storms formed and came in heavy sheets and fierce winds, keeping the ships anchored in the protective bays most of the late fall. When he cruised, the frigate's fouled hull slowed their movement and Mackenzie needed at least two weeks of dry weather to careen her bottom. Although most of his men remained healthy, he had lost six to yellow jack in the Lesser Antilles. Fevers still hit a few each week, but in the tropics, they considered that normal.

For a period the sky cleared, and the *Renown* put in to one of Port Royal's two careening docks. Tipping her sideways, slaves burned away the growths on her hull, scraped it clean, and applied coatings to protect it. After doing the same to the other side, the ship lay keel down again, and the crew and slaves reloaded the stores and cannons.

With the frigate regaining her speed and calmer waters returning, patrols started up again. Mackenzie was to cruise for smugglers and French warships with another ship under a Captain Maitland.

Before their first patrol together, a crewman rowed Maitland from his sloop, *Wager*, of twenty guns, to acquaint himself with the older captain.

Open gallery windows allowed the rare dry air to waft in as the two sat. "The *Renown* must have put up quite a fight when we took her," said Maitland, a taller and younger man by about ten years, and also a Scot.

"Aye, she did." Mackenzie knew nothing about him except he was the son of the Earl of Lauderdale and acted it. "Washington Shirley took her on the *Dover*. He followed her all night in the moonlight and captured her the next day."

"Captain Shirley, you say? I know of him. He's the one who constructed a sloop and rooked the navy to pay for it."

"What? A sloop, you say?" Mackenzie's eyes widened.

"Aye." Maitland leaned forward like a prattler over a fence. "It happened when Captain Shirley commanded the frigate *Mermaid* in the American colonies as I recall."

"I'd not learned of this." Mackenzie bent toward Maitland, his curiosity aroused.

"It's true. Years ago in Boston, Captain Shirley built a sloop, the *Nautilus,* to some outlandish design of his to use as his tender." Maitland stabbed the desk between them with his finger. "He forced vendors to charge all the outfitting and materials for the new ship to his *Mermaid's* refitting costs."

"Nae!" The brazen scheme made Mackenzie's mouth open and he shook his head. "What did the Admiralty do when discovered?"

Maitland's left eyebrow rose. "Captain Shirley had dismissed his light-fingered chicanery as a bagatelle to the admirals and said he intended to repay it later. His prestige with the navy being so great, they ignored issuing an official reprimand. Although I bet from then on they made careful checks of his accounts."

Mackenzie put his hand to his forehead in exasperation. "How do they expect us to respect our admirals in London when they allow such conspicuous fraud to go unpunished?" This tidbit validated his viewpoint that Washington was an unscrupulous and arrogant man, undeserving a rank of commander.

His surprise turned to indignation, and he frowned. "It turns my stomach to think of the efforts we responsible captains make to save the navy every shilling when others like Captain Shirley pump guineas like bilge water overboard with swindling."

"Aye, he's a rascal, that one. But he must be an able commander to snatch the *Renown* for our flock." Maitland grinned.

Be it his flagrant violation of the rules, his overbearing personality, or his dismissive regard for the value of others' property, Mackenzie couldn't pin down any one particular foible. Everything about Washington set him on edge.

Mackenzie believed in discipline and embraced guidelines and strict adherence to the official naval practices. Deviation from set rules fostered discord and confusion, ending in failure of objectives. He followed protocol with diligence and expected others to do likewise. Occasional minor infractions did not upset him, but dedication to a career required lockstep submission to its demands, unbound by personal sentiment, goals, or needs. The stability he felt by following these dedicated inclinations gave him a confident outlook on most matters.

A week later they patrolled together for the French fleet north of Saint-Domingue but separated after a storm. Maitland spied a fast-running Jamaica sloop heading east and gave the order to intercept. With an abetting wind and tranquil seas, he sped across the waves and was soon within hailing distance.

"Ahoy, heave to and be boarded!" Maitland was sure the ship was a smuggler with a load of sugar or rum.

"*Oui, oui.*" The captain of the old sloop nodded and waved, but changed his sails in an instant, wearing starboard and attempted to flee.

"Lieutenant, put a warning shot over him."

A cannon thundered and the ball skipped once on the water and slammed into the midships of the small sloop at the waterline.

"Good God, man, I didn't say to hit him!" Maitland frowned at the darkened hole.

The sloop's captain, afraid of more damages, reefed sails and hove to for boarding.

"Topsail to port!" A lookout called as they neared the sloop and Maitland spotted the billowed canvas of a warship approaching above the waves.

"Lieutenant, take four marines to the sloop. The other sail is likely the *Renown,*" Maitland pointed to the distant frigate, although a threat until he identified her. "Keep an ear for my call to return."

When the lieutenant reached the Jamaican sloop, he hurried to search for contraband.

"Captain Maitland, they've dropped off the load already and she's filled with empty rum barrels! But she's taking water fast from our shot! Can we get some of our carpenters here to help?"

"Get the crew off her, Lieutenant. Let her go under." Maitland waved his hand a few times toward the *Wager* to hurry the lieutenant back.

The smuggler screamed profanities in French over the loss of his sloop as he and his small crew boarded the launch. Maitland's sailors rowed them back to the *Wager.*

The British flag flew on the oncoming frigate, and spyglasses identified her as the *Renown*. By the time the sea rose to the top of the sinking sloop's gunwales, the *Renown* drifted close to the *Wager.*

From his quarterdeck, Mackenzie saw the sloop low in the sea. "Heard the cannon. Do you need help to save the sloop, Captain Maitland?"

"No, we'll let her go down. She's decrepit." He waved away the suggestion. "We're hunting whales, not mackerel."

Mackenzie turned away and frowned. Regulations stated they must take a seaworthy ship into port. A single shot hole could be easily repaired. Plus the crew could have received a share of its worth. His mouth twisted at the thought of Maitland disobeying orders and ignoring a financial gain for the crew.

That evening, Maitland called across to him. "This cruise hasn't netted anything worthwhile! Time to return together to Port Royal! I'll come aboard and we can plot the course… if you agree!"

Mackenzie shouted back, swallowing his pride once again at the demanding tone. "Aye, come!"

The younger officer had peerage rank over Mackenzie, who wasn't of noble Scottish Lowlander rank as the Maitlands from Edinburgh. Mackenzie was Highland Scottish and spoke Gaelic when needed, although he no longer wore the belted plaid or tartan truis at clan gatherings because of the new prohibition laws. And he still preferred bagpipes. Lowlanders like the Maitlands always had worn breeches, listened to chamber music with their noses in the air, and considered Highlanders uncivilized. It rubbed him wrong.

The two captains laid out the chart in the *Renown's* cabin, and sat to discuss their course for Jamaica.

"We can continue eastbound around Saint-Domingue and take the Mona Passage back to port. We might even run into a few more smugglers that way." Maitland smiled at the idea.

"Mona Passage will be four days more against the current. We're running short of water and foodstuffs now. It's too far going all the way around Saint-Domingue. Best we return by the Windward Passage. It's a direct route and the winds are in our favor." Though the captains had plenty to eat, the crews would be on hardtack and bad water taking the longer route, Mackenzie thought.

"We can ration. There are too many eddies and contrary winds along the Windward. Besides, big smugglers and French fleets use the Mona Passage."

At this time of year, the varying currents and opposing breezes between Cuba and Hispaniola were at a low along the Windward Passage, and Mackenzie realized Maitland knew this. Although Maitland was a new commander on the station, Mackenzie obliged his social superior, gritted his teeth, and agreed to the longer journey lasting past Christmas.

After an uneventful week passing south and west through the Mona Passage, the two patrol warships returned to Port Royal. The crews had suffered onboard, but their officers had not.

Heavy seas flowed as *le Défenseur* and Admiral Bompar's squadron neared the French coastline on a gray, cool November day in 1759. Louis and Pierre watched a British frigate shadow the ships all morning, but the size of the fleet staved off any opportunity for it to attack. Whenever their frigates ventured out to challenge her, the lone scout took flight, only to return later.

"She's hoping the rest of the enemy's blockade will meet with us so she can join." Pierre glanced east to the hazy thin gray-green stripe on the sea's edge—home.

"That gale sent their patrols away. She'll get the privilege of watching us make port, I believe." Louis's face lit up at the thought of arriving home. "We should put in by this evening, I imagine."

"Yes, you'll be stepping on Brest's quay stones within a few days, or maybe tonight if the admiral gives you leave. What will you do first?"

Louis smiled and needed no time to wonder. "Settle in at my family's place in town, eat a decent meal, and sleep in a soft bed until noon tomorrow."

"I'll rent a room at the hotel for mine. Ten months at sea transforms a man into a squid, wiggly legged and feeling as if always in motion. I need solid earth below me or I may soon grow gills." Pierre flapped his hands on the sides of his neck and laughed.

"Why stay there? Come to our house." Louis offered with a grin. "No one lives there except servants when we're at sea."

"Nice of you to offer and I accept. Your cook's food promises to be better than the hotel's!" Tilting his head, he gave a chuckle.

As they expected, no British warships blockaded the approach. On the Raz de Sein, the main channel, they saw no topsail ships. The entire squadron clustered and anchored to await pilots for the final route into the Bay of Brest.

Louis and Pierre waited on the poop deck, looking shoreward for the pilot to arrive. After an hour, a boat headed for *le Défenseur*. The pilot boarded, and walked straight to the quarterdeck.

He had a confident presence. "Gentlemen, I'm André Façonneur.

The tide has just begun to rise and we may proceed."

"We'll prepare, then." Pierre went to order raising the anchor and setting topsails. Louis sped off to tell the captain that the pilot had come aboard.

When he returned, Louis stared at the man for a moment. Something struck him as familiar. "Monsieur Façonneur, have we ever met before? My name is Louis de Saint-Alouarn."

André turned to the young officer and eyed him. "Ah, de Saint-Alouarn." His face hid a grin. "I've piloted and known your father and uncle for many years, sir. I believe you visited my father's house when you were about ten."

Louis paused for moment and then the realization came to him. "Of… of course, I'm sorry. I forgot Mademoiselle Yvette's family name—Façonneur." His face flushed and he bit his lip.

"When your Uncle René courted my sister, you, your father, and uncle came to my father's birthday dinner." André, long over ill feelings toward René, welcomed the memory.

"I do recall it clearly." Louis smiled sheepishly. "Your recounting the difficulties of piloting mesmerized me that night. Strange I hadn't thought of it since, although it gave me a great appreciation of pilots' skills. How is your family?"

"In good health. My father still shipwrights at the yard."

"As is my family. My mother, well, she tends the estate like a mother hen." Louis laughed. "My father captains *le Juste* with my Uncle René as second in command."

"We, and even the enemy, will long remember those two for what they've accomplished for our country. When things looked the worst in the last war, their victories at sea gave the nation, and especially us in Brest, the hope to endure."

"Yes, even the admiral praised my father and uncle." He shook his head. "It'll be difficult for me to leave such an impression."

"You have a long time to try, if that's your goal." André patted his shoulder and nodded, smiling. "But your life needn't match theirs. Follow your own path with passion, wherever it takes you."

Soon the crew readied the ship, and the slow steady passage through the narrows carried them to the Road of Brest for anchorage. Warships and transports crowded the large bay outside Brest's fortress. Admiral Bompar's fleet struggled to find steerage between berthed vessels to drop anchor.

When they harbored, Louis and Pierre rushed the crew to make the ship secure in hopes the Admiral might give them shore leave. In luck, before evening came, Admiral Bompar granted half the officers leisure time ashore. Louis and Pierre hurried to the de Saint-Alouarn house, high in the center of Brest overlooking the Penfeld River.

As they came to the large stone house, Louis wondered if his father had arrived there, ridden to the winter home in Quimper, or gone to their manor. He hadn't seen *le Juste* in the bay, so François might even be still at sea.

The servant answered their knock and Louis asked him if his father's ship had docked.

"Indeed, sir, your father arrived a week ago. During the day he works aboard his ship. He should return before nightfall."

Louis's face brightened hearing the news and he informed Pierre. "Oh, this is perfect! I saw my father last on the night before we left for the Lesser Antilles. They held a ball at the officer's pavilion and we talked well into the evening. Most of the night I talked to Armand de Kersaint, there with his father. He's four years my junior and should make lieutenant soon. Did you ever meet him?"

Pierre and his family, not as wealthy as either the de Saint-Alouarns or the de Kersaints, shrugged and replied, "No, their social circle ranges a long way from ours."

Louis gave a fast nod, too late to remedy the faux pas. He had forgotten Pierre's lower ranking in the Breton nobility.

The sky darkened quickly as the late fall sun sank below the horizon. Louis and Pierre, sitting in the salon and sipping warmed hard cider, both rose to their feet at the sound of the front door opening.

"Father?!" called Louis already walking toward the foyer.

"Louis?" Hearing his son's voice, François rushed toward the room. "I saw your fleet arriving this afternoon and guessed you'd be home!"

They met in the hallway and embraced, François kissing his son's cheeks. Pierre stood to the side, tickled by the warmhearted scene. After Louis introduced Pierre to his father, they drifted to the salon once more.

"Did you see the bays? Very impressive isn't it." François's face beamed. "Nothing has gathered this large since the last war."

Louis nodded. "I've never seen so many ships at anchor. They're organizing something big, I believe." The number of vessels implanted in Louis not only awe, but concern as well. "It appears to be an invasion fleet assembling. Do you know where it's headed?"

"No one said and the rumors, of course, pinpoint the places we'll probably *not* invade." François laughed. "Although, I suppose someone will have guessed right." He had his own thoughts on the destination.

Pierre tapped his lips with his finger in thought and added, "A few other officers on *le Défenseur* mentioned recapturing Quebec. It brought to mind Louisbourg, too."

François shook his head. "Last time, when we lost Louisbourg, the king and the Admiralty attempted bolder strikes at the enemy to force them to the peace table. They're not likely to change their ways. I presume it must be dramatic and devastating. I'd assume an invasion of England itself might be too audacious." François shrugged. "We'll find out at sea."

"So, you'll be going with the fleet, father?" The fear Louis had earlier again loomed.

"I'm assigned to Marshal de Conflans's fleet, yes. Of course, he's so experienced, I believe whatever our objective is, he'll achieve it. But I'm concerned if the army generals can manage the task." He knitted his brows.

"Wasn't Marshal de Conflans on *la Renommée* when they captured you?" Louis asked. "You sailed with him before, then."

"That ended in the only warship I ever lost in battle. I can go without being reminded." François laughed. "True, he sailed onboard on that voyage. We were taking him to his new posting as governor in Saint-Domingue. They gave the governorship to another afterwards. I always wondered if he ever forgave me."

"If he places you in the vanguard or rear of the fleet, he has. If you're stuck in the middle somewhere or on the sides, look out, you're still in trouble." Pierre jested, tilting his head and chuckling.

The nautical conversations continued until supper time, and then their discussion turned to their manor and Madame de Saint-Alouarn, Louis's mother. Although military talk had taken up most of their evening with bold statements, when the father and son spoke of her, their demeanor softened. The comments now reflected the high respect, love, and regard for the single most important woman in both of their lives.

François had regretted leaving her more this time than others. He knew, however, she'd handle everything at the estates well. She had a gift for managing the workers and an even better one for overseeing its finances. So, too, her understanding, charity, and compassion extended far beyond those close to her; the people throughout southern Brittany knew and thought kindly of the esteemed Madame de Saint-Alouarn as well.

Less than two weeks later on November 14, 1759, Louis watched from the deck of *le Défenseur* as *le Juste* departed along with the rest of the transports and warships, one by one, to carry his father and uncle away on southwesterly breezes. The great and much expected invasion campaign had begun after storms that pushed the British Admiral Hawke away from their coast. Louis raised his hand as *le Juste* passed by his ship, and François and René, near the railing, waved back. René amusingly removed his hat and bowed low to Louis. "On to victory, my friend!" he shouted and threw up his arms, laughing. His father simply smiled at René's jovial mockery and waved at his son.

Six days later, Admiral Hawke's fleet caught up with Marshal de Conflans and during a terrible storm, trapped the French in a large, reef-strewn bay. With little space to maneuver into a line of defense and strong countering winds, a close quarters battle ensued. François's *le Juste*, in the rear guard of the fleet, became one of the first to fight, attacked by the *Temple* and *Magnanime*. Hours later, another British warship joined them. *Le Juste*, having taken a horrible pounding from the three, hove leeward toward shore to withdraw up a river.

As the French warship turned, an officer on the deck fell, struck by a musket ball. It was François, alive but wounded. René took command and sent volley after volley into his foe's ships until he could pull *le Juste* away from the fray. A final onslaught from the *Temple* at the fleeing warship cut down crew the entire length of the French vessel, including René.

⚬⚬⚬

The first news came from a mounted messenger, sent from a small port near Quiberon Bay. The account was dire. Thousands had died, and many vessels had gone to the bottom. When the report spread in Brest, so did panic among the naval command. The catastrophic results of the clash trickled in over a period of days in late November. The French lost close to 2,500 seamen, seven ships of the line, the intrepid Captain Guy de Kersaint, and also, the famed de Saint-Alouarn brothers.

The news burned across the port in hours and Admiral Bompar called Louis into his great cabin before the young officer had heard. "Lieutenant de Saint-Alouarn, I fear I am the bearer of a most dreadful report. During the battle, both your father and uncle, François and René, were cut down aboard *le Juste.*" The admiral paused to let Louis fathom the sorrowful fact.

Louis, without asking permission, crumpled into a chair before the admiral's desk, his hands over his face. Ashen, he returned a blank stare to the admiral. After a moment, he recovered enough to ask, "Both?"

"You have my deepest sympathy, Lieutenant. They engaged the *Temple* and *Magnanime* and fought for hours. In the end, both fell upon the deck after valiant efforts to save the ship and crew." His eyes lowered.

"Did *le Juste* make it to harbor, sir?" Tears rimmed Louis's eyelids.

"No. She struck reefs later and sank with most of her crew. Only a handful survived." The admiral, stunned over the losses of the battle, placed his hand on his brow and shook his head. "These have been days of great despair for all of France. Yet, the fate of those two officers will go down as a historic loss. Your father and uncle will receive nothing but the greatest appreciation and respect for what they have done for their country and for sacrificing their lives in its defense."

Louis, his head bowed, looked up and saw a tear fall from the admiral's eye. His mind had rid itself of all other concerns and thoughts, trying to un-hear the admiral's words, *"François and René were cut down...."*

After Louis gathered himself, the admiral gave him leave and he rushed home from Brest on horseback to lament with his family.

Madame de Saint-Alouarn, at her house in Quimper, had awaited the news of her husband's death as soon as the first reports of the disaster came. Often she suffered cold suspense, dreading his demise after a major battle. This time turned out different. He did not walk into the foyer to ease her fears with his warm embrace. Instead, a smartly dressed naval officer rapped the door to deliver a letter.

Her daughters grieved and consoled one another while Madame de Saint-Alouarn quietly mourned François's passing in her chamber. Although he had never feared dying at sea, she had always expected it. In her room she wept, but never in front of her children.

Later that night, Louis rode into Quimper and trudged to the salon in the house. All his family turned their heads to him when he entered. Madame de Saint-Alouarn sat with his weeping sisters surrounding her. Her eyes, lined by reddened lids, rose to meet his. She gave a weak nod as she folded and refolded the handkerchief in her hands.

His mother's stolid, resigned poise did not fool him. "Mother, can we comfort you?" Tears fell and streaked his cheeks.

"No, Louis. The hurt will never go away, but fond memories sweeten the pain's bitterness." This was all she said, showing no despondency, but feeling it to her heart's core.

King Louis, upon hearing of the tragedy of the brothers, sent a personal note promising 1,200 livres in pension to Madame de Saint-Alouarn. Although she showed gratitude for his concern, in the salon with her family around her, she expressed her mind. "The king very kindly offered us the sounds of coins from his empty treasury chest. But we cannot eat promises. The homes, the manor, the servants, fieldworkers, and their families, depend upon us. These I must transfer now to your responsibility, Louis." For the first time, Madame de Saint-

Alouarn surrendered her affairs, vanquished not by bad crops, the wars, or age, but grief for her dear François. "My heart lies too heavy and I can manage the estate burdens no longer." Her body slumped in the chair.

"I accept that and I'll talk to the admiral about resigning my commission if they'll allow it during a war." The words drained his spirit as he spoke them.

Hearing his intention, she sat straight, her head snapped upward. "No! Like your father, the navy is part of you and you must serve. Perhaps if you take a position on land or near Brest, it would suffice." She couldn't bring herself to deny him the sea, his lifelong passion. Nor could she survive another loss if he, at just twenty-one years, also perished.

༄

Captain Washington Shirley assessed the damage the day after the battle. The great French Brest fleet sailed no more. Their ships had wrecked upon the Quiberon Bay's reef, sunk in battle, scattered, beached and burned, or foundered in storm waves. Although a defining victory, it cost the British two ships of the line and hundreds of lives. Regardless, many enemy warships had slipped away in darkness.

Washington's actions during the engagement brought tribute. He had led the squadron's vanguard and met with an opponent first. His *Temple* and the larger *Magnanime* set upon the French *le Juste*, forcing the battered and dismasted seventy-gun to flee to the Loire River. Although Washington was unaware, the next day, *le Juste* had grounded upon shoals, and storm waves destroyed her. Over 500 crewmen died in the gale's roiling surf.

Versailles had planned a series of surprise invasions of Scotland, Ireland, and England to end the war. The clash at Quiberon Bay shattered those strategies. With so many other defeats for them in 1759, the war swung far into Great Britain's favor.

"Lieutenant Griffith, set tops and mains. We're bound for the Île d'Aix to intercept those that fled." Washington smiled while reading the orders. He had fought hard the first day against *le Juste* during the melee. Afterward, his *Temple* anchored near Quiberon Bay for three days until the fierce gale that accompanied the battle weakened to gusty winds and whitecaps. Now, only searching out the retreating enemy warships remained.

"After noon we'll join a flying squadron and dead run south-by-southeast. Admiral Hawke will remain here with the bulk of our fleet."

"Sir, repairs are near completion. Three shot holes in our above-water only remain." Lieutenant Griffith pushed the carpenter and his mates to near exhaustion to mend the ship after the fight.

Washington pumped his fist in delight. "Excellent, Lieutenant. What went by the board?"

"Sir, we lost naught but the starboard cathead, the main top yard, and a bit of coaming. We'll repair most before making port."

"Keep the carpenters on the holes and have them check the masts again. I am amazed we suffered so little from *le Juste's* cannons even if we took but a third of their iron." Washington's luck had held fast for him once again, good cause for the grin he bore. "Our salvos put her to rout well enough. I wonder if they escaped south, too?"

"Sir, your command to the marines wounded her captain. I saw the rascal fall like a bag of corn. Until then, their shots looked well placed. With him gone, they aimed high, doing little to the *Temple.*"

"Aye, Lieutenant, they targeted our rigging to delay pursuing their flight. It worked well enough after losing our topsail and running afoul of one of our own. We may yet catch up with her and finish our scuffle if she escaped to Basque Roads."

By two o'clock the pursuit squadron formed, and the *Temple* sailed along the coast southward with strong winds.

As the sky dimmed at the end of day, Lieutenant Griffith knocked upon Washington's cabin door.

"Enter." Washington expected someone to announce they had arrived at the channel outside Rochefort, the Basque Roads.

"Sir, frigates are signaling enemy sighted near Île d'Aix."

"Thank you, Lieutenant, drum to quarters." Washington put on his sword and climbed topside.

"We'll hear the cannon roar soon enough if we've found them. Too bad night approaches. Darkness may confuse the fight once again." Washington and the other British captains, after fighting three days in stormy seas and murky skies, wished for a fair-weather, daylight battle. "Have the carpenters check the pumps, Lieutenant."

"Aye, aye, sir. Should sharpshooters take positions aloft?"

"Not yet, wait until we hear cannon."

As the *Temple* approached, they observed two French ships of the line hugging close to the shore batteries protecting the mouth of the Clarente River. The fortresses on Île d'Aix and the Île d'Oléron would keep the British from approaching nearer.

Lieutenant Griffith pointed, frowning. "Captain Shirley, did those two come from Quiberon Bay?"

Washington stood at the portside rail, peering through his spyglass. "Yes, I believe so. One of them looks to be the *Dauphin Royal,* and the other a sixty-four. The *Dauphin Royal* fought at the battle. The other sails I can see likely sailed in their fleet as well. Only shallow draft warships can enter up the Clarente, though, so these will anchor in the harbor."

He explained to the lieutenant. "The shore guns will protect them as well there. We can't engage them within range of their shore and island forts. The ships leading our squadron are now anchoring just north of Île d'Aix."

When the *Temple* arrived by its moored companions, signals summoned the captains to a meeting aboard the *Torbay,* commanded by Captain Keppel, leader of the squadron.

"They're penned in well at Port-des-Barques for now. But at the first chance they'll slip out southward beyond our guns. We must keep them there indefinitely. To that end, we will take Île d'Aix as those cannons can reach them if they try to escape." Keppel then proposed to take the island just as they had two years earlier. "We destroyed their stone forts during the last capture and they have only earthen works protecting the guns. We'll begin the bombardment tomorrow at dawn and when signaled, each warship will send its marines ashore as planned."

The next day as dawn's light silhouetted the hills on shore, each ship arrived at its spot to batter the island fortifications. The French ashore shot first as the ships of the line and frigates were dropping anchor. However, the squadron's return volleys struck many times greater and within two hours destroyed the last enemy cannon emplacement.

"Lieutenant Griffith, the signal is flying on the *Torbay*. Launch the marines!" Washington rushed across the quarterdeck, motioning toward the midships and boats.

As they stood on the poop deck, they watched the troops in their boats form a long line and row toward the shore. No infantry opposed them and soon the marines marched inward to put down any resistance. The island's cannons could now keep the French warships from sneaking out of their protective haven, the same tactic the British had used the entire war, which kept the enemy ships imprisoned in their ports.

Within a week, replacements arrived and Washington set off to Plymouth for repairs and to his wife, Anne, in time to celebrate the Christmas of 1759.

Admiral Hawke had praised Washington's actions, and he believed this pegged the height of his naval career. Nonetheless, whatever fortune had bestowed upon him that wondrous year, it was nothing compared to the glory of what was to come.

The Infamy of
Earl Ferrers

The day began warm and beautiful, which gave a false impression that the rest of the day might be the same for Yvette. As she waited for Abraham to return from the shipyard, she sat at the kitchen table and reread the letter she'd gotten that afternoon from France. Gaëlle, her brother André's wife, had sent word of the disastrous Battle of Quiberon Bay. Her sister-in-law, aware of Yvette's earlier engagement to René, shouldered the task of letting her know of his demise.

Yvette again read the rattling sentence: *"… both René and his brother François perished in the battle."* After so many years, she didn't expect the news to affect her as it did. In her mind, René had never changed from the last time they stood together in the street when she ended their betrothal on that cool New Year's Day.

For years, she vented her anger at him in secret, inventing fantasy scenes where she picked better words than she had actually used.

Whenever she had recalled his smooth-talking lies, she fumed in private. Abraham seldom had caught on to her chastising herself for falling in love with René or her anger at the cheater.

Now those lingering emotions lay in the past, buried over the years by more meaningful experiences with Abraham. When René's name surfaced, she paid it little regard, ignoring the nagging desire to feel resentful over his actions or guilty over hers.

The letter changed that. The words whipped her pacified mind into a whirlwind of emotions. Sorrow, regret, anger, disbelief, and even love, blew in through the window of her conscience. He had died, but her repressed and unresolved vexations had lived on and again surfaced.

For two hours she meandered from one feeling to another. Drained by them, she took hold of her rock, whose love lasted, steadfast, and she concentrated on what her future held with Abraham. Yvette told herself to accept René as the past, and not what might have been. She put it away, where it belonged, ebbing beneath the love of her husband. Her intuition told her to keep it there, never to be released again.

Soon after sunset, Abraham opened the door and walked into the kitchen where Yvette stood making their meal. He kissed her neck and put his hand on her back. "How has your day been?" he asked softly in French.

"Fine, dear. Nothing happened today worth telling you." She smiled as she looked at the scrap bin that held the letter's ashes.

༄

The course of a life can change in the extreme by a most unlikely event. Only a few months after his valorous fight at Quiberon Bay, Washington's life turned. It began with the news of his brother Laurence, the Earl Ferrers, whose wife had left him two years earlier.

In the divorce decree, Countess Mary received part of the rents from the earl's estates and properties that the court assigned trustees to oversee. Although both Washington and Anne knew of the earl's vileness and wrathful disposition, neither could have foreseen the news they would read one quiet morning upon opening a letter.

"My God, Anne. Laurence is in jail! A letter and a broadsheet came from my brother Robert. This is what is written in the London Gazette." His hands trembling, Washington read the newspaper aloud to her regarding what had occurred less than a week earlier:

> *On January 18th, a Friday, the Earl Ferrers of Staunton Harold near Leicester ordered John Johnson, the steward and a trustee of the Earl Ferrers's properties, to visit him for business matters. The Earl Ferrers, in preparation, had sent away for the day the male staff and even his mistress and her children. Only five maids were serving the earl. After Johnson arrived, the Earl Ferrers, who disliked the powers given to the steward over his finances, accused Johnson of giving fifty pounds to his former wife without permission. He also blamed Johnson of being in league with her and conspiring against him over a contract and a loud squabble erupted.*
>
> *The Earl Ferrers had locked the study door, but one maid overheard the exchange. Inside, the Earl Ferrers shouted at the steward, "Get on your knees and say your prayers for you have but a minute to live!" When the frightened steward complied by placing a knee on the floor, the Earl Ferrers demanded, "Down on your other knee! Declare that you have acted against Lord Ferrers. Your time has come—you must die."*
>
> *At that point and without pity or compassion, the Earl Ferrers pulled a pistol from his belt and shot the steward in his belly below the rib cage. The maids summoned a doctor whom the Earl Ferrers threatened with death if he told anyone about the shooting or failed to cure the steward. Doctor Kirkland, upon seeing the mortal wound, lied to the Earl Ferrers, saying the wound appeared slight and that Johnson would be well in a day.*
>
> *The doctor left to get the steward's daughter, eighteen-year-old Sarah, who arrived and hurried straight to her stricken father. The Earl Ferrers, fearing for his own neck after his fiendish deed, told the doctor and Sarah that the steward was more afraid than harmed. He claimed Johnson deserved death and said to Sarah, "Now that I have spared his life, I desire you to do what you can*

for him. If the rascal should die, and you do not bring me to justice over it, I will give you and your brother a stipend for life." She replied, sobbing, the people will bring his lordship to justice if she did not. To this he said he'd shoot anyone who came to arrest him. However, even with medical care, Johnson died the next morning.

The following day the doctor, assisted by a band of local men, assembled before the manor demanding the Earl Ferrers come forth. The Earl Ferrers appeared at a garret window, shouting no man could take him. Then he asked them to come inside for food and drink, hoping to dissuade them. They declined and ordered him to surrender. After a few hours, with the crowd growing in size, the Earl Ferrers appeared outside on the bowling green in the garden armed with a brace of pistols, a dagger, and a blunderbuss.

After a confrontation, Earl Ferrers surrendered while proclaiming his justification in killing the poor steward. The men seized him and held him in a nearby public house overnight. After an inquest, the coroner's court found Earl Ferrers culpable of murder, transferring him to Leicestershire County jail.

He dropped the letter and paper article on the desk, visibly shaken. "Pack trunks for a trip," Washington turned to Anne, still wide-eyed. "Poor John. What a catastrophe." He sat at his desk, picking up a quill. "First, I must write the Admiralty and then we'll leave for the Midlands tonight."

Anne stood beside him, shook her head and picked up the newspaper sheet. "Murder? I can't believe Laurence could do such a thing, regardless of his odious temperament. To offer to take care of the man's family as if money absolves the crime is beyond conceit!" Anne added, astonished and shaking a fist in front of her. "Has he not a speck of moral sense?"

Washington wavered between the emotional shock at the news and coming up with a logical explanation. As he scribble his letter to the Admiralty, he often stopped to try to understand what had happened.

"Our family had employed John for so long, since a boy. How could he do it?" Washington mumbled quickly, frowning and waving his quill. "Besides self delusions, he's twice-cursed; Laurence's intermittent madness overtakes him."

Anne's eyes narrowed as she scanned the report. "Laurence humiliated servants with curses and thrashings, including beating poor Countess Mary, but to kill someone?" She tapped her shoe repeatedly trying to come to terms with the crime.

"The whole family worried he might kill someday." Washington shook his head and shrugged. "But we clung to a hope that everything might turn out fine. In a sense, we're guilty of not preventing this crime." He pointed the quill's end to himself with a grimace.

Anne's mouth dropped open. "Oh, Washington! Don't take an ounce of his guilt and put it upon yourself. He's a full-grown man who knows right from wrong and controls himself when he wants. Laurence knew of his anger and false suspicions and chose not to control them." Anne, practical and outspoken, didn't have his blinding filial emotions.

Washington nodded in agreement. "Anne, nothing he's done, however, erases the fact that I have blood ties to him. I shall support him as much as I can within the law." His voice slowed to a less frantic tempo while he finished his letter to the navy.

As she reread the broadsheet, she paced before the desk. "I understand that. Just don't prevent him from receiving his punishment. If you feel guilty over what has happened, imagine your guilt if they released him and he did it again."

By the end of the week, they reached Staunton Harold Hall, Earl Ferrers' manor, and confronted the situation's high emotions. Washington's mother, withdrawn and silent, wouldn't discuss Laurence's crime, while his Aunt Selina, the Countess of Huntingdon, couldn't stop talking about it.

The family had gathered in the library to discuss how to help Laurence. Selina stood while the others sat in chairs around the room.

"Aunt Selina, they'll never release Laurence. There's such overwhelming proof of his guilt. Yet, I hope they don't execute him for murder." Washington wrung his hands anxiously and turned to his aunt. "Perhaps a long prison sentence suffices?"

"Washington," Selina's voice was gentle, "he must pay for his felony, but I agree with you, no conviction should end in death."

Washington stood and walked to Selina, and raised the possibility no one else in the room dared. "You've had the king's ear in the past, Aunt Selina. Could you approach the king so he might intercede for us?"

Selina tilted her head and shook it. "This is out of the hands of King George. Should the House of Lords condemn him, the king is unlikely to spare him." Her eyebrows rose. "You already know this."

Washington raised his finger to make a point. "Maybe the truth of it, that he's insane, will save him. Everyone knows of these ill bouts."

"He'd have to declare himself innocent and plead insanity." Selina explained to Washington. "If he does, his brothers must testify in that defense."

"No, I cannot and will recuse myself." Washington shook his head forcefully and walked away from her. "Assume he's found guilty and put to death, I'd inherit the title. People may suspect my testimony as a way to get him hanged for my benefit!" He gazed out the window in thought. "Walter, being a preacher, and Robert should testify. We must convince Laurence pleading insane is the only defense that will keep him alive."

Within the month, a jury of his peers at the House of Lords readied to try the Earl Ferrers. They had moved him to the Tower of London. To be closer, Washington and Anne stayed at Selina's house in London while trying to call on Laurence. Robert also came, hoping to convince him to proclaim his insanity. After a week of repeated requests, Laurence agreed they could visit him in the Tower.

"I regret not one bit of my actions," Laurence began, sitting on his prison bed. His boyish face hid his deep loathing for the victim. "John deserved to die for his disloyalty to the Shirleys and for consorting with my former wife against me. Had John betrayed any other person as he betrayed me, he'd have done the same." His gaze darted from one family member to the other, seeking agreement to his abominable felony.

Selina, in her ever-gentle voice, spoke first. "Laurence, the steward didn't want to take your life nor did anything worthy of his death. When you reflect in your heart, you must realize the seriousness of your crime. How it stands as a sin against God." She stood directly in front of Laurence, her finger pointed to heaven.

"Aunt Selina," Laurence responded in a loud voice, unmoved by her spiritual persuasion. "Neither did I engage in crime nor does God see punishing the scoundrel a sin! Even if so, it's a forgivable one. In Leviticus, it is written…"

"Laurence, if I may interrupt," said Washington firmly, not wanting the conversation to turn into a theological debate. "Killing John remains a crime by our legal system regardless of biblical quotes. How do you plan to counter the charges?"

"I'll plead guilty if the court sees me as such. Nonetheless, I'll argue it is never a misdeed to dispatch a man so vile." Laurence closed his eyes, making a fist.

Robert rolled his eyes, put a hand on his hip, and held his other palm forward. "Laurence, you don't understand! The court will find you responsible for the murder and sentence you to death!" Then he jabbed his finger at Laurence. "If you wish to die, affirm your guilt. If you wish to live, you must do better than hope you can sway them to accept that you acted as a lawful executioner."

Washington joined Selina and Robert standing in front of Laurence, and frowned with squinting eyes. "We've agreed the best argument you can make to stay alive is to plead temporary insanity." He used his captain's voice, deep and commanding.

"What?" Laurence's mouth dropped opened, his face flushed in anger. "I'm not a lunatic!" He stared with clenched fists at Washington.

Selina took a step back, smiled at Laurence, and attempted to calm their emotions. "Many held your Aunt Barbara and Uncle Henry, the former earl, to be mad." She spoke calmly, in a soft voice. "By referencing them as a source of temporary inherited lunacy, you might build a defense."

The change in tactic defused his temper and he turned to look at her. "That will bring shame on me. I can't do it," moaned Laurence, his hand covered his eyes.

Washington sighed and moved away, also speaking quietly. "It comes to pleading innocent by insanity or you can plead guilty of pride and get hanged!"

The emotions had tired everyone and they fell silent for a minute, each in their own thoughts on the crisis.

Laurence rose from the edge of the bed and slowly paced. A few minutes later, he spoke in a restrained manner. "Let me deliberate the choices for a few days. A life of people regarding me as demented seems as dreadful as the noose. When I've made up my mind, I'll tell you."

Weeks later, he entered a plea of not guilty in front of the House of Lords. His brothers Walter and Robert both testified him insane, as did several others. Laurence, representing himself as the law prescribed for murder, spoke eloquently in his own defense. Every word leaving his mouth proved with logic his behavior over the years was mentally unsound. Witnesses confirmed almost to a person that the Earl Ferrers often behaved in bizarre ways with inexplicable rants and deeds. The Earl Ferrers had always suspected others of conspiracies against him, and carried hidden weapons on his person. That other close relatives had been or still were mad, gave credence to his argument.

On the second day of the trial, however, the prosecutor's closing statement gutted the family's hopes. He showed Laurence, perhaps insane at times, planned the crime over days with forethought in meticulous detail. He recounted Laurence had celebrated killing his steward on many instances while fully sober and rational. Plus the Earl Ferrers's very unemotional and cogent defense itself gave evidence of a capable and sound mind.

On the third day of the trial, the House of the Lords convicted the Earl Ferrers of premeditated murder. One at a time, the Lords, dressed in their long red robes, rose and swore upon their honor they held him guilty. Horace Walpole, the noted writer and Member of Parliament, summarized Laurence's defense: "It was a strange contradiction to see a man trying by his own sense to prove himself out of his senses."

The next day the Lord High Steward, showing no pity, sentenced Laurence to be taken from the Tower to Tyburn Prison to be executed by hanging on May 5, 1760. Afterward, his body was to be dissected, anatomized, and displayed to the public.

The last night he spent only with his jailors, perusing *Hamlet*. He read aloud over and over the soliloquy of "To be or not to be" trying to draw meaning from the phrase as he uttered it. Now and then pausing, he'd ask the guards how they liked the words.

The following morning, he dressed in his wedding suit of all-white silk breeches, vest, and a coat of satin and silk, telling the guard with a shrug, "This is the suit in which I was married, and in which I will die." A constable led Laurence outside to his personal landau drawn by six black horses with the chaplain of the Tower and the sheriff joining him. The procession inched through the packed streets of onlookers, taking three hours to go five miles to Tyburn Prison.

At a quarter to noon, they arrived at the prison. After a prayer, Laurence ascended onto a raised dais higher than the main platform. The executioner removed Laurence's neckcloth and put a white hood over his head. He bound his wrists with a silken cord, and lowered and tightened a hemp noose around his neck. As the sheriff gave the signal, a trapdoor opened, and Laurence fell.

However, the noose rope, too long, allowed Laurence's toes to just touch the scaffold flooring. He struggled, slowly strangling, until the executioner pulled down on him to quicken the end by breaking his neck. The entire execution took eight minutes.

They dissected the corpse to see if he had any diseases that would have ended his life prematurely and exhibited the body for the public to see how a villainous crime will shorten one's life. Later grave diggers buried the murderer Laurence Shirley, the Fourth Earl Ferrers, and last noble ever executed in England.

∽

While in the West Indies, Maitland, like many other British and French officers, had taken on a mistress, Mary Arnot, a twenty-eight-year-old free mulatto. They met three years earlier in 1757, soon after he arrived in Jamaica and moved into a house near Kingston, across the bay from Port Royal. Such arrangements in the Caribbean happened often since the law forbade white men to marry women of color outside Great Britain. Just over a year later, she gave birth to their son James.

The threat of Bompar's fleet to the Jamaica station unnerved the commanders. More men poured into the forts surrounding the harbor to prepare for a French attack. This occurred in each British possession.

Just as Pitt's descents had caused alarm along the French coast, the British responded in like manner to word of the menacing enemy presence.

Ships on patrol cruised in twos and Maitland and Mackenzie often sailed together, with the latter avoiding speaking to the former when he could. The commanders met one day to discuss their next cruise.

"You've been commanding the *Renown* here for almost two years without getting yellow jack once." Maitland smiled at him. "I'd say that's a bit of luck." He had gotten sick the first time he set foot on Jamaican sand but never since.

"Aye. *Whit's fur ye'll no go by ye,* as they say back home—what's bound to happen, happens." Mackenzie hated thinking about the illnesses and wished Maitland hadn't mentioned it. "I've had my fill of heat, diseases, hurricanes, and rum. Jamaica can do without me. I'd bid the islands a farewell forever if I could. Although my duty demands I fight where the Admiralty sends me, I'll be glad to be in home waters." He gazed off, missing his family.

"Now that the Frenchies have left, that could happen." Maitland, sympathizing with the older man, had never minded his own stay in the isles. For him, it became the home of his family and new business venture. Many officers assigned there saw it as a lucrative opportunity to invest in the sugar, rum, and indigo businesses. Maitland had purchased ten slaves on Saint-Thomas and contracted them to a sugar plantation to work. Renting out slaves made for a tidy side income to help pay for the mansion he was building on a plantation.

"And because we control Guadeloupe, peace may come sooner." Mackenzie said hopefully, keeping his answers short to end the discussion.

"The war goes poorly for the French. You may be right." The thought darkened Maitland's face. "If they suffer a defeat on the continent, that will surely end it, I suspect." Unlike Mackenzie, Maitland preferred his stationing in Port Royal near his new son and wife.

Neither turned out correct. No peace came, and the French suffered no great blow in the field. In December, reports arrived in the islands of the terrible destruction of the Brest fleet at Quiberon Bay. Everywhere, with the dread of invasions having flown from the British colonies, life returned to normal. Their navy controlled the seas, and the war again seemed far away.

But before the next year was out, the optimism shared by everyone slipped away from Maitland. His son, not two years old, died of the fever, and grief deprived him of any joy in life or work.

When Mackenzie learned of his rival's gut-wrenching loss, he felt sorry for Maitland. He imagined how he might react if Tommy passed away in Scotland, thousands of leagues from Jamaica. It amplified his compassion for Maitland and drew him closer in trying to understand the man.

In October, Mackenzie was cruising alone near Saint John in the Leeward Islands, when he spied eight ships heading west. He crept closer until he identified their flags as French and turned and ran with the wind back to the station to recount the sighting.

Maitland's *Lively* joined the admiral's fifty-gun *Hampshire* along with another frigate, the *Boreas,* to investigate Mackenzie's report of the enemy fleet. Four days later, just north of Saint-Domingue near Cape François, on the northeastern corner of the island, the three warships spotted the French vessels at sunrise.

The *Hampshire* hauled to fall upon the enemy but the steady breezes that had given the British an advantage suddenly dropped. Light winds slowed them and an enemy frigate was successful in forcing the *Boreas* to withdraw after it lost its main royal, only to surrender to the *Boreas* the next day.

The *Lively* had trailed another frigate, *la Valeur* of twenty-four cannons that Maitland followed during the night. Most of the next day, a light breath of wind pushed both ships to the east.

Maitland, sweating in the stifling warm air, regretted what was needed. "Break out the sweeps, Lieutenant." A groan rose from the crewmen close enough to hear his order.

Men grumbled, rushing to launch the boats to pull the frigate, and took their positions to use muscle where breezes had failed.

"Pull! Pull!" The boatswain called cadence as the men hauled on the blades, lifting them up out of the sea and back in unison.

Spyglass to eye, Maitland expected his prey to do the same. Within a quarter of an hour, he saw the French frigate lower their boats into the water. Still, the *Lively* had more men and sweeps than the enemy.

They made progress at a slow rate, closing the distance. The crewmen labored like galley slaves. Sweat poured off their bodies as they dragged oars back and forth in the hot, humid air. Maitland worried that they might be too exhausted to fight if they caught up to the enemy in the morning.

He calculated it would take six hours before they reached the fleeing warship. "Lieutenant, change the crew on each boat for the men to rest for two hours. Then repeat until everyone gets sleep." More concerned over the men's fitness to fight than their fatigue or discomfort, Maitland had never engaged a ship before with a chance to capture it. This opportunity had opened to draw attention to his abilities, and neither the lack of wind nor the crew's discontent would stop him.

As the sky lightened before dawn, *la Valeur* struggled westward less than a half league ahead, not far off the eastern tip of Cuba. If the French captain has not relieved his crew, Maitland considered, they'll be in no condition to fight. He estimated another hour before his *Lively* could engage, so he ordered the cook to prepare food for the crew to strengthen them before they went into the clash.

La Valeur slowed markedly as her crew either broke to eat or the men were tiring. The *Lively* closed on her stern and steered to the enemy's starboard side. At the last moment, Maitland ordered the boats to return, as did their opponent. The moment his bow crossed in front of the French ship's aft gun ports, cannons roared.

Both ships now depended upon the light puff of air in their canvas for maneuvering and belched metal upon one another in an unending series of cascading blasts. Marines aloft fired volleys on the cannon crews, and the bloody exchange of men fighting for their lives continued. As the *Lively's* higher bulwarks provided more protection than the other's lower sides, Maitland expected fewer casualties.

After the first hour, *la Valeur* showed signs of much greater damage and a high loss of life. Then in one fierce exchange with musket balls ricocheting off the decks and rails and cannon iron putting holes in its sides, the French officer on the quarterdeck fell. Another rushed to replace him, the ship's master, and half an hour later, he too lay upon the deck.

With both officers gone and the enemy boatswain wounded, the smaller frigate, torn up and taking on water, lowered her colors.

"She's ours, Lieutenant! Haul to and make her fast to us. Take over here and I'll go with marines onto her." Maitland's face glowed with pride. At last, he thought, a prize!

When he returned after the surrender, he called the lieutenant. "How many did we lose?" Too many killed may diminish his glory, he worried.

"Two dead and no wounded." The lieutenant stood before the captain, eagerly waiting his response.

"What?" Maitland's eye widened. "Only two and none injured?" He reveled in the low tally.

The first officer smiled. "Correct, sir."

Maitland grinned broadly and slapped the quarterdeck railing. "That amazes me! They lost their captain, master, and boatswain. Moreover, forty crew dead and half as many wounded. This is a rare victory." He anticipated how well this would play in England.

"They print this kind of thing in the broadsheets at home. You'll be in the reports to the Admiralty, sir," the lieutenant announced gleefully.

When the fleet returned to Port Royal, the station commander honored the three triumphant crews with a ball. Mary, on Maitland's arm, walked proudly beside her new luminary and drew the envy of many other ladies that evening. Mackenzie attended, too, not in the least disturbed by his fellow Scot's sudden popularity for duty far beyond expectations. Maitland's undeniable naval accomplishment absolved him of any transgressions in Mackenzie's eyes.

The next day, Mackenzie put his pen to the long-promised report on Guadeloupe and the glorious triumph of the Windward Passage Battle. To make sure Lord Fortrose understood the rarity of such an engagement, he wrote, "... *if the intrepid bravery of Captain Frederick Maitland had been present at Martinique in Commodore Moore, we could have vanquished the enemy's defenses and yielded another island to the rule of Britain.*"

Both captains continued to cruise the Caribbean in search of French warships, merchants, and smugglers, sometimes together, and often alone. In April 1761, the station commander received orders from London; the Admiralty had reassigned both captains.

As Mackenzie counted paces to decide how to fit his walnut dining table in the captain's cabin of his new warship, a knock came on the door. "Come," he said, turning to the door.

Maitland entered, his hands held up in defense, and laughed. "Captain Mackenzie, you won't throw me overboard for taking over your old frigate, will you?"

"Oh, welcome aboard, you scoundrel." Mackenzie returned, laughing and shook his fist. Two years of sailing together had faded his aversion toward Maitland. "How do you find my *Renown?*"

Maitland's eyes twinkled, thinking of Mackenzie's advancement. "I suppose as much as you enjoyed commanding her. You've discovered the *Defiance* has more room, I see. Your quarters here are three times the size than on the *Renown.*" He held his arms out across the cabin width wise and beamed.

The Admiralty had transferred both captains to larger vessels. Mackenzie commanded the *Defiance,* a ship of the line, while Maitland, because of his capture of *la Valeur* in such a grand manner, took over the *Renown.* Neither of the commanders regretted the new arrangements, although Mackenzie had hoped to return home.

A disappointment for both, Maitland departed for England in September on the *Renown* to patrol the Channel. Mackenzie remained in Jamaica.

∽∾

Washington and Anne moved into Staunton Harold Hall shortly after the execution of his brother. Years had passed since he last visited the manor after a fallout with Laurence. In accordance with peerage inheritance, he became the new Earl Ferrers, entitled to all that the position conferred. The Admiralty placed him on reserve status so he could assume his new title and responsibilities at the House of Lords.

Washington, sitting at the desk in the library, worried Laurence had a great deal of debt as he inspected the books. Upon perusing the ledgers, he smiled and exclaimed, "Well, the figures look good. Rents and profits from livestock, crops, and mines continued to increase with little sold off. Laurence owed a few outstanding debts, but they amount to only a few thousand pounds. He got an offer for one of his racehorses that we must settle, and we have some leases to renew. Overall, the properties appear in excellent shape. The holdings bring in around 11,000 pounds a year."

Anne chuckled. "If the king grants us the estate patent then we'll do well. If not, the king will do well." The finances didn't concern Anne, still in shock to discover she had become a countess when Washington became the 5th Earl Ferrers. People treated her with more respect and friends adulated her. Moving into Staunton Harold Hall with its intricately designed gardens and elegant rooms turned earlier fantasies into reality. She loved them when visiting and now she enjoyed them every nice day.

Washington told her although he now gained the title, the estates legally belonged to the Crown, reclaimed after Laurence's hanging. They'd act as trustees and someday take possession if the king approved the patent and Parliament confirmed it. His good standing in the navy and the Shirley family's centuries-old support of the monarchy almost assured reinstatement. Still, a small doubt remained. King George II had never been one to grant new peerages. Washington hoped the king didn't see the old title of Earl Ferrers in that light.

Washington's transition from a navy ship commander to manor owner at first displeased him. Predictably, once he moved to the manor and the lure of the sea faded, he adapted to the aristocratic lifestyle. He found it gave him more opportunity to follow his real love, to read new scientific theories, attend lectures, dabble in new interests, and explore nature. After buying a telescope a few weeks later, he ordered an orrery made of gilded brass with ivory and exotic woods representing the six planets.

One day in the library, he searched through the messy stacks of documents that sat in piles Laurence abandoned willy-nilly around the room.

"Oh, dear." Washington chuckled as he sorted the papers. "Here's a tied bundle of letters addressed to me in the drawer." He held them up for Anne. "I wonder why Laurence didn't send them to me?"

Anne crossed the room and picked up a letter and scanned the contents. "After the terrible fights the two of you used to have, revenge pops up as my guess." She dropped it back on the stack.

"De mortuis nil nisi bene." Washington grinned and raised an eyebrow.

Used to him spouting Latin phrases, Anne smirked and asked, "Which means?"

"Never speak ill of the dead, dear. I'm sure it just slipped Laurence's mind. Or maybe he planned to give them to me on my next visit," reasoned Washington.

She giggled, a hand going to her mouth. "That would've resulted in a long wait. After he tried to shoot you in one of his tirades, you promised never to return. Are they important?"

"Let me see," he said as he riffled through them. "Nothing very urgent. Oh, here's one from my carpenter on the *Renown,* mailed from France. Abraham must have moved back to Brest to marry Yvette, his French fiancée."

After reading the letter, Washington smiled and laughed. "Abraham also asked if I bought a telescope. We discussed astronomical theories throughout his time on the frigate. Abraham had an affinity for science and would be thrilled to find out what I'm planning."

"Exactly what are you planning?" Anne smiled. She had seen him preoccupied with charts and drawings.

"Scientific preparations, my dear." Washington pointed his finger skyward. Anne laughed and let the question go unanswered.

"Go ahead and prepare, or whatever you wish, just don't dip into the estate money. You're responsible for it until the king decides whether you can keep it." Her warning ended in a smile.

He waited now on word if he'd be living as a noble landsman or a titled naval seaman.

The Ravaging Blaze
and the Ragged Bundle

The shipyard at Blackwall found itself again in a tight place with the British navy now in total domination of the seas. After the Battle of Quiberon Bay and gaining in the war against France in the Far East, the Americas, and the West Indies, the Admiralty cut back on shipbuilding. The East India Company, likewise, slowed requests for ships. The sudden drop in construction meant they had to let many workers go.

"Tomorrow's my last day of work at the shipyard," Abraham reminded Yvette as he slumped into his chair. He added, "But don't worry."

"Not worry? We have bills to pay! How much savings is set aside?" Yvette stepped away from the pot on the small stove and faced him, hands on her hips.

"Enough for a while." He threw his head back and closed his eyes. "I'll try to find a position at the shipyard in Woolwich or at the docks."

"How much means enough?" She pressed, frowning.

He thought a moment, sighed, and opened his eyes. "Around twenty pounds plus a few shillings. It should stretch at least half a year. I didn't receive my final salary at the shipyard yet, so that adds another pound and six."

Abraham didn't tell his wife the higher taxes on their house in France plus the rent on the flat in London created a disturbing shortage of funds.

"After we returned to England, I felt sure I could find work, too. So far—just an illusion." Yvette exhaled loudly. "As French, everyone sees me an enemy. I might find something in the Spitalfields again, but the mobs are too dangerous to work there." She hated dejection and let it drift from her mind.

"They'll hire me somewhere." Abraham's fingers drummed the table.

Yvette moved to the other side of the table and sat, staring wide-eyed. "Do you think you're the only one being sacked? If Blackwall is getting rid of carpenters, then they all are letting go of them. To kick out a shipwright as experienced as you, prospects must be decreasing everywhere." Her tongue clucked, dismissing his optimism.

Abraham never could hide things from Yvette, her analytical brain wouldn't be fooled or patronized. As he settled into his routine for the night, an item in the broadsheet caught his attention.

He had read about the Earl Ferrers's trial and execution but didn't realize that Washington Shirley was Laurence's brother and had inherited the title and estates.

"Yvette!" Abraham held up the newspaper and waved it excitedly. "Do you remember my captain, Washington Shirley, on the *Renown?* He was three years my junior, the same as you. That would make him thirty-eight now. When they hanged the Earl Ferrers, he got the title."

"Oh, so now *you're* friends with nobility." She mocked him and laughed.

He frowned in jest. "No longer a friend, just a past acquaintance, I suppose."

To speak of aristocrats once again reminded Yvette of her

unfortunate past with René de Saint-Alouarn. She said nothing but continued cooking, and her thoughts drifted to Gaëlle's letter months earlier. She hadn't mentioned René and François's deaths to Abraham, mindful of his sensitivity. But now was not the time to tell him.

"When we lived in Brest, I wrote Captain Shirley, asking if he ever got the telescope he wanted to buy. Actually, I wanted to find out if he stayed in the navy after the war, but he never answered. We had such interesting talks." Abraham sighed, smiling at her, delighted in his memories. "I always liked him. Captain Shirley had a good scientific mind and treated his crew fairly. Our relationship, however, bothered a few of the other officers. They disliked him for favoring a mere ship's carpenter." He chuckled.

Two days later he hiked to Woolwich hoping to find work, but learned, as Yvette had guessed, all shipyards were dismissing workers.

After the long trek home from the yard that night, he slouched in the chair at the kitchen table. "It seems life won't allow us to thrive." Once again, he confided in her, seeking solace.

She lifted a shoulder and tipped her head. "You're viewing it wrong. The war returned you to me unharmed and with wonderful tales." She smiled at him. "The navy taught you far more than just working at the slips could have. Perhaps this will present an opportunity, too. Have faith." Yvette was convinced of a divine plan.

"Faith?" He smirked. "I'd rather believe, regrettably, our actions brought us to this point, and God had little to do with it." His eyes rolled over Yvette's penchant for connecting religion to everything.

Yvette paid a visit to her closest friend in London the next day. "Abraham is having a hard time finding a new shipwright position. I don't know what to suggest." Yvette's face sagged, thinking of their financial situation. "He's so skilled, yet the yards don't hire him for lasting jobs. Every day he sinks further into melancholy."

Madame Goubert's new, ongoing courtship with Jacques stemmed from helping Yvette earlier. She wanted to repay Yvette for that blessing some way. "Then ask those whom you know. Countess Selina may find a position for him if she believes she still owes you a favor for handling those French soldiers at Donnington Hall. The next meeting of the

Calvinists comes this Saturday. She'll give a talk and you can attend with me." Madame Goubert grabbed her hand and smiled. She admired Yvette's audacity and personality far more than her friend knew, and wanted to help solve the problem.

Yvette agreed and a few days later, she sat and listened to Selina speak, as many times before. At its conclusion, she sought out the countess.

"Your presentation is inspiring as usual, Lady Selina." Yvette flattered when they met in the common room.

"Yvette, thank you. It's nice you could join us again. I hope those who heard my message will practice it." Selina smiled. "Charity is a cornerstone of our beliefs."

"Madame Goubert told me of Earl Huntingdon and your youngest son leaving us. I want to tell you how sorry I am." Yvette voice and face expressed sympathy. "I recall the time I spent at your manor in the Midlands and how I enjoyed the earl's conversations at dinner."

Selina resumed her assured bearing after a brief sad look down and nod. "They're at peace now with our Lord. My oldest son, Francis, assumed the title of the new Earl of Huntingdon. Donnington manor became his now. I live most of the year here in London." She smiled.

Yvette spoke in a serious but low tone, so others in the crowded room wouldn't hear. "Lady Selina, I also wanted to ask you something. Abraham is having great difficulty in obtaining work. Might you be aware of someone needing his skills? I've been unable to find a position since returning to London and with his paltry earnings, I'm afraid we may become desperate!"

Selina stared intently, listening as Yvette told her sad dilemma. "Hmm, I can't think of anyone." She paused. "But now, I remember something." Selina's voice rose and a smile grew on her face "It's not ship work, and I don't know if shipwrights can repair houses. Francis mentioned needing work done on some of our buildings at the manor."

Yvette's hopes rose and exclaimed, "Oh, Abraham is good at any carpentry! He rebuilt most of our cottage in France."

"Then I'm sure your husband would fit our needs. The task may not last long, but it will provide at least some income." Selina, known for her generosity and caring, delighted in aiding Yvette. "I'm returning to Donnington Hall in two days to visit my son. I'll tell him I've found someone reliable." Then she stopped and cocked her head to one side.

With a smile, Selina proposed a different idea. "Better still, if you and your husband wouldn't mind accompanying me in my coach, we'll make the trip together. It will save you the fare and save me from hours of boredom." She grabbed and patted Yvette's hand.

Awed at how easily the countess had resolved their burden, Yvette gushed, "Oh, Lady Selina, how can we thank you?"

Selina, wide-eyed, acted shocked. "Me? The chance to help others is bestowed as a gift from God. Besides, I will forever owe you a debt of gratitude for what you did for me with the, uh… French *visitors* at our manor." She gave Yvette a quick wink. "They could have shot us all! My knees shook the entire time and you took control."

Madame Goubert, overhearing the mention of the Frenchmen recalled the story and acted ignorant. She grinned and considered her good turn getting Abraham employment as only a partial repayment for Jacques, Yvette's gift to her.

Two days later, Selina, Yvette, and Abraham climbed into the countess's coach for the trip. More important than just a few days of work, Abraham thought, their association with the countess might even find him a permanent position.

As the coach bounced along the road, Selina tapped Abraham's knee with her fan. "Abraham, I'm so glad we've met. Yvette used to keep me informed of your marvelous adventures at sea." She widened her eyes, smiling. "She's so proud of you. Do you find living on land difficult?"

"Well, I much prefer it, my lady." He chuckled and patted his stomach. "Seasickness in rough weather much afflicted me, and the terrible battles make equally horrid memories at times." He pursed his lips with a slight shake of his head.

"My nephew served as a captain in the navy until recently. I presumed he'd have a difficult time adjusting to living on land, yet he's now content to leave the sea for the Midlands." The countess finished with a smile.

Curious, Abraham asked, blinking. "Oh? Although unlikely, I may have met him. What is his name?"

"Now his title is Earl Ferrers, but before, Captain Washington Shirley." She said with her head raised, proud of her nephew.

"Captain Shirley?!" Abraham's voice rose. "He's related to you?" His broad smile indicated his pleasure and he slapped his thigh over the surprise.

Selina again smiled. "Yes, before I married, my family name was Shirley."

"Lady Selina, I thought you were born a Hastings?" questioned Yvette with a slight frown, confused.

Selina nodded and chuckled. "It changed to Hastings when I married the earl and I also gained my peerage title, Huntingdon," she explained. "How are you familiar with my nephew, Abraham?"

"I served as his carpenter on the *Renown*, a ship he commanded. Not long ago I wrote to him, though perhaps he didn't get my letter."

"When we reach Donnington Hall, I'll send him a message. He lives nearby. If he can break away from his new tasks, he may come for a visit." Her eyes lit up.

Abraham opened his palms upward in amusement. "You can't imagine how over the years I've missed his brilliant thoughts during our conversations on science. I look forward to seeing him again. How far away does he live?" To see his old captain again delighted him almost as much as getting work at the manor.

"Oh, seven or eight miles in Staunton Harold Hall." Selina laughed. "The earl continues his interests in science and recently bought himself a new spyglass or something for watching the stars."

His mouth opened. "A telescope?" The kind countess had delivered even more wonderful news. "Now you have me bent on getting together. We both are fond of astronomy."

During the tedious, three day trip, the adults took turns entertaining one another. Abraham told tales of his experiences at sea, while Yvette described life in a French sea port and surviving the harrowing Cornhill fire the first time she lived in London. Selina spent much of her time expounding on the Calvinist religion, which she supported not just in spirit, but funding.

When they reached the estate in late morning, a splash of multi-colored vistas woke their senses. The gardens' floral designs exploded with warm mid-summer hues. Rectangular lakes, edged with yews and other shrubbery, reflected the blue sky above, each spaced between trimmed green lawns connected by broad walking paths.

The horses and coach wheels, crunching upon the graveled road, came to a stop before the façade of the old Tudor manor. Coachmen helped the ladies out and everyone stopped to stretch their legs.

Upon entering, Abraham began to study the structure. The first manor hall he'd ever visited, the interior piqued his interest, and he inspected the building methods and materials used.

"Francis, come and meet my friends." Selina pointed to the guests as her son entered the room. "Dear, I didn't have time to write to you. I'm sure you don't mind if we stay a few days, do you?"

The thirty-one-year-old Earl of Huntingdon, stood tall, his narrow face and high brow similar to his mother's. Like his father, he carried himself with confidence as he strode across the foyer.

"Mother, need you ask?" He greeted the strangers, used to the commoners his mother often brought with her. Francis found his mother's growing radical beliefs wearisome, yet, he tolerated her out of duty.

The party strolled out to the main garden where they explored the paths. They chatted about the plants and manor while Selina pointed out rare flowers. The countess had imported them from everywhere in Europe and the Americas. Soon they stopped before a bronze statue of a kneeling archer with his bow pulled back.

"That's Robin Hood, an Earl of Huntingdon, too," said Selina, with a slight smile and nodding at the sculpture.

Yvette widened her eyes. "Robin Hood? Abraham told me the stories. I recall he used to rob people, no?" She walked around it and studied the face.

"Robin Hood stole like a highwayman, but was generous to the poor and noble in his causes." Francis smiled, reflecting. "Much the same as my mother." He took pride in his ancestry, and in his mother, regardless of her extreme take on religion.

"Yes, I'm charitable, too, but I don't steal from people!" Selina giggled and shook her head as the four continued their walk. "Tell me, is my nephew, Earl Ferrers at his manor?"

Francis thought a moment. "I believe so."

"Fine. I'll send a message this afternoon that we have an old friend of his at our hall." She smiled. "Abraham served under him in the navy."

Later that afternoon after receiving the message, Washington spent the rest of the day blabbering about the *Renown's* carpenter and Yvette to Anne. He dashed off a response and invited Abraham and Yvette to come to his home the next morning. A driver fetched them in a coach for the short trip a few hours after sunup.

Staunton Harold Hall and the estate buildings appeared in the distance; the geometric-shaped gardens and lakes surrounding the hall highlighted the landscape. Towering trees bordered the roads and reflecting pools glinted in the sunlight. A small, Gothic-styled church stood a short distance from the main residence.

As the carriage pulled up outside the entrance, the double doors swung open. Washington came trotting out past a servant, smiling and waving.

"Welcome, welcome! Aunt Selina, you've brought happiness in your coach today." He ran forward and grabbed at Abraham's hand. "A good day to you, my old friend. I assume this lovely woman is your dear wife." He bubbled with excitement and pumped Abraham's hand.

"Captain Shirley—I mean, Earl Ferrers, sorry. I suppose I'll have to remember." Abraham laughed while helping Yvette down with his other hand. "Yes, this is Yvette."

Yvette climbed out of the coach and curtsied as Washington bowed slightly to her and hurried them into the house. Selina bussed Washington's cheek and joined them as they made their way inside.

In the foyer, Washington curled his finger. "Come in and let me introduce you to Anne, the new Countess Ferrers."

Abraham bowed low and Yvette again curtsied to Anne, coming to them. They made their way to the main parlor, filled with the trappings of nobility and tall windows.

The room offered a wonderful view of an English garden before a reflection pool. Beyond the pool lay an extensive meadow with treelined lanes that reached beyond and ended in a forest of great oak trees. Yvette took in the sunlit expanse. "Oh, what a scene. It's beautiful, like a palace."

"Yvette, you embarrass us." Anne laughed and placed a hand to her mouth. "Royalty build palaces and we don't share that status. I'm still getting used to the idea of being a countess. But I've looked forward to meeting you. My husband says you're quite an adventurous woman. You fled France with Abraham during the war, pretending to be Scottish?" Anne's eyes sparkled inquisitively.

"I've only been so daring since knowing Abraham," she answered with a nod at her husband. "It's his life that's forced me to traipse between France and England."

Soon they were catching up on events in their lives, relaxing in the parlor. Washington detailed his acquisition of the title and lands and his transformation into a landsman, and Abraham and Yvette related their life in Brest and return to London.

Anne and Yvette took to one another, while Abraham and Washington reverted to their old ways. The men talked and even argued over science and ship designs. Selina interjected updates to the local news and what she heard in London.

"Abraham, I must show you what I've purchased—a telescope!" Washington grabbed Abraham by the sleeve and pulled him toward the library.

"Lady Selina mentioned you bought one. Reflector? Refractor?" he asked as excited as Washington in the rush to the room.

With a broad grin, Washington removed a draped cloth from the long tube. "A refractor with achromatic lenses. I used it to view Jupiter and the moon, so far. It produces spectacular images!" He wrung his hands remembering the sight of the giant planet.

Abraham eyed the equipment and stroked a tripod leg. "I'm so envious of you. From where do you view them?"

"The church's belfry roof. The tower has a fantastic view with few obstructions." Washington had an idea and rushed to add, "Oh, you must stay the night! We can go out later if the sky stays clear and observe the planets. Will you?" Washington smiled eagerly as Abraham continued to inspect the telescope.

He looked at Washington with a small smile, chuckling. "You don't need to ask twice. Of course, we'll stay. I wish the clock struck midnight right now."

Washington threw up his finger for drama. "For more exciting news, I want to get a precise chronometer for the transit next year."

"You intend to measure Venus's transit?" Abraham raised his eyebrows.

"Why not? If I have the equipment and if the weather permits, I'll capture the exact times it crosses the sun's surface. See, I made a transitarium of Venus." He motioned Abraham over to the bookshelves that lined the walls on three sides of the library.

Washington took a small wooden box off a bookshelf and proudly opened it. It contained a mechanical representation of the sun, earth, and the orbit of Venus; a small orb represented the planet. By turning the handle, the ivory earth revolved and Venus orbited the sun. A little plate placed in a slot displayed where Venus passed in front of the sun and its angle in relation to the earth. The intricate mechanism showed in three dimensions the concept of the transit.

Holding the instrument, he squinted at the small delicate parts. "Where did you get this?" Abraham smiled in wonder.

"From Benjamin Cole's in London, the watchmakers. They made it from my designs. Every time I tried to explain what the transit was, no one understood." He shrugged and shook his head.

"When is Venus transiting next summer?" Abraham asked, his brows knitting.

"Just as Halley predicted, it'll occur on June 6th. With good conditions, we'll see it in England."

Abraham returned the box to the shelf and then patted the telescope's tube in admiration. "We live in such an exciting time. It hasn't happened in over a hundred years. I wish I'd be here to witness it."

"Well, why not?" Washington's face lit up. "If you're here, you could assist me. I'll need help. I haven't figured out everything yet, and before the transit, you can set everything up with me and take notes." He made a quick nod, confirming the plan. "Good idea, Abraham, you've solved a problem."

"Great, if I'm not working at a yard. Since opportunities have dropped for permanent positions, I just might be your assistant then." He replied, but unspoken, he wondered how he could afford such a luxury.

"If you're not in a shipyard next June, then I insist you come. Regardless, we can watch Jupiter and, I believe, Saturn tonight." Washington reached around and pulled an ephemeris out from a desk drawer and checked the charts. "Tonight, both will appear." He closed the book with a quick snap and banged it down on the desk in triumph.

Abraham's excitement had yet to dispel. "How lucky, at last I'll get to view them in a good telescope. What constellations?"

"Both rise in the east, Jupiter in Aquarius and Saturn in Pisces, and both are best viewed after midnight when they move well above the horizon." Washington answered turning for the door to leave.

He and Abraham thanked Selina as she left for her estate and settled in the parlor for an evening of catching up. Anne and Yvette, sitting across from one another, exchanged their stories as well.

Later in the night's chill atop the church's bell tower, the two men stood gazing in wonder at the two planets. The moonless and cloudless sky provided them with exceptional viewing as the Milky Way stretched its halo of silver across the star-pierced black dome.

Soon, the wives joined them, climbing up the ladder and carrying glasses of sherry in exchange for views of the planets.

"*C'est incroyable!*" Yvette placed her fingers on her cheek as she looked at Jupiter in the telescope.

"Yes, incredible. See its moons? Just wait until you view Saturn." Washington moved the finder scope to Saturn, focused, and got out of the way for the women.

Oh's and *ah's* followed as each took turns in observing the rings around the giant orb. Washington allowed them to get their fill of the spectacles until the cool air chilled them. Then he and Abraham lowered the telescope off the roof, and they warmed themselves with a pot of hot rum back inside the hall.

"For the transit, I still must buy a decent chronometer. Without one, a parallax measurement is useless. I hope the Royal Society expeditions make it to the Americas and elsewhere to take measurements for the triangulation. The society announced they plan to, yet who knows if the astronomers will get there or if the weather will favor viewing."

"How accurate must the clock run?" Abraham's scientific mind sought more.

"The whole transit takes seven hours. For a measurement to figure out the distance to the sun with accuracy, Halley limited errors to within two seconds or less. I can get a good chronometer within that limit now. Only I'm hoping clock makers come out with a better one before June of next year."

"Again, I envy you. Life grants to but few the privilege to spend time in a field you love. I've favored carpentry since a young man. But I'd prefer science if money availed itself."

"I'm spending more than just time." Washington widened his eyes. "Now I can buy instruments I delayed purchasing earlier."

A day later Abraham and Yvette departed for Selina's manor again to work on the Donnington estate buildings. For Abraham, it took minimal effort to patch the structures that had rotted timbers, uneven floors, and jammed doors. After two weeks they returned to London. At home, they searched for positions and Abraham found repair work once more on small ships while Yvette became frustrated looking for a bookseller to hire her.

"As soon as I open my mouth, they tell me they have no openings." Yvette pouted. "The bookshop owners presume French women can't make good clerks."

"Why hire any French person at all, especially a woman, when lots of Englishmen line the streets unemployed?" Abraham tried to cool her emotions with reason. "Other than street vending or being a servant, a woman needs luck to have a clerk position, let alone like the one you had at a bookstore our first time in London."

"I might claim the same for an Englishman's chances of getting a shipwright position in Brest. I could own a bookstore and do better than most of the owners I've met."

Abraham didn't want to challenge her on it since he agreed with her. In reality, they needed more money than he made. Any kind of employment for her could help.

The expenses to maintain the house in Brest, although not too much, kept them from getting ahead. He received enough to cover costs in London but their French cottage nibbled away everything else and still left them short funds.

"Tomorrow I'll try at Blackwall or Woolwich. They may have opened positions," he said, allowing himself to be optimistic.

"What am I going to do? No one will hire me and I need to work." Yvette's lack of employment made her feel inadequate. After the ease of getting her first job in London, she falsely assumed it would be easy again. "From now on, I'll seek anything that makes money."

Yvette's pronouncement, although sensible, skewered Abraham's self-esteem. Not being able to support the family was a recurring problem for him. The times were hard for even skilled laborers, yet he still expected he should earn enough for them both. However, he hoped that work could fill Yvette's void of being childless.

One morning in early September, Abraham prepared to set out for the day. "I'm taking a boat to Woolwich to hunt for an opening, and I'll be back in the afternoon," he told Yvette, kissing her cheek before stuffing his lunch in his leather bag and closing the door behind him.

The rowboat cost almost a full shilling for the ten-mile ride to the Woolwich shipyard, more than he wanted to pay. However, he couldn't waste a half day walking and arrive too late to be hired. In Woolwich, however, no jobs arose, although a shipwright told him the Portsmouth naval yard needed more carpenters after a lightning strike had destroyed many of its buildings.

That night at dinner time, he told Yvette of his plans to go to Portsmouth the next day.

"Portsmouth? That's two days away. You'll have to pay for a coach. Where will you stay?" Yvette glowered and drummed the table, concerned over the extra drain on their savings for a coach ride and inn.

Abraham glared into his mug of coffee after finishing his meal.

"Still, a position looks definite. I'll stay as long as they need me." Then he told her the worst part. "You may have to join me if you don't find work here. We can't afford two places to live; one for you and one for me."

She reacted as he thought she might. "Wait! So, if you go, I might have to go, too?" Her mind spun to digest the thought. "Portsmouth—where I can't find any employment? It's such a small town I doubt that they even have stores needing new clerks, let alone any work for a female!" she growled.

Her tirade stung. So, he tried to be logical. "It may be, but it'd be naval shipyard work for me. The pay should be steady and might be permanent. Besides, I'd earn more salary than if we both found just temporary jobs in London." He smiled trying to calm her. "Don't you believe it's worth the try?"

She rose from the table and turned away from him. "It's a try that will cost a lot of pounds and you may end up with no job and just waste money already stretched thin." She spoke more even-tempered, holding back her anger.

Abraham got up and stepped behind her, placed his arms around her, hugging her. "Dear, we have to take chances sometimes. The prospects appear good that I'll get the position. Let's try. You know I wouldn't follow a fool's errand."

Yvette conceded with a frown. The next morning he left for Portsmouth, and once again she searched the bookshops in London.

In the coach to Portsmouth, Abraham heard from a navy lieutenant openings had existed earlier. The officer wasn't too sure, however, if they still needed men. Carpenters, he mentioned, had been flocking to the yard for weeks. Abraham worried the rest of the trip that Yvette may have been correct.

After arriving, he rushed to the shipyard and pulled his papers from his leather bag and handed them to the clerk. To his relief, they told him to start work that very day.

The fire had gutted a storehouse just stocked with new supplies for ships. The flammable materials inside, tar, turpentine, and pitch, burned with such intensity that saving the building became impossible.

Breezes spread cinders to the rope-house, hemp-house, and a spinning house, destroying them. The tally of the loss amounted to over 50,000 pounds.

With the many extra workers hired to get back on schedule, the influx of builders made housing in Portsmouth difficult to find. To accommodate them, the navy pitched camps, which saved on inn and room rents, but made for uncomfortable living conditions even in late summer. The first night, Abraham found himself stuffed in a campaign tent with three other carpenters, sleeping head-to-foot.

Two days later, the shipyard put Abraham to work on a captured French frigate named *le Blonde*. To his trained eye, her lines typified French design. He soon discovered the navy had captured her near Ireland, surveyed, and determined her fit for service in the navy.

Much of the design appeared the same as the frigates he worked on in Brest. A week passed, and Abraham got into a discussion with another carpenter. "The *Blonde* is very typical of most French frigates. Look at the acute inward slant of the midship freeboard. That really reduces crosswind forces on the hull and keeps her from heeling." He grinned at the innovation.

The other replied, nodding. "I saw the same on one I repaired before. A former French frigate called the *Renown,* two years ago with many characteristics like *le Blonde.* We rebuilt her and brought her closer to Establishment standards. " He chortled. "As you can guess, it slowed her."

"I repaired her before they towed her here and assumed we'd ruin her speed." Abraham confessed and shook his head. "I built her in Brest before the war along with others."

Their supervisor overheard Abraham's conversation.

"You've had experience building the Frenchies?" he asked Abraham, an eyebrow raised.

"I worked in France on many before the war," he replied.

"Huh," the man grunted and walked away.

A week later the same supervisor offered him the crew foreman spot for the repairs and refitting of *le Blonde.* The promotion increased his salary twenty-five percent, and they moved him to a former old marine barracks with real beds.

When September ended, Abraham considered whether Yvette should move to Portsmouth but worried once the shipyard's schedules returned to normal, they might dismiss him. In a letter, Yvette told him of her luck in finding a book-sales job. The owner of a bookstore on Pater Noster Street, Mister Buckland, needed a French-speaking vendor. As a street vendor, Yvette sold French versions of Anglican religious books. The owner paid little, and she worked outside the entire day. Nevertheless, she appreciated any employment. Abraham knew he couldn't ask her to quit even if he worked the winter in Portsmouth. Yvette needed something to occupy her time and to make money.

∞

"Livre Anglican de prières!" Yvette shouted in French and then in English, "Anglican book of prayers!" She'd been having a slow day and had sold just a few catechism pamphlets for a pence or two. The day before she had sold four *Common Books of Prayer,* and she earned a good commission and impressed the store owner.

Mister Buckland told her she could sell the publications in Spitalfields for whatever she liked as long as he got his share of the sale. Although people judged Spitalfields by its rough reputation, it held a concentration of Protestant devotees and book buyers. Maybe they need to pray more than the rest of London, Yvette joked to herself.

Yvette read a few of the pamphlets and concluded they sounded similar to what she heard at the Calvinist gatherings. She wondered if selling Protestant books harmed her beliefs. Then decided, as she had about Abraham, people believe things based on their personal experiences, not hers, and what they read had no influence on her.

At first, she hated being a book-woman in Spitalfields. Not only were the anti-French mobs a threat, but ruffians, thieves, and prostitutes passed as common traffic on the streets, and they intimidated her. She quickly learned to put on an air of self-confidence and toughness in speech and attitude that kept the miscreants away. Yet, witnessing young people engaged in a life of crime and moral decay depressed

Yvette. Teenaged boys congregated on corners or in alleys plotting evil, while young girls plied their bodies for a shilling or even a few pence. She added their salvation to her nightly prayers.

Abraham had written her, but she hadn't told him where she was selling out of fear he'd worry for her safety. Had he seen the immorality she'd seen in the few weeks she worked for Mister Buckland, he'd have forbidden her to work there.

The weather turned wetter and cooler with fall well on its way. Her book bag protected the merchandise and her wide-brimmed felt hat and cape protected her head and shoulders. Just the same, the cold rains soaked the rest. The heavy book bag made walking difficult. In addition, if it rained hard her dress weighed her down even more. The few shillings she earned each week provided for food with little left.

One afternoon as she walked and barked her wares, Yvette had an old feeling well up inside her. It was difficult to pinpoint, but she had these before in her life—omens of something important. This time, a warmth grew inside. It demanded she turn at the next corner. Often she ignored these strange impulses, but not that day.

"Look, there. Now that's a pitiful sight," a soot-covered chimney sweep said, standing in an alleyway with a group of others. They stared at someone on the ground.

Yvette, curious, turned into the alley and peeked over their shoulders. On the ground propped against the cold stone wall was a young woman, no older than seventeen. She clutched rags to her chest and was as pale as a book page. Her lips had turned bloodless and her eyes focused on a distant imagined vision.

"What's wrong with her?" someone asked.

"I think she's dying." The chimney sweep shook his head.

As Yvette studied the girl, it seemed obvious. She had witnessed the slow breath and ashen complexion many times when patients died in Brest's hospital where she volunteered. The woman's face had sores covering it. "Who is she?" Yvette pitied the young woman.

"A prostitute," said one. "I've seen her around here for months now. Her name is Michelle and she's always sick. Men seldom desired her." He faced away from the wretched scene.

The other passersby also began to leave yet Yvette drew closer to the stricken young lady.

"Can you hear me, my dear? Can I do anything for you?"

Her eyes settled on Yvette and her lips, dry and cracked, spoke to her with a slight French accent. "Please, take this." She struggled to lift the ragged bundle to her. Yvette reached down and picked up the dirty clump.

She felt it move and uncovered it, her eyes opened wide, finding an infant. "This is your baby?" Yvette asked her in French, stunned. The woman nodded and weakly pointed from the baby to Yvette.

The young mother's whispers faded, inaudible, and her eyes rolled.

Another passerby stopped to investigate. "Poor creature. Dumped like garbage and left to die alone by a heartless bawd."

"She handed me her baby." Yvette pointed to the child, a tear in her eye and overcome with compassion for the poor woman and infant.

"Probably has the pox, too. It looks half-starved to death. My, how its bones show." The workman grimaced and looked away.

"She's three or four months old." Yvette assessed her by her size. She gently brushed hair from the tot's face and drew her closer.

As she did this, the young prostitute moaned and let out a final deep breath and closed her eyes, her hand still pointing to Yvette.

"Poor creature, indeed. Once an unsoiled maiden who had dreams of motherhood, home, and a husband, I bet." The workman bowed his head and walked away.

Yvette sat on the cobblestone beside the dead mother and cradled the baby. She paid no attention to the stares and murmuring of those around her and searched inward for guidance. Minutes later, Yvette bent over the body and gently kissed her forehead. "*Merci,* Michelle. Go in peace," she whispered, crossed herself, and left.

Yvette didn't know what she should do and tried to find someone to have Michelle's body removed. She carried the baby and walked along the street, looking for a constable or city marshal.

Twenty minutes later, she found and reported the death to a constable. Indifferent to the news, he logged the location of the body. When she told him about the baby, the man ordered Yvette to take her to the foundlings home in Bloomsbury.

He snickered. "They won't keep it for long. She's starved and sick. They only house the healthy ones." He didn't bother a second glance.

Yvette walked away amazed at the callousness over an innocent's life. As she carried the child, Yvette realized this was a trial from God and headed to the bookstore.

Outside the store hung a large sign above the door that read, Buckland's Fine Books, decorated with a picture of a buck deer with gilded antlers. Yvette went in through the rear entrance off the alley to avoid creating a spectacle. She set the baby on a wooden case and found Mister Buckland.

"Sorry, Mister Buckland, I must leave early today from my rounds," she said and awaited a curt response.

"Are you ill?" Mister Buckland, peered over his spectacles. He was a short, rotund man about fifty-five years of age and had been a publisher for over twenty-five years. His constant criticism of everyone showed he wasn't a patient sort.

Yvette worried he'd be outraged, but her conviction forced the story out of her. "This is strange; a dying woman thrust her baby into my arms an hour ago. I'm not sure what to do. The child needs milk and is starving." Yvette took him into the storeroom and showed him the baby.

At first, he drew back when she unwrapped the rags. Then slowly he gazed down on the child with compassion in his eyes. Sympathy overtook him and he agreed Yvette should rush the baby to be nursed by someone. Mister Buckland asked a clerk if anyone close by wet-nursed, and the man pointed her in the right direction.

Yvette hurried from the store and found the wet nurse, who fed and cared for babies for working mothers. She explained how the dying woman had given her the baby, and at first the nurser hesitated to feed a prostitute's child. Then after inspecting her, she discovered no pox or illnesses other than malnutrition and put the baby to her breast for a few pence.

"This baby can eat food now at five months, and appears small because she's eaten too little," the woman said. "Do you plan to keep her if she lives?"

Standing in the small flat with three babies in makeshift cribs, she realized the thought hadn't occurred to her the baby might die. Yvette's face flushed and she nearly shouted her reply. "I must!" Then more quietly she added, "In effect, God has given me the duty. The mother's last act was handing her to me."

Though Yvette desperately longed for a baby, a prostitute's starved baby who arose from immorality didn't appeal to her. The only thing she knew about the child was her mother's first name. Despite that, since God placed the child in her care, she believed, then God meant for her to care for the little one.

After feeding, Yvette took her back to the flat and made a temporary crib in a cabinet drawer. She didn't know how to look after a baby and sell books, but she'd think of a solution.

While changing the baby's wraps, Yvette saw how filthy the child was and washed her. As she dried the fine blond hair, the baby's blue eyes focused on her, watching every move without a sound. Yvette stared deep into the azure pools of innocence, almost expecting the baby to say *Mama*. The realization she was now responsible for the child in lieu of her real mother, swept her up into feelings of pity and motherly tenderness.

"Oh, you good little baby." Yvette whispered. Within an hour, Yvette's natural maternal responses surfaced. After trying and failing to have a child, God might not grant her another chance, she mulled. She resolved to accept what God had provided for her and tend to the baby as though she had birthed her.

As Yvette cradled the baby in her arms and paced around the flat, she grew anxious over how Abraham might react to the unexpected presence of a harlot's newborn. How could she express in a letter that she had to accept this new calling from God? Her religion, she knew, made him uncomfortable and even irritated him. Plus, babies create big changes in people's lives—and expense. Perhaps, she considered, it would be best to postpone telling her husband.

Yvette took the baby with her as she searched for clouts and a pilcher in a store. The linen clouts cost too much, so she decided to just use rags. The woolen pilcher was cheap, its size large enough to hold the clouts and accommodate a growing baby; and the ties tested sturdy. Then she looked for a used pewter feeding bottle and found one at a fair price, that and the babe's clothing were enough to get her started.

At home, she boiled a cup of milk, added flour and bread crumbs to make pap for the bottle, and then fed her. Later, when Yvette ate her dinner, she chewed a spoonful of the food and fed the baby until she turned her head away and took no more.

The child hadn't a name, so Yvette gave her the one thing her birth mother could leave the baby, her mother's name, Michelle. The gift wasn't much, but it'd last her entire life. That night, the baby lay upon the bed with her, wanting to be fed only once.

The next day before work she gave the baby to the same wet nurse. The cost of the care didn't amount to much, yet Yvette needed to sell more books to pay for it and the other necessities. That day she sold twice the amount of the previous and thanked God in her prayers for the blessings.

Over the next week she adjusted more into a workable routine. The baby spent the day with the nursemaid and each night she watched the baby until she fell asleep and woke to feed her when she cried. Exhausted in the mornings, she struggled to get through her days of bookselling.

One evening when she returned to the shop, Mister Buckland approached her as she pulled the heavy book bag from her shoulder. "How's the baby doing?" he asked with a surprising, but genuine concern. "No fevers or lesions?"

"Fine so far." Yvette bit her lip, hoping it was true. "She'll need a lot of love and food to gain more weight." She counted and returned the unsold literature to a shelf and handed him the sales money. It had been a good week. Yvette's sales rose as she learned new selling tricks.

He took the coins and smiled with knitted brows. "If the child makes it to her first year, I have a number of old things for her."

She nodded to her employer and replied, "How kind for offering and asking about Michelle, Mister Buckland."

"I brought a toy for her." He reached in his coat pocket and produced a small wooden baby rattle.

Yvette grinned at his generosity. "She'll enjoy it." She took the gift and placed it in her pocket.

He looked down and shook his head. "What you're doing is very kind and Christian of you, Yvette. Most people would've taken the baby straight to the foundlings hospital or left her in the street." Her charitable nature clashed with what he might have done, and his face flushed slightly.

"I must admit to deliberating both." Yvette smiled large with dimpled cheeks. "Even so, I feel this is no mere chance happening. I think of it as a gift coming from heaven. To reject such will insult God."

"I didn't picture it that way." Mister Buckland tipped his head and agreed. "You're right. Perhaps Huguenots have a better take on this than we Anglicans." He laughed.

She joined in the laughter and added, "Maybe, though actually I'm Catholic, not Huguenot."

"Catholic? Oh, I see." He hesitated, his mouth opened a bit, and he stared away. "I'm afraid I thought you a French Huguenot. That, ah, is why I sent you to Spitalfields to sell our publications. Ah…" Mister Buckland, flustered, lowered his eyes from her gaze.

He glanced up at her. "This places me in a very disturbing predicament, Yvette." He swallowed hard, his eyes darting to the side. "I must let you go. It's not that you've done anything wrong or aren't a good vendor. Just the same, if others found out we hired a Catholic in our Anglican bookstore, we'd never hear the end," he huffed.

His remarks cut deep and words leapt from her mouth. "Please, sir, I've been selling enough, haven't I?" Yvette pleaded, eyes wide with desperation. "With the new baby I need work! Can't we forget I said I'm a Catholic?" Blood drained from her head and her body sagged.

Mister Buckland's hand waved side-to-side in front of him. "No, Yvette. A Catholic cannot work here. Let me pay today's earnings, and then you must leave." He opened his cash box and tallied what he owed her, avoiding her eyes.

To begin another long search for a job ran through her head and made her ill inside. The position wasn't much, but it provided enough for the baby's needs, she thought. She had yet to tell Abraham about the baby. Would it anger him when she spent more for Michelle?

Adding a shilling more out of guilt, Mister Buckland reached his arm around without turning to face her. "Here's the money for your sales and a bit more." He dropped the few coins into her hand without meeting her eyes. "I'll pray you find a new position."

As he slunk out to the front of the store, Yvette's reply trailed him in a weak voice, "Thank you." Near tears, she picked up her things and left.

A Trick, a Troth,
and a Trap

The first mention of Michelle to Abraham came in the second letter he got from Yvette in late October 1760. From the baby's description Abraham wondered if the weak child would live. Such a shock could devastate Yvette. That a prostitute gave birth to her didn't matter to him as much as whether the baby might have contracted a disease and spread it to his wife. Although unfortunate she lost her position, he made more than other temporary workers in Portsmouth and enough for the extra expense of an infant.

Since the navy had diverted shipbuilding to other yards due to the fire, the few ships in Portsmouth being repaired, refitted, or under construction went back on schedule. This meant in just a matter of weeks, the local shipwright guild would want their men to handle the workload, and discharge the new temporary workers. Abraham hoped his former guild membership might influence them to keep him on through the winter months.

By December, however, the shipyard posted a notice of a thinning of the recent-hired shipwrights, and the first ten left. By Christmas, a second batch left. Only Abraham and two other temporary men remained on the job. Abraham assumed this was because of his advanced skills in ship repair and foreign shipbuilding knowledge.

The local guild also had an opening for a new member and Abraham expected they'd allow him to join since he had belonged to the guild in Woolwich. But an announcement came in mid-January releasing the last carpenters, including him. Abraham didn't understand why they refused him when a lesser-skilled man got the membership.

When he returned home to London, Yvette dragged him by the hand the moment he entered the front door. "Come see your daughter," she squealed, leading him to the bedroom.

The child lay asleep in an old wicker cradle. Abraham gazed down on the baby. It seemed right, almost as if she had always been there in her cradle. He had the immediate desire to hold her but didn't want to wake her.

"So, tell me what happened." Abraham smiled and walked back into the kitchen to sit, dropping his clothing pack and leather bag on the floor.

She related how she got Michelle and now was looking for work again. Yvette added the baby took ill soon after she lost her job, so she had stayed home caring for her. As she told him, she wondered if he had yet accepted the notion of a new daughter not of his own making. That anxiety made her speak quickly and her hands fidgeted.

He picked up on her nervousness. "Darling, I'm so overjoyed for you. Michelle is a wondrous gift for us both. Naming her Michelle is perfect as well. I'll fall in love with her by the end of the day." He hugged and kissed Yvette as she relaxed and hugged him back.

Abraham noticed how motherhood changed Yvette. She behaved more seriously with him. Everything she mentioned over the next few days revolved around Michelle. Abraham, too, became focused on the new family member, helping care for her, although he left changing the dirty clouts to Yvette. Michelle seemed much healthier than what Yvette described in her letters, and the baby had gained weight.

Yvette said she tried to find out who Michelle's dead mother was, but shrugs always answered the question. So many young girls came to London to make money and ended up as prostitutes. All that Yvette learned was Michelle's mother lay in a pauper's grave under a simple wooden cross.

Not long after, in February 1761, Abraham received a letter from Washington Shirley. He had written news about the transit of Venus, purchasing a chronometer, and still insisted Abraham come to Staunton Harold to help. Without his assistance, Washington claimed he couldn't carry out the grand experiment. The last item emphasized Washington's desire for Abraham and Yvette to return for another visit if work and time permitted as his guests for a week in the spring.

Abraham wondered whether Washington understood how commoners lived. For the wealthy, taking trips cost little. Washington's ignorance of the value most placed on money or how little of it reached the pockets of workers dumbfounded him. He wrote back that he had yet to find a lasting job and a shortage of funds forbid his return until the summer.

Weeks later, when a friend from Woolwich informed him that a membership had opened in the Worshipful Guild of Shipwrights, Abraham asked him to suggest his name for reinstatement. Soon after, his friend explained he couldn't become a guild member anywhere because the navy listed him as deserting.

"How and why would they list me as a deserter?" he repeated to Yvette for the fifth time. "Since I served over the four-year enlistment until the war ended, how can they classify me that way? No wonder I've had such a hard time finding a lasting job." He rubbed his head in frustration.

"It's just an error. Go to the navy offices and straighten out the mistake! I'd hate to see you arrested and hanged." Her chuckle hid her concern.

"Desertion can't be taken as a joke." He bowed his head, shoulders hanging. "I can't prove I'm not a deserter. There's nothing I have to avoid a navy court-martial. If I don't correct this error now, I won't find work anywhere. I was lucky they didn't arrest me in Portsmouth or Deptford."

Yvette frowned and narrowed her eyes. "You told me they seldom hunted for them after the last war since so many deserted."

"Yes, though, I can't take that chance." His mouth turned down. "It keeps me from joining a guild. The only person who can help is Captain Shirley. He's aware I served my full term and could clear this up with the navy."

Abraham wrote Washington explaining the error, suggesting a date when he and Yvette could visit him just before Venus's transit.

A few weeks later, he received a reply with fare money from Washington telling him to come to the manor at once. They'd stay as his guests until they completed the transit work and Washington cleared up the desertion mess. A few days later, Abraham and Yvette took a stagecoach and arrived in Leicester where Washington's coach met them for the final twenty miles to the manor.

As they approached the estate, Abraham, Yvette, and the baby, alone in the coach, smiled as they rode in better comfort than they had on the stage coach to Leicester. "Imagine riding like this every day instead of crammed into a coach with smelly others on hard wooden seats. The earl has a wonderful life," Abraham said, his fingers brushing the seat cushion.

Yvette smiled. "Hmm, don't get too used to it, dear. We're lucky for the next week or so to experience their luxurious lifestyle. Then it'll be back to London and our squalor." She giggled.

Once again as they approached the main hall, the door opened and Washington stepped out. Anne stood by the door as he trotted up to the coach and raised his arms. "Welcome, my friends." He greeted with eyes twinkling.

"Earl Ferrers, you are a blessing to see after bounding for days on the rutted roads. Although, I must admit it's a much quicker trip with the turnpike finished," Abraham laughed.

Washington beamed as the footman held the coach door for his visitors. "Progress happens at lightning speed these days." He tittered. "We're building canals and announcing inventions and discoveries every month. It's a remarkable time we live in!" Washington declared.

"Come inside for tea, I have to show you something afterward." He hurried them in as the footman retrieved their bags.

After a half an hour of chatting in the parlor over tea, the five split up. Anne whisked Yvette and Michelle away to the garden while Washington took Abraham to his library, a virtual Eden of knowledge with books on every subject and by most classical authors.

"We'll discuss your desertion later. Here's what I've been working on," Washington said as he unrolled a large drawing. "I want to redesign the manor in a more contemporary style."

On the drawings were many façade designs for the main hall and the outer buildings, the fashionable Palladian style replacing the old Jacobean architecture. A view from above showed the gardens and lakes in natural free-formed patterns instead of the precise geometric shapes of the old landscaping. Washington had drawing after drawing of the hall, stables, and other structures on rolls that left just the Gothic church untouched.

"Sir, these are marvelous designs. Who's the architect?"

"No architect, just a beached sea captain pacing floor boards instead of a deck." Washington's gaze was distant.

"You've done excellent work. The plans are remarkable and the overall effect is splendid! The layout is very modern and fresh." Abraham's trained eye for technical details found no flaws.

"I based them on the work of a colonial architect named Peter Harrison whose works stand out everywhere. His story I find an interesting one." He paused. "It's one you should hear. The French captured the ship he voyaged on, back in '44 when he sailed from Italy for Boston. They quartered him in the Citadel of Louisbourg in the commander's home under house arrest. While there, the commander allowed Peter to use his study to work. Peter discovered the fortification drawings for the entire citadel in the room, so he copied them." Washington's eyes gleamed wide. "Soon after, the French released him to return to Boston, and he smuggled the drawings in the lining of his clothing. After Governor Shirley got them, the invasion plans began." He pulled up a chair and sat, motioning to Abraham to do the same.

Abraham clicked his tongue in amusement. "The French caught

and imprisoned him in Louisbourg, and their largest French fort in the Americas fell because of it."

"In brief, yes." Washington grinned at the irony. "The governor used the fortification drawings to convince others of the possibility of attacking Louisbourg. Once he convinced everyone, he used the drawings against it with success." As he spoke he unrolled yet another finely detailed drawing from his stack.

Shaking his head, Abraham rubbed his chin. "History is full of little unrelated seeds growing and entangling into complex consequences." He eyed the new drawing intently.

Washington pointed to the plans. "Although these drawings show the overall effect, I need someone to handle the specific aspects. I can't start, though, until the king approves the return of the property to me. Until then, I'll begin estimating the costs for the labor and materials." He opened his arms wide. "I want Staunton Harold to be a showcase of the modern style." He gazed out the window with pride.

After discussing the drawings and how they could drain, alter, and refill the lakes and pools, their construction talk turned to Abraham's navy problem.

"Tell me, now." Washington frowned and squinted. "What's this business of desertion you mentioned earlier?"

Abraham patted the table before him with his fingertips as he related his dilemma. "It seems an error occurred. They listed me as a deserter after I left your ship." He sighed and slouched in the chair. "When I tried to join a guild, they rejected me because of it. It may be the reason why I haven't found a permanent position."

"Well, I'll write a letter to the Admiralty." Washington's brows knitted, wanting to help him. "That will settle the matter." Washington walked to his desk and wrote a letter confirming Abraham had completed his entire enlistment plus months more until the war ended. He sealed it with wax in front of Abraham and placed it on his desk.

"Should I deliver it at the naval office, sir?" asked Abraham.

"No, that could arouse suspicion to its authenticity. I'll send it in the post from here. Besides, they might arrest you on the spot for desertion. Best let my amendment precede you."

"Thank you so much, sir." Abraham beamed, sitting upright. "It'd be impossible to get a decent job without this being corrected."

Washington raised an eyebrow and stood. "Concerning that. One reason I showed you the drawings is I'll need a reliable man to assist with the project. It'll be hard for me to find a person who knows carpentry and construction methods as well as you do. I'm aware you're not a house builder. Just the same, you understand how to build something complex, the time, and the costs. You are perfect for it; someone familiar whom I can trust. Will you stay?"

"That's a kind offer, sir." Abraham said sheepishly, looking down.

"I'll provide you with a cottage and good pay in addition. Think on it over the next few months to deem if it'd fit you." Washington winked and cocked his head. "Either way, you can stay in the cottage until the transit and I'll pay you a small stipend for your help."

"I am flattered." Abraham smiled and put his hand on his chest. "I'll give it a great deal of thought. To be frank, since I'm without a job, I like to say I will. Yet, I've always hoped to use my skills in shipbuilding and advance as far as I can. When the desertion charge is cleared, I may finally be able to do that."

"Let's leave this undecided for a while with the offer remaining." Washington waved the issue away with his hand. "Tell me later what you decide," he finished in a commanding tone.

Washington returned later and put the letter in a drawer. They never discussed when he'd send it, and he wanted the carpenter to remain there for as long as possible.

The months flew by as Abraham and Washington consulted on the transit and construction techniques for the new manor changes. Abraham inspected the buildings and gave his opinions on timber joining that complemented the redesign and what parts should remain. He was more than glad to repay his friend for the hospitality.

In June, they began the plans for the upcoming transit of Venus and the critical seven-hour window of observation. As the men discussed the project in the library one day, Yvette sat alone by a harpsichord, thinking, and twisted her mouth. "I still don't understand why finding the distance to the sun is so important." It had confused Anne as well.

"To know the earth's distance is crucial, then we can determine our exact location at sea with geometric formulas." For sailors, this long-known navigation issue had caused countless losses and deaths. Abraham continued, "We lost an entire fleet on the shoals not long ago when they mistook their position by just a few miles. We're able to solve how far north or south we are from the equator, but we can't identify how far east or west we are."

"Oh, that's so easy to grasp." Anne confirmed, nodding. "Now why couldn't you have explained it that way, Washington?" She laughed

"Well, I did, didn't I?" He frowned, mocking her jest.

"Perhaps, although I didn't understand it until Abraham demystified it," Anne wrinkled her nose at Washington.

He chuckled at her. "Let me add to what Abraham said. Sir Edmund Halley discovered the solution was viewing the transit of Venus across the face of the sun from different spots on the earth and comparing the results. That's difficult, however."

"Won't your telescope let you see it go across the sun?" asked Yvette, brows raised.

Washington turned to her and nodded. "Yes, but to measure with accuracy, we need two things: a very accurate clock, or chronometer, and a telescope to observe the very edge of the planet start its passing, timed to the second along with the degree of angle. Just viewing through the eyepiece of my refractor won't magnify the size of the sun enough to see that exact moment." He wagged his finger and stretched out his arms. "We require a huge image. We'll try what others are suggesting; use the telescope as a camera obscura lens to project it large to get a better reading."

For two days, Washington and Abraham scouted the estate grounds for a suitable viewing area. The best location was a farmhouse on the hill above the manor where they installed the telescope and chronometer.

Before dawn on the day of Venus's transit, Washington and Abraham anxiously awaited the sunrise in the farmhouse. The women came up the hill chatting to join them as the sun peeked above the distant hill and tree line.

"Well, we've had a bit of luck. The clouds have cleared," said

Washington as his telescope projected the image of the sun upon a linen screen in the darkened room.

Just before nine they held their breaths to catch the black silhouette of Venus touching the sun's edge.

"Be prepared, now, be prepared! Ladies, you can witness the time for us. Abraham, be ready to keep the image on the screen, ready, ready, there—now!" Washington made a mark on the linen screen where Venus touched the boundary of the sun and drew in the planet's contact point on the linen.

"We got it!" Abraham, watching the chronometer, wrote the exact ingress to the second with its angle.

"All right, now we must time it again when Venus moves completely inside the sun's edge." Washington guided the scope.

Seconds passed, he again started. "Ready, ready—now! Wait, no, now! What's happening here? Look, there's a bubble of shadow stretched outside the circumference of Venus still attached to the sun's edge." Washington furrowed his brow.

Stumped, both men turned to one another with quizzical expressions.

"What happened?" Anne asked, her head tilted.

"Well," said Abraham. "We timed the ingress exterior. We likewise noted the time when Venus slid entirely onto the face of the sun, then we saw this shrinking band stretching out from the planet to the sun's edge...."

"Let me sit and analyze this." Washington put his elbows on his knees and fists on his cheeks as he sat in a chair. He chewed on his lip and shook his head. "I've read nothing mentioning such a phenomenon."

Abraham scratched his cheek, equally puzzled. "Do you know anyone else doing this experiment, sir?"

"Yes, scientists in England, most of them are in the south." Washington still had his knuckles pressed onto his face. "They'll present papers to the Royal Society for months after the transit. I'll ask a few of the Fellows." With that he rose and adjusted the linen panel.

"The Royal Society Fellows? You're familiar with its members?" Abraham's eyes opened wide that Washington had friends with anyone in the prestigious body.

"Yes, yes, a few." Washington brushed off the question, still dwelling on the strange dark attachment. "I wonder if it's a kind of optical illusion?"

Now somewhat bored with their excited husbands, and their own curiosity satisfied, Anne and Yvette bid them goodbye. "That's enough science for one morning." Anne waved as she and Yvette left the farmhouse.

Abraham still contemplated the oddity. "Maybe others will solve the mystery of the band. Too bad we have to wait until the next meeting to find out."

"Oh, I'll hear of it before then from the scientists who are Free Masons. Our next meeting is before the Royal Society's. I'm confident others are as excited over this new strangeness and will discuss it."

This surprised Abraham as well. "You're a Mason, sir?"

Washington assumed all men of notoriety belonged to the Masonic Temple, although it had impressed Abraham. "Yes, for years. I belong to the Grand Lodge in London. Most of our grand masters and many members of my lodge pursue science to some extent. So, I'll find out something on the surprise we saw," he said as a matter-of-fact.

After they finished their tasks on the transit, they carried the chronometer and telescope into the hall. Like two boys winning a cricket match, they were in good humor the rest of the evening. After dinner, they all moved into the parlor. They stood, looking at a portrait of Washington's grandfather.

"I was wondering whether you had decided yet on moving to the manor until I complete the reconstruction?" Washington asked.

"That sounds marvelous!" Yvette smiled. "I'm in love with Staunton Harold." Abraham hadn't mentioned the job offer to her.

"We should first discuss our options before we jump to any decisions. Once they amend my record, I want to go back to a Royal Navy shipyard. I'm sure if they have an opening and review my carpentry experience, they'd allow me to join the guild again in a permanent position."

Yvette knew Abraham's desire to advance and his need for

recognition for his skills. On the estate, though, Washington and the countess treated them almost as equals. She and Anne had become close friends, and Anne had taken to Michelle like an aunt, giving her the best of everything.

Disgruntled over the answer, Washington worried. He needed the honest carpenter's eye and knowledge of construction.

"Abraham, until we get the desertion claim resolved, it makes sense for you to stay here. I'll begin paying you a full wage. You'll live in the cottage for a peppercorn rent, say, a pound a year to make it legal. When the navy corrects your discharge confusion, you can decide whether to move back to London."

"That's tempting." Abraham walked to the fireplace, thinking. "Hmm, all right. A few weeks or a month is a small delay to my plans. It's a persuasive offer. Not to mention, two against one is unfair." He wagged his fist at Yvette and Washington.

"Make that three against one." Anne rose and ran, standing next to her husband and Yvette, putting up her fists in a boxing pose. "She's my closest friend in the Midlands. I shall not lose her without a fight." Everyone laughed.

∽

By the end of July, Abraham still hadn't heard from the navy. Yvette, however, was living a dream. She had a baby, a wonderful home on a country estate, a working husband, and a new close friend, a countess no less. It was hard for him to take that away from her and he hesitated in pressing Washington for news about the desertion claim.

Abraham worked on the construction drawings with a salary of over sixty-five pounds a year. That would earn him more than if he were at Woolwich and enough to cover the expenses of the cottage back in Brest. Although the new position undermined his shipwright goals, he embraced the idea of climbing out of the debt they had faced with enthusiasm and thankful glee.

Late in the fall, Washington sent his record of the Venus transit and transitarium to a friend in London who presented it to the Royal

Society in December. Without hesitation, they considered Washington a candidate for a fellowship. The organization endeavored to garner respectability and privileges, and voted in titled men regardless of the real value of their scientific contribution. They elected the Earl Ferrers into the distinguished group that month.

Washington and Abraham learned few transit times surfaced accurate enough to establish the sun's exact distance. No one, to their disappointment, had an acceptable theory on the cause of Venus's pesky shadow.

Soon after, Washington's brother paid a visit to discuss finances, and the proposed building costs.

"Abraham, this is Robert, whom you may recall handled your investments when you served on the *Renown* in the navy," introduced Washington as they stood in the library.

"So, you're the carpenter he praises so much." Robert smiled pleasantly. "Did the navy change your discharge error? I checked your old account to make sure you didn't leave any money, but the naval pay master couldn't have deposited it to your name if they listed you as a deserter."

"To date, the navy hasn't informed us of my status. It bothers me they're taking so long. It's been six months." Abraham's head and shoulders drooped.

Flushed, Washington said nothing and nodded at the navy's tardiness. He had yet to mail the letter and now regretted stalling, even if it had kept Abraham at the manor. Later that night, Washington confessed to Robert his devious postponement.

"That's scandalous, Washington!" Robert pointed an accusing finger at his brother. "You've no justification to keep him here by misusing your authority that could have corrected the issue. You betrayed his trust in you! Too often you overlook the importance of others' money and rights." He put his fists on his hips and strode to the other side of the room, his back to Washington.

"Yes, I'm ashamed of myself." Washington's face reddened again. "I'll give you the letter. Please right things for me on your return to London. Won't you?"

"More to amend the navy's error and help Abraham than to absolve your failings. I swear, such terrible decisions made by the Earls Ferrers. Are we cursed?" He threw his arms up and shook his head. "May God strike me if I ever become an earl!"

"If he does, He will have struck me first." Washington laughed. "You're next in line for the title."

Three days later Robert left for London, carrying the letters to reverse the navy's assertion. In London, he rushed straight to the Admiralty, presented the papers, and explained the mistake. The navy clerks told him they'd look into the matter.

Louis de Saint-Alouarn remained on station in Brest after his father's death. The French Admiralty assigned him to a smaller port vessel rather than to a warship to prevent Madame de Saint-Alouarn from losing another of her family. The tragedies of his father and uncle's deaths had rattled his spirit and desire for victory over the enemy. Like many French, he simply wanted the war to end. His assignment to a non-combative ship pleased him.

The first appointment placed him on a wood hauler and afterward a tender. Then as the navy needed more experienced officers for the fleet, he transferred to a pram, a two-masted ship with twenty cannons and two mortars. The intended plans for the invasion of England, however, had vanished after the defeat of the Brest fleet, and he cruised along the coast, scouting for the enemy in relative safety.

A family friend, Marie Drouallen, whose father also perished a year earlier on *le Juste*, called on his mother one day. She was two years younger than Louis, whom she had known since childhood, playing with his dog and dapping stones on nearby ponds during warm summer days.

As Marie grew into womanhood, Louis found her charms increasingly appealing. She possessed an air of gentility, was accommodating in her behavior, and always pleasant. Her mother had died when she was small and her father, a naval lieutenant before his death, had often been away at sea. Reared by relatives, she learned to depend upon herself.

Louis's mother sat upon a divan in their parlor with the young Marie. "As François used to say, 'In high seas, one must find shelter in a deep port.' Any time that you need a friendly ear, mine is waiting. You're family to us, Marie. My daughters consider you a sister, and I see you as another daughter." She smiled gently at Marie.

Marie pushed her light-brown hair off her face, and put her hand to her bosom. "I've considered the de Saint-Alouarns my second family since a child, Madame de Saint-Alouarn. It's so strange that after all these years we now suffer the same grief. Father is smiling above that we can find consolation in one another." She touched Madame de Saint-Alouarn's hand. "How are your children dealing with the loss?"

"They are recovering from it, just as I am. Our hearts remain scarred, but they heal faster knowing others share the same wounds." Madame de Saint-Alouarn's eyes dropped and then gazed directly into Marie's. "Have you made plans for finding your own home now that you have an inheritance?"

"I still puzzle over the endowment my father provided for me. Relatives have managed my finances until recently, and I'm at a loss as to what I should do with the funds." Marie lifted her eyebrows, leaning in. "You have always been keen with investments, Madame de Saint-Alouarn. How should I proceed?"

Madame de Saint-Alouarn dipped her head and grinned. "Most say to place it in banks for safety. But I prefer to put money to use. Caution is the key. One must consider it a device for profit rather than for entertainment, and for service to all instead of only oneself. It is powerful when used well."

As they discussed investment strategies, the salon door opened and Louis entered. He had returned to Brest from a cruise and had ridden the entire autumn day to the manor, still smelling of horse.

"Oh, we have Marie here?" He beamed and rushed to them and hugged Madame de Saint-Alouarn. Then he bowed to his longtime friend and greeted her, kissing her hand. It was the first time he had ever been so formal with his friend. She had occupied his mind for weeks more than any other concern and his joy in seeing her there eclipsed everything in the last six months. Their conversation spanned family concerns, the war, the memories of their lost ones, and ended two hours later when Madame de Saint-Alouarn left the room to rest.

Louis rose and closed the door after his mother departed and returned to sit beside Marie. His next action seemed as harrowing as facing cannons in sea battles.

"Marie," Louis paused, his face serious, "our fathers' passing has changed the family order and responsibilities for us both in our households. This new role has urged me to consider taking the next step in maturity." He swallowed and licked his lips. His hands were sweaty. "We've known each other most of our lives, and I've always admired your beauty, perceptiveness, and intelligence." He hesitated, trying to figure out what to say, although he had practiced it for weeks at sea.

"Thank you, Louis. I respect your sense of responsibility. At our age, it must be difficult for you to head the de Saint-Alouarn estates, care for your three younger sisters, and serve aboard a ship." She waited for him to go on, her hidden left hand nervously creasing her dress folds. Marie had long prayed for this day.

He cleared his throat, and continued. "I spoke to my mother earlier, and she agreed, that if you were to join our family, it would benefit us both. I realize this notion may sound brash or sudden to you. But I have given it consideration for some time. You and I seem mated by fate, for which I'm grateful. We've walked through life much on the same road together, each a wheel on the same wagon, traveling in parallel." He immediately hated his metaphor, wishing he had planned out what to say better. "When we met again at the requiem mass for our fathers, I decided then to explore the possibility of a union." He stopped and looked up, eyes wide in anticipation.

"The same has taken hold in my mind." She heard blood rushing loudly in her ears. "If you are, as I assume, suggesting marriage, then proceed. The idea is wise and my aunt suggested it to me just weeks ago." The guarded words came out automatically, but inside, she felt exuberant over his proposal and wanted to scream out her answer.

"Mother did the same. Do you think they've been conspiring to bring us together?" He chuckled at the obvious and she added a nod, giggling. "Then if we agree to such an arrangement... would you be my bride?" Louis, his insides tingling with joy, needed but one word to complete the oft-dreamt fantasy.

"Yes," she said, restrained, trying her best to be a proper lady. "I can imagine no other I'd rather wed than you. We've endured the same for so many years. I've imagined our union often." For Marie, marriage to Louis gave her a family of her own and a direction beyond living with aunts and uncles. To marry a wealthy de Saint-Alouarn would also provide her with additional financial independence. But more than that, she had always admired Louis and had grown very fond of him.

Louis had begun to question his choice of a naval career after the death of his father, but out of the ashes of his remorse, he discovered the spark of a happier future with Marie. On a cool day in January 1761, they married in the chapel at the Chateau of Kerazan, ten miles from Quimper.

Mackenzie, now commander of the *Defiance,* a large sixty-gun warship, hadn't tempered his loathing of the tropics over the past year. Although he sent the latest naval rumors to both his wife and Lord Fortrose, his clan laird had not returned correspondence and his wife and son were still not by his side. Neither of these factors provided any relief from the steamy torment of the Caribbean.

In a lamenting message to his wife, he wrote in part:

My Dearest Beloved Alana, How much longer must I endure confinement to this abominable isle without my family? It has worn on my spirit and withered my humor. The rainy season has begun once again and men fall like its drops, most never to rise again from the yellow jack. Not a day passes that I do not question the sweat of my brow may be a fever. Though I am resolved in my duty, when every ship arrives without a new assignment to home waters, my mind darkens....

Mackenzie, banished to the backwaters of the war, also envied those captains on patrol near the enemy. Little chance of advancement existed in snagging small rum-runners when others captured French warships in combat. Opportunities for notable actions slipped away the longer he remained in Port Royal.

As a last resort, he approached his only powerful contact within the government, Lord Fortrose, with a plea:

> *To that end, my gratitude would be unbounded if your Lordship were to use influence at the Admiralty to bring my afflicted soul back to English seas.*

The reply from Lord Fortrose, however, discouraged his hopes:

> *My Dear Captain George Mackenzie, Please pardon the brevity of this note as both my health and duties work heavy on my time. Your reports from the Port Royal Station have well served to fortify the defense of our esteemed Pitt in the expansion of his military aims. Goals that we both embrace. As you are yet unaware of this most recent tribulation, occurring but days ago, Pitt has resigned his position. The cause of this calamity arose from Our Royal Highness King George III's desire to end the war with France post haste. Our honorable Pitt, in deference to the new government's objectives, has stepped aside. This bit of news is no doubt as shocking to you as it afflicted me. At present we must prepare for any attack against Jamaica and our other colonies as both our king and the enemy king will seek to gain as many conquests as possible before going into treaty talks. It is in the nation's interests to have its best captains and admirals serving duty on the fringes of our empire. I shall approach a friend in the Admiralty concerning your request, however, later when I return to my offices upon regaining my health. Your most Humble Servant, Member of Parliament, and Mackenzie Mòr, Lord Fortrose.*

Not a month passed before he received yet more sad news coming from Alana. Lord Fortrose had died of his illness. This broke Mackenzie's sole influential link to remedy his predicament.

Fame and Fortunes

By the start of 1762, the war blossomed for the British and faded even more for the French. At sea, their superiority kept the French ships inside their ports, pressing upon their enemy's morale; on land the various armies fought battles that pockmarked the face of Europe with no country a clear victor.

This kept Abraham and Yvette from returning to France, although they were content with their circumstances, and baby Michelle was thriving. Abraham found his new vocation interesting; learning building construction became a different carpentry and masonry challenge for him.

Washington loaned Abraham books from the library on masonry, which Abraham soaked up. Most of his education, however, came in the actual inspection of the buildings on the estate and watching repairs done to the structures. He volunteered his skills often and joined the repairmen whenever time permitted.

"Abraham," said Yvette, pulling him from his thoughts, "how soon after the war do you think we can return to France?"

"Right away, I assume. We've enough saved to pay for passage and to live on for weeks, maybe even months." He answered without inflection as he polished his boot. "I miss your family, too."

"We left so long ago. I've had these bad notions lately as if someone were in trouble at home," she said, with a frown. "I believe it's my father."

"Now don't upset yourself until they send news from Brest. No sense wasting tears over whims." He stared at her and put the boot down, concerned.

"Abraham, when I get the intuitions, I pay attention. They don't strike often, but when they do, I'm certain something is happening or will happen." She stroked a ringlet that had fallen from her hair bun, eyes downward. "It's as if I'm drawn to something or someone with strong emotions."

"Ah, the Great French Sibyl, my personal seer," he said laughing to lighten her feelings. Fortune-telling fell alien to his scientific mind. The thought of it seemed ludicrous, but he'd listen.

"Go ahead and laugh!" Yvette stared hard out the window, her mind far away. "I know the signs. Something happened," she replied.

To Abraham, her spiritualism overpowered her reason and he ignored it without another comment.

Two days later, he caught Yvette crying when he returned from work. Regardless of his tactics to dissuade her from her unfounded assumptions, she felt sure something had happened to her father. He believed the extended stay in England was taking a toll on her.

Not long after, they received a letter from her brother telling them of her father's near-death illness. Anton had caught a bad lung infection and high fever. The doctor said it almost killed him on the very day Abraham found Yvette crying. Although he was recovering, the doctor warned hard labor might weaken and finish him, so he couldn't return to the shipyard.

At first, Abraham thought the timing between Yvette's warning and Anton's illness only a coincidence. But a lingering doubt remained over his disbelief of omens and the supernatural. If such prescience is possible, he reasoned, it jeopardized scientific rationale for all history based on cause and effect; how can one predict outcomes before they happen or from afar?

Abraham told Washington, one day, of his wife's foreboding. They took a scientific approach to solving the phenomenon and discussed it at length as they pored over plans in the library. In the end, neither could explain the premonition.

"Whether by divination or by chance, what she felt happened," Abraham stated. "I can't imagine how to explain it other than coincidence or an unknown natural process we haven't discovered yet. If a coincidence, then it is astounding, and equally so if a natural process."

"Well, the way I can tell if something will happen," laughed Washington, "is by peeking ahead a chapter in the book I'm reading."

They shrugged the mystery away and returned to their work until moments later a servant brought a sealed packet to Washington.

Disappointed, he waved the papers, pretending to be excited over the news. "Ah, at last, good news. The Admiralty has looked into your desertion case. To correct the crew list, this says you must go to Plymouth where the navy keeps *Renown's* records. They've enclosed my statements for you to deliver, too." Washington held in his disappointment, "Do you wish to leave right away?"

"That's great news. Yes, sir, as soon as possible." He grinned.

"I'll have someone take you to Leicester to catch a coach tomorrow." He returned a smile, but inside it worried him.

Days later, Abraham climbed from the carriage in Plymouth and walked to the shipyard. He had missed the sight of the sea and the smell of salt water over the last few years. Taking his time, he strolled to the records office, pulled the letters from his leather bag, and showed them to the attending naval official.

"Here's what you'll need," said the clerk after a bit, handing a paper to Abraham. He smirked. "Your captain could have prevented this if he hadn't signed off on the purser's roster error."

"Well, it's corrected now," replied Abraham in a gleeful tone.

"By the way," the clerk mentioned, catching Abraham before he walked away. "That *Renown* you crewed, was she a frigate?"

Abraham paused at the door, turned, and smiled. "Yes."

"Well, she just moored by the eastern dock if you care to visit her. The *Renown* brought in two privateer captures."

"I'd like to see her again. I helped build her," chuckled Abraham.

"Oh, she must be a different vessel." The man gestured with a wave of his hand. "This *Renown* is a captured Frenchie."

"The ship's the same." Abraham grinned and left the clerk to wonder.

Abraham walked along the quay and recognized her by the figurehead of the Goddess of Fame. She lay thirty feet from the dock. As he got closer, he could see how repairs and the rebuild over the years had changed her shape, although her profile still stood out from the English warships around her, as always.

Abraham's eyes took in his favorite build and noticed a sailor at the ship's waist. He tried to get the sailor's attention. "Ahoy there, *Renown!* From where did you sail?"

The sailor pivoted. "Ahoy! We returned from Spithead after a Channel cruise, taking *Conte d'Herouville,* a twelve-gun snow, and a few days earlier *Saujon,* a six-gun cutter." The sailor pointed to two French ships anchored opposite in the harbor with British ensigns hoisted above their French flags.

"I used to serve on the *Renown* and the *Dover* that took her in '47. Who captains her now?" asked Abraham, his brow knitted.

"The captain is Frederick Maitland. A good captain he is, sir," added the sailor with a broad grin.

"Maitland, huh?"

"Aye, sir. Captain Maitland's been commanding her for a year now since the other Scot, Captain Mackenzie, left."

Abraham studied the damage done to the hull from her recent engagements. "Has she seen much action?" He said pointing to the holes in her side.

"Aye, both in the West Indies and in the Channel. The *Renown* is a good sailor but a damn wet one." The sailor laughed and shook his head.

"I remember that, too." Abraham joined him in laughing. "After we captured her, I was her carpenter."

"You helped in the capture?"

"Aye. She almost went under before we got her holes plugged." Abraham pointed to her waterline and smiled.

In his cabin, Maitland overheard the two men outside shouting to one another, and quickly strode midship.

Maitland stood at the waist calling and smiled. "So, you're the carpenter who helped Captain Shirley take the *Renommée,* huh? I know of you. Come aboard if you have the time, sir. I'll send a boat."

"Aye, sir, it will be my pleasure." Abraham stepped into the gig when it got to the dock.

Standing beside the mainmast, he and Maitland discussed the seafaring characteristics of the frigate. Abraham explained the construction differences between the original *la Renommée* and the rebuilt *Renown* in detail. Then the conversation turned to its capture and Washington.

"How did you find Captain Shirley, Abraham?" He asked with a raised brow. He had only known of him through Mackenzie.

"Sir, he's a most generous and righteous man, fair and clever." Abraham nodded to confirm his beliefs. "I'm living in a cottage on his estate in Leicestershire and helping him rebuild his manor hall. He's planning it in the Palladian style to replace the older design."

"I've learned a good deal about him from an officer who commanded the *Renown.* His description differed somewhat from yours." Maitland sported a restrained smile.

"Ah, Captain Mackenzie, sir?" Abraham, familiar with the previous commander, wondered what he had said.

Maitland's eyes opened wide. "You know of Captain Mackenzie?"

"Aye, from a fellow sailor who'd shipped with him, sir. He said Captain Mackenzie's blood flowed with regulation ink and he ate uniform starch for breakfast." Both laughed. "I can understand why he might find Captain Shirley different to his liking. Captain Shirley goes against the wind rather than runs with it, if you know what I mean, sir."

"Yes, Mackenzie follows orders to the letter. He used them as an anchor whereas I've heard Shirley fancied to cut and run." Maitland snorted. "I suppose it's fitting that Shirley is ashore living a lubber's life and Mackenzie is on the Jamaica Station."

"Still there, sir?" He'd heard earlier Mackenzie sailed out of Port Royal. "That was where my friend told me they stationed him years ago."

Maitland chuckled aloud. "Yes, and no sign they'll relieve him to return home soon. He told me he had crossed an admiral. He detests the islands. Whereas, I love them."

They exchanged tales before Abraham left to find an inn. The next morning he left for Staunton Harold, after seeing his old frigate again, he reminisced the entire way home.

The frustration Mackenzie experienced over his stay in Jamaica subsided when the Port Royal squadron learned of a coming expedition. He prepared the *Defiance* to take part in an operation against Cap François, a French port in Saint-Domingue, getting a chance once again to display his military skills. Great Britain had declared war on Spain, France's ally, in January 1762, just months earlier. With a treaty in the making between the countries at war, if the French fleet in Saint-Domingue joined the Spanish one in Havana, the Admiralty feared a joint descent on Jamaica might give their enemies political leverage during negotiations.

The *Defiance* left in May with five other ships of the line, a forty-four-gun, and two smaller frigates to blockade the French harbored there and keep them from joining the Spaniards in Cuba.

While on duty a league from the port, Mackenzie invited other captains over to the *Defiance* for supper and drinks. "Gentlemen, let us toast our king and success in this campaign." Mackenzie held up his glass of wine. Rumors had spread that their blockade served a second purpose, a much more important role than preventing the French from leaving the port—an eventual invasion of Cuba itself.

The officers drank to a chorus of hurrahs and then sat to eat. One captain, newly arrived at the station, spoke. "If a descent on Havana proves true, as the talk suggests, won't the Spanish await our fleet in the beat-back to Cuba?"

Mackenzie nodded. "Aye, that may follow if we take the customary route; running with the leeward winds west from Jamaica south of Cuba, and then northeast along the Yucatan Channel southwest of the island. Then we'd fight the currents and winds in a beat-back up the western side to Havana. Even worse, sailing windward to Havana allows time for the French here to unite with the Spaniards. The combined force could stand as a wall against our few ships. Or worse, the Spanish before us and the French behind our fleet." He pointed to both the left and right.

Another added his concerns, frowning. "If the Spanish came here from Cuba now to drive away our blockade, we'd face enemy on both sides then, too."

"Let's also pray a hurricane doesn't blow all our plans to the winds. The season has yet to begin but one may come at any time in these latitudes," Mackenzie warned with a slight shake of his head. "So far, the French fleet sits in the harbor, sheltering under the port's guns and dare not venture out. The Spanish present a worry, but should another French fleet come, they'd also outgun our small squadron."

"Another French fleet? From where might those ships come?" an officer contradicted, mockingly. "We're blockading the last of the West Indies squadron here at Cape François. We've sunk or captured their Brest and Mediterranean fleets and what little they had left we dispersed. They'll be no other arriving."

The rebuttal reddened Mackenzie's face. "Overconfidence is a dangerous thing, sir. It's true we've diminished their fleets. But we are not privy to what strategies they exchange in Versailles." He held up a finger in warning. "Even a dead snake may strike."

A few of the older captains slapped the table repeatedly in agreement, experienced in having the unexpected ruin presumed sound plans.

After weeks keeping the French corralled in the port, the squadron commander held a council. "I'm sure most of you have given ear to scuttlebutt that our real goal is not to maintain a blockade of Cape

François but to strike at Havana. I can confirm it's true. We shall make sail tonight at midnight for Cape Nicholas in the Windward Passage. There we shall join others to attempt a descent. Our route to Havana, however, will not be south of Cuba or in the Yucatan Channel, but through the Bermuda Channel." He paused then for the expected gasps—and they came.

After a moment of nervous whispering, an officer spoke up. "Sir, the Bermuda Channel? The Spanish don't even use that passage! For good reason, the route hides shallow reefs that rip keels from hulls, low-lying cays to crush bows, and perilous currents sending ships into reefs. They say by day it's dangerous and at night, treacherous!" His eyes were wide.

"Indeed, it's a fact," Commodore Pocock replied calmly. "Without skilled pilots and accurate charts, it's foolhardy. Yet we have both and we shall proceed along that waterway. The Spanish will expect us to go along the southern side of the island to attack from the southwest. Few dare sail the Bermuda Channel. We shall, and reach and run with the wind westward on the northern side of Cuba and arrive in far fewer days." He grinned slyly. "This will prevent the French here from having time to combine with their fleet or attack our rear." The commander's voice was confident as he assigned the captains their positions in the squadron. "Gentlemen, return to your ships and prepare to get underway."

The warships hauled off leeward in the middle of the night to meet with a fleet assembling near Cape Nicholas on the far western tip of Saint-Domingue.

The *Defiance* approached the promontory the next morning as the sun broke into the sky. Hundreds of dots of white sail scattered across the sea, stretching to the horizon in small groups and heading northward. Mackenzie whistled and turned to his first lieutenant as he pointed. "Now there's a sight few have ever beheld. We join one of the greatest shows of naval power in this war, Lieutenant, remember this scene." He had, for the moment, forgotten about his long stay in the islands and desires to return home. The sight before him gave him a sense of duty, purpose, and pride.

The entire flotilla of warships, transports, hospital and storeships dropped anchor near the cape to wait for stragglers and other squadrons from the West Indies and even America to join them. Once the vessels gathered, Sir George Pocock, the commodore of the fleet, assembled the captains.

"Commanders, Havana takes claim as the most strategic port on the Spanish Main, their largest trade center, and the best harbor in the Caribbean. The enemy has a shipyard there capable of producing first-rate ships of the line. As both a military and commercial target, its capture is of great importance to Britain's political goals, especially with the impending peace negotiations to end the war at hand."

"This naval force must succeed in its capture and we shall carry out the orders from the Admiralty *to the letter.*" His commanding bearing inspired the captains. "Our fleet has seven divisions. The first will lead as our vanguard with divisions six and seven taking positions behind to guard against any French engaging our rear."

He continued as he unrolled a map of the route. "Over 12,000 regular infantry fill the transports and more than 14,000 officers, seamen, and marines man our invasion force. In total, over two hundred vessels compose the squadron, including twenty-one ships of the line and twenty-four lesser-armed warships with every sailor and soldier standing ready to bring this mission to a victorious end." His palm slapped the table.

"The frigate *Richmond* has returned from reconnoitering the Bermuda Passage as far as Cay Sal and found our sea charts correct." Commodore Pocock raised an eyebrow and pointed to Cuba's capitol. Every captain craned his neck to view the map. "Spies report the enemy has twenty ships of the line anchored in Havana Bay. With their powerful fortress del Morro protecting its entrance and another overlooking the bay, surprise rates as the key factor in our success." The admiral looked steadily around the room at the officers. "Concerns, gentlemen?"

He took a few questions and the throng of captains left to ready their vessels for the departure northward. Within hours, the ships hoisted their anchors and formed their assigned groups as they traveled behind the lead division.

The orderly column of ships, miles long, rode gentle swells as night fell under a waning crescent moon. It was Mackenzie's turn to inform his officers. After eating, he pulled out a chart of the Bermuda Channel and returned to the dining table and his officers.

"This shows the hazards we face." He spread the map on the table as the lieutenants and warrant masters stood and gathered around it. "I had a great misfortune several years back to be blown into the channel by a storm. It is the devil's sea with hundreds of miles of shallow bottom. We'll cruise northwest in a straight line along the coast for four hundred and fifty miles before heading west-by-southwest to Havana." He pointed to the route with a stern expression.

"The most dangerous part of the journey lies near Cay Lobos and Cay Confite, close to half the way there. They border a narrow passage almost two hundred miles long and merely eight miles wide that our fleet must squeeze into and cross with the greatest care at a sea turtle's speed." His eyes held a steely gaze and he marked the cays' locations with his finger. "A gale coming upon us during its crossing could result in the loss of many ships. A hurricane—all of them." His hand swept across the map as if brushing away the fleet. "It'll surprise me if this voyage doesn't see a few vessels founder, ground, or wreck. Still, we gain a tactical advantage on the route." Mackenzie tapped Havana.

∽∾∾

It had taken them three hundred and twenty miles and three days of sailing for the convoy to reach the southeast end of the beginning of the narrowing waterway. The massive group of vessels followed the first division's lead with fast frigates shepherding in ships that wandered too far to the sides. The warm evening breeze offered no relief to the crews as the sun's tip sank in the west. Blood-red clouds spread outward across the sky from its last fading rays. The ominous darkening tones heightened the sailors' dread of what lay ahead—the narrows of the Bermuda Channel.

Before, it had been easy sailing with clear skies and good winds.

The previous night, a sliver of a moon had graced the starry night, but this night held no such promise. It would be dark with no moon to give lookouts help and a sky full of patchy clouds to obscure even the little light the stars might provide.

Commodore Pocock, realizing the dilemma the fleet faced either in a new moon crossing or by waiting to sail it in daylight, had sent a frigate ahead earlier. Her captain sounded the bottom as he slowly sailed along the edge of the channel. The shallows extended out from the cays and shoreline of Cuba for miles in some places and then dropped off into great depths. The irregularity of the coastline and shallows made navigation perilous. Wherever he found the bottom close to the surface, he sent his boats off, taking long timbers with them. There they pounded three timbers into the sand and affixed tarred sail cloth to the top of tripods. As night came on and the fleet approached, the frigate sailed ahead and the men lit the beacons as a guide for the deeper route between the precarious islets.

Mackenzie stood next to his helmsman as the ships slowly gathered into rows of four or five abreast for the narrows. "Keep your eyes on the stern lantern of the ship ahead and follow it." He told the helmsman, showing no sign of fear, although his fingers opened and clenched continuously as the *Defiance* gradually hove toward the clustering vessels.

"Should his lantern grow brighter, he's stopped or beached. Haul sharply starboard but care for those abreast of us. We mustn't run afoul of them." He cautioned.

If the ships collided with one another, it was their doom. None could stop to help in a repair while traversing the channel or hold up the miles long line of ships that needed to get through it.

The darkness swallowed all sight of the other warships as Mackenzie stared hard ahead. Only the flicker of the lanterns let them know they were in a vast armada. Like fireflies set upon a course, the glimmering lights danced on the waves around them.

Mackenzie turned to his lieutenant and pointed to two flaming wedges far ahead. "There, see the beacons! Those are the beginning of the channel." Then he said in a loud commanding voice so all could hear. "Take care men—it begins!"

Every seaman stood by the railings or on the shrouds peering into the darkness. They listened for breakers and scanned for stopped lanterns, the shadows of nearby vessels, anything that might endanger their passage. When the watches ended, those who should have slept, stood upon the deck, unable to close their tired eyes on a hammock, afraid of being below if foundering.

To make matters worse, the waves had begun to grow as the wind increased in strength. The *Defiance* dipped in the four-foot waves and Mackenzie quickly trimmed the sails, slowing her speed so not to run into the ship ahead. Unable to see the clouds in the black sky, he prayed it was not the beginning of a gale. The winds gained for over half-an-hour and then slowly decreased to a gentle, steady blow.

In the distance, the loud thudding of two ships colliding carried to them, shouts and curses followed as they cut tangled rigging to free them. This happened numerous times throughout the long night as the dangerously close ships plodded on into the blackness.

With the lightening of the morning sky, the eastern clouds turned silver and blue. As the sun reappeared on the sea's horizon, the billowed forms turned brilliant reddish-golds and violets. The glorious scene offered hope to the crews after their fearful night but warned of a threat still far away and coming fast, storms that could push them into reefs or ground them in the shallows.

All day and into the evening, the ships in columns and rows passed through the narrows with the winds increasing. At last, just as rain fell and whitecaps splashed against hulls, the last of the rear guard sailed safely out of the dreaded passageway. Mackenzie's fears for his ship passed, and although many ships had crashed into one another, not a vessel ran aground or sank.

Seven days later, the invasion formation passed by Cay Sal, the last island, into the Straits of Florida with only a hundred miles of open water to Havana, southwest. They had accomplished their daring feat saving a week of sailing time, even though they had crawled at only two-thirds a league each hour in the channel.

Early the next dawn, the British vanguard's lookouts spotted the faint outline of Castillo del Morro on the Cuban coast. No battle line of Spanish warships formed before it. Their plans to surprise the enemy had succeeded.

The entire front half of the squadron lay just twenty miles from land by eight o'clock that morning. Crews could hear the alarm bells ringing in the distance as their foes awoke to the unbelievable realization that they lay under attack. Within an hour, everything went silent again and as the fleet approached nearer, no infantry lines, ships, or cannons had formed outside the fortress.

Not until early afternoon, when the British ships approached a scant six miles from the shore, did the defenders rush to man their guns and walls. In a feint tactic, Commodore Pocock sent transports and warships west to lure their infantry to the wrong side of Havana, as he intended to land troops on the east side. A storm, though, stopped any further advancements until nightfall came.

The next day, the British troops debarked onto landing boats near two small outposts east of the port sending a wave of marines ashore. As night came, the invading army of thousands camped in and around the now deserted gun emplacements.

When the army marched on the great citadel guarding the bay's entrance, it soon discovered that Castillo del Morro stood on solid rock, impossible for digging siege trenches before its walls. For days, the British troops explored the Spanish defenses and concluded that they could not attack the Castillo by infantry alone. They concentrated on taking the high ground behind the fort that overlooked it and the entire harbor. The defenders of this high ground, in time, retreated, and the British set up artillery batteries to hammer the Castillo and port from above them. In control of the superior position, they then took the eastern flank of the entrance channel to the port and set up more guns to bombard the city.

On June 27, the commodore ordered Mackenzie's *Defiance*, along with the *Hampton Court*, a sixty-four-gun, and nine smaller craft, to search out a safe harbor westward to shelter ships from possible storms.

Mackenzie, in the lead ship, drew near Mariel, twenty-five miles west of Havana.

"The charts show this to be a promising harbor, well enclosed with high hills around it. There's a fort at its mouth, though." Mackenzie peered through his spyglass next to his first lieutenant. He signaled the *Hampton Court* and then took his gig to her to discuss the possibilities.

Mackenzie inspected a map in the captain's cabin. "On my chart, it doesn't show how large of a bay. We could investigate its potential, although we'll have to end the fort's threat first." He hoped Captain Innes of the *Hampton Court* agreed.

"Hmm, it seems to be what Pocock is looking for." Innes nodded. "In the morning, we could attack the defenses and try to gain access to see what lies in the harbor."

Up to this point, the *Defiance* and the *Hampton Court* had patrolled as guard ships on the eastern end of the anchored fleet. Now Mackenzie and Innes were being given the chance to prove their mettle. Both captains wanted to enter the action.

"How shall we proceed?" Mackenzie had his own ideas. A foray into the harbor as quickly as possible was needed before more guns could be placed to defend the entrance.

"We should both begin the assault at dawn and advance once we've quieted them, I should think." Innes cocked his head, and looked at Mackenzie.

"Aye, that might work. It may take time before we can silence their guns, though." Mackenzie pretended to mull over the plan with a long pause, staring at the chart. "Perhaps we should do as you say but if we see an opportunity, one of us can slip past the fort into the harbor to determine if it's worth the effort."

Innes smiled and agreed to Mackenzie's plan as he rolled up the map.

The next morning the two warships closed in on the stone fort and shelled it for two hours. Mackenzie noticed a lull and set his sails to slip past it into the channel leading to the harbor and past two scuttled ships that almost blocked the entrance. Minutes later, Innes prepared his sails likewise, just as the fortress opened up again on him. The *Defiance*, however, was underway and slipped into the passage, out of range of the fort. The *Hampton Court* stayed to bombard.

As Mackenzie left the narrows and rounded into the bay, a docked frigate and scow shot at his ship. The frigate showed a flurry of action on its deck, with men rushing back and forth. On the scow, a fore-and-aft rigged ship, the same was occurring.

The *Defiance,* from across the harbor, showed her thirty guns and sent paced blasts from her weapons upon the two smaller ships. They returned uneven volleys that puzzled Mackenzie, wondering why their gunners did not use every cannon. This exchange lasted for some time with little damage to his vessel but extensive damage to the enemy's. Then their firing stopped altogether.

The vessels unfurled their sails and set to embark. They had the wind in their favor and Mackenzie turned toward them across the bay. Together, the two foes hugged the distant shoreline trying to circle and race for the exit.

When they plodded halfway across, Mackenzie bore away, and catching more air in his larger sails, came down upon them. Only a mere forty yards separated them and he again turned to show his cannons. In seconds, both lowered their flags without a fight.

"Lieutenant, send boats to the captures and I'll return to help Captain Innes."

Just as he spoke the words he detected stillness at the harbor's mouth. Minutes later, the *Hampton Court* floated into the bay. The fort had either surrendered, or the cannoneers had abandoned it.

With both large warships sitting silently in the bay, a few citizens ventured from the buildings to see the result of the battle. Soon, boats returned from the two captured ships and the lieutenant hurried to Mackenzie.

"Sir, the scow and frigate had only ten men on each. Their captains debarked with most of their crew when the fight began. They had just arrived from Veracruz after escorting a convoy of Spanish merchants and were out of supplies with many ill."

"That explains the strange returns of their cannons. Send the captured frigate out to the rest of our squadron and tell them they may enter." Mackenzie beamed and wiped the sweat from his hat brim and brow. It foretold another warm tropical morning, but a successful one.

They had taken Mariel with no lives lost and in just half a day.

Within two hours, the nine other vessels entered the bay and docked to unload troops to occupy the port and fort. Innes congratulated Mackenzie and suggested he return to Pocock and give him the news. The *Defiance* left for the main fleet in the afternoon.

Although they had taken Mariel as a haven, the greater goal, Havana, was still held by the Spanish. Castillo del Morro proved invincible, even after being shelled by the batteries on higher ground.

Commodore Pocock then sent warships to shell the Castillo with some success until three sustained so much damage they withdrew.

As the siege continued for weeks, an epidemic of fevers hit the British regulars in their encampments. In the beginning, hundreds took ill, then thousands, and deaths became common.

More troops from the colonies in North America arrived over the weeks to bolster the ailing infantrymen in the hospital ships and ashore. With little progress in capturing the Castillo, Pocock's hopes depended on the sappers who were burrowing through rock under the seaward wall. On July 30, they detonated explosives under the bastion and the entire corner of the Castillo crashed to the sea. The British regulars stood ready and flowed into the fortress by the hundreds through the breach. By day's end, the British flag flew over the mighty Castillo del Morro.

Then an incessant bombardment from the Castillo, the high ground batteries, and cannons along the entrance channel rained iron upon Havana and its harbor from across the bay. The city, inner fort, and their anchored ships suffered tremendous damage.

The brave Spanish put up a strong but useless fight. After a massive pounding for days, they surrendered. After the capitulation, they learned the Spanish governor had assumed a Spanish convoy was arriving the day the British fleet reached Havana and had canceled the alarms, only to discover his error much too late. Oddly, the Spanish didn't scuttle or burn their fleet within the bay, and the warships fell into British hands.

⁓

In the spring of 1762, Washington set out for London with the goal of attaining another laurel of fame. His fellow Masons had nominated him as a candidate for the next grand master for the lodges in England and colonies. They held the meeting at the Vintners Hall on Thames Street in London. Over three hundred Free Masons attended, and to a man, elected Washington the Grand Master of England.

After becoming Earl Ferrers and a Member of the House of Lords, as well as a Fellow of the Royal Society, becoming the Masonic Grand Master crowned the glory of his civilian life. Washington enjoyed more wealth than he ever imagined and had attained social, political, scientific, and nobility titles. Little recognition remained he could strive for that he hadn't already received within three years at the age of just forty. Now he focused on rebuilding his estate.

Abraham yielded to the actuality that work on the manor was slowly replacing his plans to return to a shipyard. He still missed his hands' grip on an adze, but became accustomed to a pen in his fingers to sketch roof details and door frames. Washington gave Abraham unlimited liberties to keep him on the manor. Anne, whom Abraham found most appealing, had become more friendly, often stopping by to chat, prompting a nice break from his work.

"Abraham, a letter arrived from France for you," Anne said one day, handing him the folded paper.

Yvette's father wrote someone had broken into their country cottage in Brest and stolen pieces of furniture. Later, he scowled while reading it to Yvette. "What shall we do with the cottage? I'd hate to see it vacant until we return. The taxes and repairs already burden us, and now thieving? Perhaps we should sell it."

"We put so much effort into making it a place we love. Can't we hold onto it and have my father and André watch it?" Yvette suggested.

"They can't live in Brest and take on the responsibility of repairing *and* guarding it."

"Then we must concoct a better plan than selling it," groaned Yvette. "Perhaps my parents could move into it."

"They seem to like it as much as we do." Abraham reflected on how Anton enjoyed it and fishing from the river bank. "Ask them the next time you write."

"Now that Papa doesn't work, you may be right," offered Yvette. "I'll send a letter tomorrow."

A month later, Yvette got the reply. They agreed to move to the cottage and sell their own house, and Anton promised Louise to buy a horse and cart to get to church. Living in Brest had indeed lost its appeal for them after he had lost his job at the shipyard. In addition, crime rose each day as more unemployed men roamed the streets.

Yvette mentioned the whole issue to Anne, who felt sorry for her and Abraham. She had grown up in relative wealth, and financial troubles most faced seldom plagued her. Moreover, now as estate caretakers, she and Washington became wealthier and more prominent in society by the month, it seemed.

Anne told Washington about the problems that evening. As Abraham worked on a roofing plan, Washington stopped to see him.

"Abraham, I heard of the difficulties you encountered with your cottage in France and I'm glad your in-laws solved it for you. We'd hate to lose you when the war ends to ward off burglars in Brest."

"Sir, I'd hate to leave before the rebuild starts, too. You've done so much for me. Without your help, I might be in prison or hanged for desertion."

"That error by our purser still bothers me. I can't imagine how I signed *Renown's* crew roster and didn't notice your name marked as a deserter."

"Well, sir, it's resolved now. Did I mention when in Portsmouth two months back, I visited the *Renown?* Captain Maitland had returned her to port after capturing two French privateers."

"Maitland is a good commander, and I suppose Mackenzie's performance in Havana got him a fine position as a reward."

"He told me Captain Mackenzie is still in Port Royal and hates the islands. But he had angered an admiral who's keeping him in Jamaica."

"I didn't know that. Perhaps I'll mention something to a friend at the Admiralty to reassign him on home waters. Captain Mackenzie deserves better than punishment after his capture of Mariel and the warships. He's always been friendly to me and is a good captain."

Back in London a week later, Washington again took up his residence in a posh section of the city. The year before, he'd leased a house on Great George Street. It sat only a stone's throw from the Parliament building he attended as a member of the House of Lords. The brick building was four stories tall with an oval window in the pediment's tympanum above the entrance; it stood out from the other properties on the block. Corinthian columns and pilasters, and fine-polished woods and marbles adorned with friezes and carved ornaments decorated the interior.

"I've decided I spend enough time in London that I'll need a place here," Washington said to his brother Robert, sitting satisfied in the elegant parlor. "I plan to buy this home."

"Hmm, it'll be an expensive year when added to your estate costs. We may have to sell land later to pay for it." Robert winced over the thought. "What progress have you made on your plans for the manor?"

"Superb headway, more than what I had hoped. Abraham and I have drawn up the final details for most of the construction. Although this whole project will take much longer than I originally expected, years more, I'm afraid," responded Washington with a cocked smile. "Abraham's insight continues to be invaluable to me."

"Do you think he'll go back to France after the war?" asked Robert, concerned for the project.

"I suppose it depends on the incentives. Abraham has his mind set on being a shipbuilder."

To keep Abraham on the manor became a challenge as well as a high priority. The salary he gave him was substantial, more than others paid. Regardless, Abraham's love of shipbuilding threatened the reconstruction. Yet, the war held him back from leaving. Washington knew it wouldn't last forever, but for now, he was delighted to have the carpenter.

⚖

Within six months after their marriage, Marie's passion for Louis helped ease the loss of her father. One day, she approached him in the parlor with an unusual question.

"Did you ever consider training a cadet?" Marie smiled with a raised eyebrow as Louis sat in his chair reading.

"I'd rather command seamen than the spoiled sons of counts at the academy if that's what you're asking." He didn't raise his eyes from his book.

"Hmm, not quite. If a very young cadet came aboard, would you then?" She grinned and turned sideways to him.

Now Louis looked up, bewildered. "I suppose so. Why are you asking me these things? Did someone suggest their son come aboard with me?"

"No. No one else's son needs you to tutor them." She lowered her hands, below her belly. It revealed a very slight bulge in her abdomen.

Oblivious, Louis frowned and stared at her.

Marie shook her head and lowered it, staring at her stomach.

Louis followed her eyes and gasped. "My Darling! You're with child!" He sprung up and embraced her, and she pulled him close, pushing her womb into him.

She giggled and patted the top of his head as if he were a boy. "My brave lieutenant has the blind eyes of a potato. Yes, you will have a child. If a son, he'll learn your skills, and mine, if a girl."

"When?" He asked hurriedly. "What month is it coming?"

"In late June, perhaps in early July." She looked up into his eyes and kissed him.

When June 1762 came, Marie gave birth to a healthy boy and most of the de Saint-Alouarns attended the baptism two days later. Louis swore he'd never leave her and to be there for his son. It seemed convincing and even reasonable. The British blockade had kept him in the Road of Brest for months. Sometimes when storms pushed the enemy patrols away, he sneaked out for a short patrol along the coast. For the most part, his service had stayed peaceful and in Brest.

That month, he prepared to transfer to a new warship. *"Le Royal Louis* has 116 cannons, the biggest we have, and larger than any enemy ship," he bragged to Marie but hesitated in giving her the destination of the ship's next voyage.

"I suppose you'll remain here in Brest then. That warship hasn't raised her anchor from the Recouvrance side of the river since she launched five years ago." She didn't concern herself over Louis's safety. After all, he had yet to see combat since their marriage the previous year.

Louis shifted his weight, eyeing the floor. "The Admiralty seldom sends first-ranked ships out unless on very important missions."

She shrugged. "It's good to know you're safe here in Brest."

He hesitated, then confidently continued. "Actually, we'll be setting off on a short voyage with the new captain who wants to test *le Royal Louis* before going on any long voyages."

"You'd be leaving on a long cruise afterward? When?" Marie's brows knitted.

"Not for some time from now. This first one will be short." He hoped she hadn't heard of the rumors the navy considered a mission to Brazil if the ship proved seaworthy.

Marie trusted the size of the colossal warship could ward off any attempts to engage her in battle and Louis surely must be safe aboard her.

Before putting out to sea, Louis oversaw the loading of cargo and supplies. "Sir, we now have twenty-five tons of powder in the magazine. We'll take on the remaining ten after returning." Louis informed the captain his third day aboard. He stood in the captain's quarters, surrounded by elegant panels of carved walnut and ornate, gold-leafed rococo furnishings.

"Check with the boatswain to make sure we have all the munitions we can carry onboard by departure." Captain Beaussier Isle, an older commander of many expeditions and offices, glanced up from his desk at the young Louis.

"May I ask, are we expecting engagements outside the bay, sir?" Louis stoically lifted his chin.

"Not if we can avoid them, Lieutenant de Saint-Alouarn. No, we'll need as full a loaded hold as we can carry to resemble the actual draft and weight as if on a voyage." He glanced up at the young lieutenant again and smiled at his show of bravery. "We have plans for later if *le Royal Louis* is sound enough. This trip will decide that."

Two days later they departed from Brest, and a day later, they ran into a strong gale that tested their ship. As the winds blew, every man on board felt the ship keel leeward too far.

The first lieutenant stood on the lower gun deck with a device to measure the excessive angle of tilt as the ship rolled in the high blasts. "She's around six degrees from the center of gravity, sir. I'd say another fifteen knots and she'd go over." The results had shaken him and his voice showed it.

"Well put her with the wind then. That's enough testing for one day." Captain Isle grimaced at the news; the designer had erred on the ship design.

Later he announced the finding to his officers at dinner with disappointment in his voice. "She's top heavy. I'll request that they lower the cannon weight on her upper decks but I'm not sure that will even be enough."

By the time Louis returned from the cruise, the elegant premiere-ranked ship had come close to capsizing twice in storms. Sailors complained and vowed never to sail her again. One officer said he'd resign his commission if ordered aboard her without modifications.

At home, he confessed to Marie his frustration with the navy. "She rolled so much that I doubt she'd be fit for battle. Imagine, the expense and time to construct a warship just to look impressive but never leave the dock!"

"The voyage benefited us then if not the navy." Marie sat knitting baby clothing and nodded. "Now they realize not to use her without changes. Otherwise, you might have gone down with her." She giggled. "That would leave our two little ones without a father."

"Two? Another is coming?" Louis grinned.

She squealed out and put down the knitting needles, laughing. "If babies counted as ships, you'll soon be an admiral." The next year

Marie gave birth to a daughter.

Versailles had planned for *le Royal Louis* to lead a fleet against Brazil, Portugal's prize colony in the Americas, in a manner of Pitt's descents. The attack would strain the alliance between Portugal and Great Britain and force the British to send reinforcements to protect their ally. Also, the mission might restore Versailles's and the public's faith in their navy after so many defeats. However, with the report that their largest ship was defective, she sat dockside for the rest of the next year, and King Louis prayed for an end to the war....

Days of Revelations

By February 1763, all the combatants signed treaties, and peace silenced the last musket and cannon. The Seven Years' War had resolved many controversies, forcing the French to give up their holdings in eastern Canada, Nova Scotia, and Cape Breton, along with many possessions in the West Indies, Africa, and India.

Washington Shirley and Abraham began to renovate Staunton Harold Hall and the surrounding manor lands soon after receiving the land rights from the king.

One evening, after Yvette finished washing clothing, she approached Abraham sitting near the fire, and asked him the question she had put off. "Now that the war has ended, do we have money to return to France?"

Abraham remembered his promise. "We do, but the earl needs me more that we've started tearing up the gardens and removing trees." He had wondered when she'd ask him about it and hated giving her the answer. "I want to return to France, too, but your father says there's little work there. So, we'd have to come back to the manor."

"Abraham!" said Yvette, glaring.

"I know. Give me a few months to complete my projects here. Then I'll approach the earl and ask him if I can leave for a while."

"Two months," Yvette agreed, frowning. "This spring we'll be in Brest. My parents haven't seen Michelle yet. She'll turn three by then!"

Abraham assured her by vowing, "I promise we'll go, and by then we'll have saved more money for the trip. If the shipyard in Brest will take me back, we'll stay in France."

Weeks passed and he took on more responsibilities as the projects increased in scope. Each stage required more of his time and supervision. The housing of itinerant workers, pay schedules, shipments, all took careful attention.

In May, he oversaw the changes to the landscaping that were well underway. The spring rains softened the ground and laborers moved earth to create the free-form bank contours of the new lakes. Tools and supplies had arrived and others needed to be purchased.

"Abraham." One day Yvette cornered him as he returned home. "You swore we'd return to Brest." Her eyes glinted and she stood arms crossed, primed to force a resolution to the issue.

He slumped into his chair, not knowing what to tell her. "We shall, in a few weeks. Right now I've dozens of tasks to finish. As soon as I can see a break where they don't need me, then we'll leave. We must be patient."

"I've been patient! For seven years I've waited," she argued and tugged on his sleeve. "I want to go to Brest, *now!*"

Abraham hung his head. "Yes, you're right." He wanted it as much as Yvette did but money had always tipped the scale. Their delay in leaving depended on his work, yet now, he saw, his work must give way to his family's needs.

The next morning in their makeshift office, Abraham put aside his pen and stood before Washington. "I was hoping to discuss something of importance with you, sir."

"What is it?" Washington raised his gaze from his paperwork.

"Sir, I must return to France for a visit and wondered how I should proceed with plans to cause the least disruption to the project."

"How long do you expect to stay in France?" He asked, worrying he might lose Abraham to the shipyard.

"Right now, I'm hoping less than a month, although it may be longer."

"I see." Washington looked down at his desk at the many lists for the project. He came up with a quick response. "This comes as a setback. My brother Robert and I sold estates in Astwell and Brailsford to pay for construction materials. I hoped you'd oversee the purchases."

"Well, I could stay another week or two and get things in order before we leave," Abraham offered to lessen the blow of his absence. "The workmen started the landscaping, which should last months before they run out of lakes to dig."

Washington upped the pressure. "Oh, I didn't mention I'm planning on hiring more stone cutters, masons, and construction workers to start right away on the buildings. Is it possible to put off your trip?" Washington expected a threat of being replaced to compel Abraham to stay. "I suppose I could always hire someone else to supervise while you're gone." He looked down at his papers, feigning disappointment.

Afraid of losing his job with none promised in Brest forced Abraham's hand. "I didn't know you planned to rebuild so soon. That takes priority over a visit to France." He gave in to the empty threat. "I can travel another time. I'll change my plans."

When he got home that night, he dreaded what Yvette would say.

"Dear, I talked to the earl today about leaving for France…" Abraham mentioned, preparing for the coming storm.

His pause had already told her the answer. "And what did he say?" she asked while holding a spoon of honey for Michelle to lick.

He cleared his throat. "Well, we're starting on the rebuilding of the hall right away. He needs me. If I leave, he'll replace me with someone else."

"Abraham, you gave me your word," she said firmly but not loud, surprising him with the gentle reply.

"I did. But I may lose my position." He felt pressured between pleasing his wife and his boss. "You know how good we have it here and there might be no work in France."

"More waiting? I realize making money comes first, but…" She hadn't the answer either. "What can we do?" she asked, her mouth turned down. "My parents *must* see our daughter and I want to see *them!*"

"Perhaps we can wait until I have their schedules and plans set up for a few months ahead." He offered his plan, tensing his face. "When winter comes, the work will slow, and we'll leave."

"That's too far in the future, and winter makes traveling with Michelle too difficult." Yvette closed her eyes tight. "She may fall ill."

"Then I don't know how to solve this." Abraham shook his head in disappointment.

Yvette mulled it over for a moment, wiping Michelle's mouth clean. "There's no reason I couldn't go home without you. I can manage a three-day crossing straight to Brest." Her eyes brightened.

Abraham considered if Yvette took a ship straight to Brest, it should be safe and he could escort her onto it. He agreed. "Fine, that sounds reasonable and I'll accompany you to Dover. I'll ask the earl for a two-week leave instead of longer. He'll allow it."

The next day, Washington approved Abraham's proposition rather than lose him forever.

By the time Abraham and Yvette arrived at Dover, the spring's showers had ended, preparing for the glorious month of June. The seas calmed allowing unhindered voyages across the Channel.

Yvette and Michelle boarded the vessel and waved goodbye to Abraham on the dock as good winds filled the spread canvas. When the shoreline disappeared in the distance, they went below to the small passenger compartment shared with four other travelers.

On a stroll around the deck that evening, Yvette leaned against the railing. As the ship's rocking lulled the child asleep, she cradled Michelle in her arms, her head resting on Yvette's shoulder. Orange clouds surrounded the sun as it touched the sea on the horizon.

"Now that's a pretty scene," declared one of the other passengers in French. "Your silhouettes stand out beautifully against the sky's colors. I heard you speak Breton to your daughter earlier."

The stranger had a stocky build and walked toward her with a slight limp. He introduced himself and said he came from the small village of Saint-Nazaire on the mouth of the Loire River.

"Did you travel from the colonies?" she asked, curious.

"I pilgrimaged to Louisbourg to visit my brother's grave." The middle-aged sailor leaned upon the starboard rail with her. "He died during the siege at only twenty-six."

Michelle stirred but did not waken and Yvette turned to him. "I'm sorry to hear that. Did he serve in the navy?"

"The army. He died defending the fort." He paused, putting his arms on the railing. "I sailed with the navy until the war ended."

"Did you get hurt in any of the battles?"

"No, just minor things. The worst happened to my ears because of the guns." The sailor pointed to his head. "The few scars and stiff joints from wounds I can tolerate, but losing one's hearing steals one of our best senses."

Yvette noticed his head turned to the side, so she spoke louder. "My husband told me how gunners lose it from the cannon booms. Such a loss and one that's permanent, too. We should thank God that you came back. So many gave everything for France."

His face drooped at hearing her words. "Most of my crewmates died when my ship sank. The few who could swim and avoid the rocks made it to shore. The surf took the rest," he looked down sadly into the sea with a survivor's guilt.

"What warship did you serve on when that happened?" She asked, hoping to lift him from his pain.

"*Le Juste.* We lost her at Quiberon Bay in '59. If she hadn't sunk, we'd have anchored near my village. Only bodies and wreckage remained at the Loire's mouth."

As she recalled, René and his brother François commanded *le Juste* during that tragic event. Yvette's heart stung at the thought, and she asked him to tell her the circumstances of their deaths. The sailor described the details of the battle, although he had helped with a gun crew below deck when the brothers received their wounds. But he told Yvette they commanded as good and honorable officers to the end.

He'd seen the men bring René below before he died.

Yvette tried to picture the horror, mix of emotions, and pain René must have endured at the end. The sailor described more than Gaëlle's account in her letter. Although she hadn't realized she held unanswered questions about the event, his narration resolved the final concerns she had for René. She now hoped he truly lay at rest.

Two days later, the familiar outer bays and the Goulet sat before them as the vessel plied into Cameret Bay to await a pilot. Yvette's heart pumped faster as the pilot boat approached, hoping her brother André might guide them into the harbor. Disappointed, she watched another climb onboard to navigate.

Once ashore, Yvette hired a man with a horse cart to take her and Michelle to their country cottage. As they rode through town to the far city gate, she noticed how shabby Brest appeared. Buildings had fallen into disrepair, and the townsfolk looked poorer. The war had taken an appalling toll on the port. She sighed when they left the port along the road to her country cottage.

When she arrived, she walked along the path to the front door with the spring garden in full bloom. "Pick some for your grandmother, Michelle." The three-year-old-stopped every few steps to tug at a flower with one hand and add it to her small bouquet.

"Papa! Anyone home?" Yvette hollered, excitement coursing through her body more with each step.

"Wait a minute," replied her mother Louise's muffled voice.

"Momma, open up, it's me!" Yvette called.

The door swung wide, banging against the inside wall as Louise rushed out, her arms open for Yvette's embrace. "Oh, praise God! Oh, praise God! Oh, oh!" Her mother threw her arms around her.

Moments later, Anton joined them at the entrance, hugging and crying and talking over one another's questions and greetings. Then Louise spotted Michelle and swept the girl into her arms, kissing the child. Anton grabbed the tot's hand and shook it while smiling and gushing compliments over her. Michelle, unafraid, enjoyed the gaiety and laughed.

The cart driver dropped off their bags by the door and left as the elated group entered the cottage to sit. Yvette filled them in on the trip and their affairs in England. They focused their attention on Michelle as Yvette told them how well she behaved on the crossing and how Anne considered the child almost as her own.

"I didn't expect the countess to embrace a child of her history with such a strong attachment. She keeps company with Michelle at times as much as I, but she's without children of her own," said Yvette, running her fingers through her daughter's blond hair.

"History? Why shouldn't the countess love her, too?" questioned Louise, curious over Yvette's wording.

"Oh, I suppose I never related how I came by Michelle in full," Yvette replied, not noticing their concerned looks.

Anton suspected something not right immediately. "Didn't you receive her from the foundlings hospital in London?"

"No, no. I wrote she came to me as an orphan, but I suppose if I hadn't gotten her as I did, we might have gone there for a child." As she sat admiring her child, Yvette still had not seen Anton's serious expression. "Oh, the story is far more miraculous."

"Miraculous?" Eyes wide, Louise expected a divine revelation. "How did you get her?"

"A poor wretch of a woman, probably no older than eighteen, lay dying in an alleyway when I came upon her. She offered her baby to me." Yvette smiled as she faced her mother. "As the last act she did before passing, it was a sign that God wanted me to care for the child."

Anton's head jerked back. "She expired in the street? Had this young lady no home in London, no family?"

"Well, no, she had neither a husband nor relatives to provide for her," replied Yvette, tilting her head with a sad look. "There are so many like her."

Anton caught her meaning first, frowned, and leaned back in the chair. "I see... you mean her mother died as a harlot?"

Not suspecting a negative reaction, she continued. "Yes. Look at what a wonderful child she bore!"

"Oh, my," whispered Louise, astonished her daughter could rear a whore's child.

"Isn't she the most beautiful child? Those blue eyes..." praised Yvette, still unaware of her parents' shock.

"Is she stricken?" Louise, with her brows knitted, inspected the tot's skin, lifting her sleeves.

"Stricken?" asked Yvette.

"With the pox or Neapolitan disease?" Anton eyed the child also, and wondered if clothing covered the symptoms or scars from view.

"With Neap... ? No, she's a very healthy child." Yvette smirked at the thought they assumed she might have syphilis. "Don't you think she'd have died or become much sicker after two years? She appeared in good health when I got her, although thin. Her mother hadn't been able to feed her because she'd been so ill." Surprise more than anger accented her voice at the questions.

"So the young woman died of the condition, then?" asked Anton, placing his hand on his mouth.

"She may have died of Neapolitan or gaol disease, consumption, or cholera. I'll never find out the cause. It makes no difference now. The child has grown without infirmities and remains in good health. That's all I care." Yvette frowned at the insinuation the mother's life choices had contaminated the child.

Her parents still believed that Yvette might give birth someday to her own child, and their minds repulsed at having their new granddaughter the unholy issue of a prostitute. Michelle stood as a symbol of carnality and neither Louise nor Anton said more.

Their questioning and hesitation to accept her daughter openly hurt Yvette, who had expected her parents to embrace Michelle without qualms. She realized later she'd have to explain Michelle's parentage differently than she did to her parents. Others might ask the same questions, and too many of the parochial-minded held strong biases. She decided to say the child's mother died unexpectedly as a widow, a probable falsehood, but perhaps one that could have been true. She concluded, as great minds can only be fed small lies, small minds can be fed big ones.

Everyone she talked to asked about Abraham and his work. When she described his working for nobility with an important position, it impressed them. Yvette felt proud of Abraham and told friends how Anne, a noble, had befriended her. Yvette didn't need to exaggerate her close relationships with both the Countess Ferrers and the Countess Huntingdon, and she reveled in the prestige.

During her stay in Brest, Yvette mentioned how poor the port looked. Anton related more examples of the city's decrepit state. Warship construction had dropped almost to a complete halt with workers seldom paid.

After the war, Brest fell into a state of dilapidation and severe unemployment. Then destitute sailors and idled workers grew in numbers and crime engulfed the port. The wealthy fled to other cities or to their country manors. When merchants left, taxes increased to compensate for the loss of revenue. The high taxes forced the poor out of their dwellings and the spiral down continued.

Yet along the tree-lined river, outside the high stone walls of Brest, the family's bucolic life thrived. Their peace in the cottage contrasted with the terrible happenings within the walled port. Relatives and friends often rode out to the cottage for gatherings to escape Brest. Summer overflowed with picnics, walks through the fields, impromptu celebrations, and fishing along the riverbanks. As pleasant as it seemed, Yvette missed Abraham and told her parents she'd return to England in the first week of September.

Once everyone learned of her coming departure, they agreed to a party for the week she planned to leave. Her mother prepared the family's favorite dish, a fish stew with lobster, clams, scallops, monkfish, and potatoes with carrots. Gaëlle brought fruits, while Yvette contributed her famous crepes filled with apples and cheese. They rested by the riverbank after eating, and everyone listened while Anton played his fiddle. As the sun set, the guests left in couples and groups until, by nightfall, only Anton, Louise, and Yvette leaned back staring at the starry display. Michelle slept beside them on a blanket.

"Well, that's that," Louise said. "I'd better start cleaning."

"We'll help, Mother."

"No, you just stay. I enjoy putting the house in order," Louise told her as she walked back toward the cottage carrying Michelle.

Yvette and her father sat gazing at the beautiful darkened landscape with the lights of Brest in the distance and the river murmuring below the trees.

"Yvette, you have a wonderful family now, a good husband and a child. Does your life satisfy you?"

"Father, I'm so content being married to Abraham and having Michelle."

"Well, far better married to Abraham than that rascal René," Anton mumbled, lowering his brows.

"Father, that's not something to dwell on anymore. René's gone. Let him and our history rest in peace." Yvette gently slapped his hand.

He smiled to himself. "Sorry. A father has a hard time when remembering somebody who hurt one of his children, more so if a daughter." He changed the subject. "When do you expect to come back to France for good?"

"I'm not sure. Abraham must get employment wherever he can find it. With the current slowdown in Brest, he won't be able to get a shipwright position here." She paused and closed her eyes. "It may be years before we return."

"Regardless, you must remember this, Yvette, I love and miss you, so much." His eyes had already spoken as much.

∽

The end of the war provided France a chance to remedy the poor performance of its navy. Britain had returned a few of the islands they captured during the war in exchange for lands France had taken, but most, like Canada and Nova Scotia, were lost forever to their enemy. Louis, still assigned to *le Royal Louis,* realized his chances of seeing naval action vanished when they signed the treaty. His days now became dull aboard the great, flawed ship fettered to the mooring.

Near midyear, Marie gave birth to their daughter, and Louis prayed he'd stay in Brest instead of going on a voyage. He wished to help rear his two children, remembering the longing for his own father when away. But fortune shifts to irony at times; he learned of plans to put out to sea.

The admiralty assigned *le Royal Louis* to a less demanding mission of escorting a fleet to resupply the regained French colonies in the West Indies. Louis told Marie as soon as he heard of it.

She had become used to his being close to home. "Oh, no, not that long!"

Louis tried to make light of his absence. "Time will fly for you while caring for the baby and I'll be back probably before next summer. Don't fear for my safety or regret my absence." He'd miss home, too, but reminded her, "I've been so lucky not having to voyage longer than a week or two on patrols since getting back from England. Yet, it's my duty, just like our fathers. You'll be fine and my sisters and mother will help you fill the days."

"Yes, your mother and sisters could tend to the children, but none of them can replace your company." Marie's eyes welled with tears.

Her sadness made it hard to leave her. He offered what little comfort his words could. "We'll have to take each mission as it comes. Some will turn out longer than others and we'll make the best of our time when together." But he expected no trouble on the voyage and to return in little time.

The next week they took a carriage to the de Saint-Alouarn country estate where Marie and the baby were to stay with his family. After she settled in, Louis reported back onto *le Royal Louis.* Before embarking early in May, the armory took off half of her cannon, greatly lightening the upper decks. The reduction of iron allowed the ship to navigate better, although she still tended to overly heel leeward.

Five months later, Louis returned to France from Saint-Domingue and the Windward Islands. The captain declared the warship still unsafe, even when *en flute,* with reduced cannons. She never sailed on a mission again and remained berthed for the next ten years until the navy demolished her in 1773.

The materials for the reconstruction of the main hall trickled onto the Staunton Harold estate. Abraham recorded the inventory and located storage areas for the supplies. Bit by bit the new landscape layout took form. Two of the lakes created a natural vista and workmen filled in the remaining old reflection pools and canals. They removed the long lines of trees bordering the roads while craftsmen began work on the hall.

The architectural plans for the main building doubled the length of the front. It gave the façade a longer, more pleasing rectangular look than the blocky original Jacobean style.

Abraham's duties kept his mind off of Yvette, but the evenings sitting by himself in the farm cottage brought loneliness. Washington's library offered Abraham hundreds of books to read; still, thoughts of his wife and child interrupted his reading. The monotony of his meals and daily routines caused Abraham to fantasize his boredom away.

One of the few distractions he allowed himself often came in his imagination and even sometimes in dreams that had taken hold of him months earlier. His mental seraph, Anne's charm and beauty, had seeded a schoolboy's crush. Abraham didn't let it interfere with his love of Yvette. The daydreams only provided infrequent relief from dreariness.

With the quiet solitude wearing on him, Abraham appreciated that Anne, who also missed Yvette, often stopped by to talk to him.

Anne came to Abraham one day in the library. "You must be terribly lonely. Have you received news when Yvette and Michelle will return?" she asked. "Their absence must torment you."

He quickly stood up from the table, heaped with drawings and papers. "No news yet. I presume before autumn as we agreed when she left. I suppose you're as anxious as I for their return."

"At least you have Washington around to talk to, Yvette is the only close female friend in whom I can confide. Although she's in France, I'm thankful, at least, for you being at the manor, Abraham." Anne found his company a nice change from servants and her husband. "We're so far from towns, a friend nearby provides distractions from the humdrum. I so enjoy your company while she's away."

"The same goes for me and your visits." His gratefulness grew with every memory of their indebted life in London. "You and your husband have been more than kind and generous to us. The two of you treat us beyond our position."

"Abraham, Washington and I see you as an equal," Anne admonished and giggled. "I must tell you, Washington is having a bedroom made into a nursery for when you visit with Michelle. The furnishings he's purchased for it exceed any I've ever seen for a child. Washington has taken to Michelle as much as I."

Her admission made him blush. "I don't know how to thank you, my lady. The earl provides us with more than my talents or friendship are worth. Every convenience is made available to us." Their stay at the manor would have seemed unthought of just a few years earlier. "Lately, I've considered how privileged living here has changed our fortunes."

"I'm hoping it's enough for you to stay here a long time. I rely on your company to brighten my day, Abraham." Anne patted him on his arm and smiled before leaving him to his work.

During Yvette's absence, Anne's femininity and gentle character provided a pleasant diversion from overseeing burly, sweaty workmen. Her friendliness and wit titillated him. Abraham looked forward to seeing her pretty face around the hall with her red hair, a pennant, signaling a welcome break. At times, he caught himself imagining what she looked like in bed. He rationalized that Yvette's temporary absence and lack of intimacy prompted such tempting desires.

The very next day a letter from Yvette announced her return.

My Dearest and Beloved Abraham—Time has sped and before the leaves alight onto our fields, I shall return. The sailing comes in two weeks' time, but you need not meet me in Dover. I found our friend, Madame Goubert in Brest one day. She, too, had returned to visit her kin when the war ended, bearing joyous news. She's engaged to wed Jacques, who also is here with Lucie. We four shall return together to London. From there, it will be but a few days on the coach to Leicester and into your arms. I do, however, also have some unpleasant news. The shipwrights in Brest, who now receive no pay from the navy, are leaving for other work. Many do common laborers' tasks in the fields or unload fish along the docks. The port has fallen into terrible condition with poverty everywhere. I fret we must postpone the dreams we had for our return. Yet we can delight in your current situation, and until my eyes gaze upon yours, be steadfast that I shall soon be embracing you. Your Loving and Obedient Wife, Yvette

The news of the port's deterioration depressed Abraham the rest of the day. His desires to return to the shipyard in Brest had dominated his thoughts during Yvette's absence. Now, a shipwright future after the manor project turned doubtful.

Shortly after, Washington provided Abraham with his own workroom in the main building, and a few weeks later, as he studied at his drawing table, he heard footsteps in the hallway.

"Abraham." The familiar voice made him twirl around in his chair. Yvette stood in the doorway with Michelle in her arms.

"Yvette." He rushed to her, and after embracing for a long moment, he asked about her crossings of the Channel and the visit. Yvette gave him a summary of their trip.

"How's the cottage in Brest?" He had worried if Anton could manage with the upkeep.

"Father cares for it fine and the garden looks as hearty as when we planted it. He felled trees along the edge of the garden for winter wood, so when we return we can expand the garden. Although I love our cottage here, the country cottage in Brest I regard as our real home. Michelle had a wonderful time playing along the river and in the woods with me."

Abraham laughed. "Michelle stole your parents' hearts, I'm sure."

Yvette paused, looking away, recalling their first reactions. "They're old-fashioned and hold her mother's profession against her. Neither said anything mean nor treated her poorly; even so, Michelle may never be a real grandchild to them. It broke my heart at first for them to reject her, although they warmed up to her by the time we left. I can't understand why they reacted that way. Michelle was an orphan for heaven's sake! God wants us to love all."

Abraham, stunned, had expected them to embrace Michelle as one of their own grandchildren. "Don't be angry with them. When we move back, they'll have missed her and will realize her life is what they should judge, not her mother's." Their rejection unsettled him. "Although, it surprises me Anton has that attitude."

"Papa stays old-fashioned and my mother, priggish. They haven't experienced enough new events there." She snorted. "Little changes in their routines for their conventional beliefs to expand."

Suddenly Anne's voice coming from the hallway broke the tension. "Yvette?"

"In Abraham's workroom." Yvette spun with a broad grin.

Anne rushed through the door and kissed Yvette and Michelle on their cheeks. "Oh, I've missed you so. A servant told me you returned."

"I've missed you, too. Michelle has asked for you so often." Yvette handed the child to Anne to cuddle.

She hugged the tot and stroked Michelle's hair, smiling. "You must tell us how you enjoyed your trip."

"I'll tell you this evening after supper, if you'd like." Yvette no longer paid her formalities. Although a countess, Anne had gladly given up the pretense of titles in private for her relationship with Yvette.

"Please, I don't want to steal you away from Abraham," Anne said. "Both of you join us for supper tonight. The earl should return around eight. I'll watch Michelle until then. After we eat, recount your voyage."

"Fine, we'll come for dinner. Now I have to unpack and shall see you at home, Abraham." She kissed Abraham and left.

Anne, holding Michelle, remained in the workroom for a few seconds longer.

"You're so lucky having these two. Well, I'd better tell the cook to prepare dishes for five for supper this evening. Don't be late." Anne headed for the kitchen.

That evening after dinner the couples sat in the library and listened to Yvette describe her trip to Brest. Then Yvette mentioned she had met a sailor from Saint-Nazaire aboard ship.

"Where's Saint-Nazaire?" asked Washington, sitting with his legs crossed in his favorite upholstered chair.

"Close to the Loire River mouth," said Abraham, recalling the town. "West of Nantes around a twenty miles. It's a very small village."

He nodded, uncrossed his legs, and leaned forward. "Oh, I'm familiar with the mouth of the Loire. During the Battle of Quiberon Bay, my ship drove the *Juste* into the river shallows where she struck reefs and waves destroyed her. Almost the entire crew perished along with the captain, François de Saint-Alouarn. Abraham, you remember him, the French captain of the *Renommée* when we took her."

Yvette controlled herself and said coldly, "And his brother, René, died there, too." She decided it was time Abraham know the truth.

"René de Saint-Alouarn commanded on board and died, too?" Abraham's jaw dropped. "No one told me he passed."

"Both brothers. They died from our action before the ship broke up," Washington added matter-of-factly.

The scene flashed back into Washington's mind, triumphant as each officer fell upon the deck. It was a grand moment in his career. As he related the story and his commands to the marines, Abraham looked at Yvette.

"Yvette, I'm sorry." It was all Abraham could say, realizing she must have taken the news with remorse, regardless of the years and their marriage.

"Sorry?" Washington questioned after Abraham interrupted the story.

Although Yvette had fancied herself to be free of emotions concerning René, the talk filliped her heart when she realized Washington caused René's death.

"The *Juste* hove leeward toward the Loire, when..." Washington, oblivious to his effects on Yvette, had continued to describe the battle but stopped when he noticed her vacant stare.

No one said anything. Washington stood silent and confused until Anne spoke. "Dear, we'll talk later."

"Shall we retire?" interrupted Abraham. "Yvette needs to recover from her long trip." He glanced sideways at her, still seated, motionless.

"Of course," mumbled Washington, still wondering what he had said wrong.

Abraham and Yvette walked back to the cottage, Michelle fast asleep in her father's arms. He laid her to bed and returned to sit with Yvette.

"This is the first I've learned of his death, Yvette. You've been aware for some time, haven't you?"

Her hand fidgeted with the hem of her shawl. "Yes, not long after it happened. Gaëlle wrote to me." She looked over at him, sympathetically. "I didn't want to burden you with any of those memories."

Abraham closed his eyes for a moment. "It kept me from comforting you when you needed it."

"You shouldn't have to. René should mean nothing to me." She returned to looking at the shawl hem.

"But he does and I can't expect you to ignore the feelings you once had for him, regardless of how your emotions changed after we married." He felt bad she had kept the truth from him. "I understand you must carry fond memories of him."

"I thought I was over my feelings for him after I first heard of his death. Then on the ship to Brest, I met that sailor who'd been on *le Juste*. He told me how they died. Then tonight, learning the earl's involvement overcame me. I'm sorry. It's not that I love René any longer, it's just...." She was at a loss for words.

Abraham said, "Don't try to explain or rationalize emotions, dear. They simply are."

"It's more than that. Learning the earl's crew caused the de Saint-Alouarn brothers' death shocked me. It's changed the way I view the earl. I don't think I can ever enjoy his company again, at least not as I did in the past." She shrugged. "It's irrational, I know. But in effect, Washington killed both René and François."

Abraham put his arm around her. Yvette, committed to her carpenter over any English earl or French captain, said nothing.

As Abraham lay in bed that night he recounted the many times René's memory had brought Yvette to tears. And how she had spurned his love in favor of René. He wondered if she hadn't discovered René's infidelities, would she have preferred René to him? Even though it was stupid to be jealous of a dead man, René's long-lasting effects still haunted them. Her feelings over René's death, although understandable, made Abraham upset. He tossed in bed over this old wound until asleep.

The next day at the manor, Abraham assigned men to their tasks and walked through the work sites doing inspections, taking inventory in his head of the material usage. He circled to a part of the hall where construction had ended for the time being with no workmen present.

"Oh, Abraham. I didn't expect you to be here," said Anne, surprised.

"Countess, you shouldn't be in this section of the house," he warned. "Nothing is secure yet. We're still putting in roof beams." Abraham pointed up, smiling. "Something might fall on you."

"I came to view those roof beams. Abraham, you're such a creative man," she replied, approaching him. "The earl would be lost without you. It's your genius that is the heart of this project."

Abraham, flattered, brushed off the praise as Anne came nearer. "Thank you for saying so but the basic designs come from the earl. I just carry out his wishes." The room was dark with dusty sunbeams streaming through the new windows, spotlighting Anne. She glowed in it. Abraham saw why Washington had picked her, a beautiful and intelligent wife for a man of wealth and fame.

"Ideas and actions, Abraham. You're the one who accomplishes the real work and can handle the details with your extraordinary skills. Take the compliment as you wish, the results reflect the truth of the matter," Anne said, smiling, and glanced away. "Washington spoke out of turn last night to mention the deaths of the de Saint-Alouarns and he behaves so ignorant at times when it comes to people's emotions." She let out a loud breath.

"Well, I'm sure he regretted the accidental comment. I talked to Yvette. She soon let it pass." He didn't want either Anne or Washington to feel guilt for the slip although it had upset their evening.

Anne took his hand. "Abraham, you seem to understand women's emotions. That's an uncommon talent for most men."

Abraham expected her to withdraw her hand after speaking, but Anne kept it there for a few seconds before removing it.

Over the last few months he noticed how Anne eyed him, not alluringly, but as if in contemplation. The frequency of her visits to the workroom had also increased when Yvette left for France.

"Ah, I must speak with the earl about timbers in the garden." He said hurriedly, looking back at the door.

"Washington left this morning for Leicester and won't return until sometime this afternoon. Perhaps there's something I can do for you?" Anne stood close and looked up into his eyes, smiling.

Abraham leaned back, his throat in a tight knot. "Well, we may need to move timbers stacked in the back in the rear garden."

"I can handle that. If the timbers lie in the way, we'll put them elsewhere. Let's go inspect it." Anne grabbed his arm, walking toward the doorway to the garden.

She stepped forward, still holding his arm. By the time they arrived at the doorway they walked arm-in-arm.

Upon entering the garden, Abraham pointed out the stacked lumber on a garden path. "The timbers might keep people from strolling the garden. Do you want them elsewhere?"

"Well, we could put them..." She paused mid-sentence and stopped on the garden path, turning to him. Something had bothered her for weeks. "Abraham, this may seem an awkward confession. But the earl seems somewhat distant of late. I respect your candidness and confidentiality. Do you think he has found another? A new love? At times, he ignores my needs. I need a man." Anne still clung to his arm.

I need a man, rang an alarm in his head. "To be honest, I'm surprised you'd ask me," he stumbled, not knowing what to say. "I have no knowledge that he entertains thoughts of any other woman." Anne stood close in front of him. He bit his lip and blood rushed to his head.

"Besides the earl, I consider you as the only other gentleman I ever would view as a close confidant. I rely upon you for your honesty." She placed her hand on his, expecting him to tell her the truth about the earl.

"I view that as an honor, Countess," Abraham responded with a smile. "The fact you favor me, though, overwhelms me." Her attention excited his libido as much as his ego.

"Please, if you have any ideas about how I might solve my problem, tell me. As a compassionate man, you might have the insight." Anne patted his hand and continued to walk along the garden path.

After telling him where to place the timbers, she strolled back into the house. Abraham stood wondering about what transpired. Had she been flirting with him? He'd always found Anne a fascinating woman. Although any fantasies of lying with her existed just as fantasies, momentary prurient larks, it was nothing he expected or even wanted to happen. Her mention to him the need of a man and that Washington hadn't fulfilled her needs seemed too closely placed.

The rest of the day as he worked, the complexity of her *I need a man* dominated his mind. Abraham knew that would be the end of their friendship and Yvette's trust if he told her. Still, did the countess really insinuate what he thought or only what he hoped?

Abraham reasoned out the scenario if Anne's suspected proposal were true. If he complied with an affair, his guilt over being unfaithful might depress him or cause him to lose Yvette. Refusing Anne outright, on the other hand, might make her bitter enough to take revenge and cost him his position. Lastly, he'd never tell the earl of his wife's disloyalty. How he should let Anne know he couldn't have an affair was the problem, he weighed. The refusal had to be done so Anne understood she appealed to him, but he must remain devoted to Yvette. It complicated his life at a time when he felt vulnerable to pursuing something exciting and different after months of sexual frustration and boredom, and years of bedroom routine.

That night Abraham made love to Yvette physically and Anne mentally, the sin making the pleasure much greater. The guilt he carried for the imagined liaison with Anne kept him brooding throughout the next day.

Two days later, Anne found Abraham in the workroom. "Abraham, when you get the chance, please come upstairs to my bedroom. I have something to show you."

Abraham answered businesslike, "I'll be there within the hour after finishing these estimates." His mind raced at the thought of being asked into a countess's bedroom to be *shown* something. After a few minutes, he decided not to make her wait, so he put his work aside to attend to her needs.

In case Anne might try to seduce him again, he practiced rejections while approaching the bedroom. At her door, Abraham hesitated, it stood ajar an inch. When he knocked it opened wider and from the darkened hall he saw her looking out of the windows facing the gardens at the rear of the manor. The bed lay behind her.

"Who's there?"

"Countess, it's Abraham, as you asked."

"Enter. I didn't expect you to come so soon." She moved toward the door.

He grabbed the handle and stepped forward. "What is it you need, my lady?" Abraham stammered standing sideways in the doorway.

"Please, Abraham, don't be so proper now that I've expressed my trust in you," Anne said drawing nearer. "I asked you here to tell me if it is possible to have the glaziers put in larger windows in this wall for a better view."

"I'm sure it is possible. It can be added to the schedule. Is that all?" He rubbed his hands to ease the tension, wondering if there was anything else on her mind, gazing at the bed.

"Have you thought about what I said, earlier about Washington?"

"Of course. I admit I'm perplexed about it. Fidelity is a powerful thing," Abraham whispered, hoping she understood his dedication to Yvette.

Anne wondered what he meant about "fidelity" and moved in front of him. "Yes, fidelity is powerful, but at times one's needs often conflict with devotion." She hoped she was fulfilling Washington's needs and not losing his devotion.

Abraham envisaged her naked white body on the bed and stepped more into the room.

"Then this continues as something my husband need not know—ever." The knotty and sensitive subject of Washington's possible impotence or an affair would be sure to embarrass her husband. "I'm aware of your close friendship and pray it doesn't corrupt your loyalty to him. I'd like to keep it between the two of us." She had wanted to make sure he would not say anything to her husband and moved behind him.

"Naturally, no one else need know." Abraham said, his throat tightening. "I'll help you with your problem however I can." He gave a look again toward the bed.

"Until later, then," she said, opened the door, and Abraham left.

As he returned to his workspace, he anguished over his clearheaded dedication to his wife or an irrational tryst with another's.

The Sibyl's Prophecy

Three weeks later, the chill of a Midlands' late fall reminded Abraham of working at the shipyard. He spent most of his days outside and even when inside, the half-completed rooms with open roofs and windows without panes let the winds blow through. It bothered him; at the shipyards he did physical work to warm himself, but now he only supervised. In many ways, he missed the heavy labor, yet he appreciated not having swollen chapped hands or aching muscles.

The front façade wall neared completion, but the interior still had to be redone along the back of the hall. Several rooms were livable, while dust, materials, and workers filled other areas.

"The glaziers will arrive next week, sir, to start the windows on the ground floor," he mentioned to Washington.

"Fine, it looks fetching, doesn't it? A sturdy and appealing design overall. My wife says your hard work is turning my dreams into reality," complimented Washington, smiling while standing outside before the entryway.

"Thank the countess for me." Abraham wondered if she still desired him. She had not approached him on the matter in weeks.

"Yvette and you should come to dinner, and bring Michelle. Strange, Anne hasn't invited you to dine for weeks." An evening with his friend never failed to entertained him. "Could you join us tomorrow?"

"I'll ask Yvette, sir. Our quiet evenings need some excitement. She'll enjoy it." Their company always pleased him, too, and lately, especially Anne's.

The next night they joined Washington and Anne at the hall in the main dining room, while a servant girl watched Michelle in the new nursery. Afterward, they conversed and continued drinking wine at the table.

Anne looked alluring in a new gown that highlighted her figure. "Abraham, my husband said when he captured the *Renown,* your knowledge helped. It must have been exciting, building warships and surviving battles. What insights did you gain by it?" she asked.

"The first war ended as a waste." Abraham glanced at Anne nervously. "The work, the money, the materials, the loss of lives, just to appease the kings and their ministers. They could have settled the conflict with much less destruction by flipping a coin."

Washington took exception, setting down his drink and staring at his friend. "The skill in warfare decides who wins the combat and the war, whereas a coin toss is left to chance."

Abraham shut his eyes, took a sip from his glass and argued. "We believe victory results from a great leader with greater strategies. In reality, from what I've experienced, chance determines the largest part of triumph more than skill. Often a battle is won by who encounters a better wind or the flight of one cannonball than the pursuit of a better tactic. Especially in the earlier war. Besides, when it concluded, regardless of whether the generals and admirals had more skill or luck, they gave back everything. We fought for nothing."

Washington's face reddened and his voice rose. "Rubbish! Although the end of that war disappointed many, it set up serious consequences. It prepared us for the glorious results of the next." He moved his chair back from the dining table. "Abraham, you miss the significance of the historical sequence. The conflict resulted in defining the fundamentals and strategies for the ensuing one." He frowned and tapped the table with a dinner knife.

Even in his wine-dulled mind, Abraham knew arguing would only upset his friend further, so he nodded in frustrated agreement.

"Anne, we've roiled blood with our discussion, can you play something on the harpsichord to soothe it?" Washington snickered over his supposed debate victory.

Anne, having drunk the least, rose, and walked to the library. She sat at the harpsichord and began playing while the others found places to sit. Yvette rested her head on the divan pillows. Washington slouched in his chair with his legs crossed outward in front of him. Abraham took a seat near the harpsichord.

After the second piece, both Washington and Yvette fell asleep and Anne quit playing to not disturb them. She got up and motioned for Abraham to follow her.

"Too much wine for them, I suppose," she said to Abraham.

"And for me," he replied, wondering what the immediate future held.

"Let them sleep. We can talk about your exploits at sea in the nursery." Anne led him toward the foyer staircase.

"Well, the adventures were few, most of our time was filled with either boredom or hardships. I'm sure the earl's stories sound not much different than my own; weeks of tedium and bad food interjected with a few hours of terror. For me, it wasn't as frightening. I worked below decks filling shot holes, unlike those manning cannons who watched the balls flying at them with snipers firing upon them from above."

"Bad food? The earl served as captain." Anne giggled as she ascended the wide marble stairs ahead of him. "You and he experienced sea life from two different perspectives. One can't blame either for the viewpoints. Forgive him, his rank forces his opinions." She lowered her voice. "I hope we don't wake Michelle if she's asleep."

On entering the nursery, she dismissed the servant girl who had been watching Michelle sleeping in the small bed.

Anne stood at the bed's foot. "Oh, how darling she looks." Her distant gaze reflected her sadness, then she turned to him. "I'll likely be childless and unfulfilled. However, now that months have passed since we last spoke in confidence, I hope you can help me in my desperation."

"I understood your reasons then and still respect you. It must be hard for you to be frustrated and barren." For a second, Abraham wondered if he impregnated her, would the earl know it wasn't his own.

"More than one might realize. Women need things, too. The earl provides what he can, yet recently lacks in his attentiveness." Months had passed since Washington and Anne had been intimate in bed.

Abraham stood behind her and resisted hugging her. But he touched her arm and whispered, "Is there anything I can do to help."

She turned around to him. "Yes, have you discov..." she paused as a creaking door interrupted. It opened and Yvette walked into the room.

"Oh," she said when her eyes fell on them standing close, Abraham's hand on her. Yvette stepped back and stared at him, asking in French, "What are you two doing in here?"

"We came to see Michelle." Abraham hurriedly stepped away from Anne.

Anne said nothing and smiled.

Yvette walked to the child's bed, picked up Michelle, and left them, saying, "It's time she's taken to bed. Are you ready to go?"

Abraham paused a moment, looking at Anne. "We can talk later." Then he rushed to catch up with Yvette.

Yvette had climbed halfway down the staircase by the time he reached her. She said nothing and strode toward the door, holding sleeping Michelle. Abraham saw Washington through the library door, still asleep in the chair.

Abraham followed her out of the hall. "We needn't wake our host to take our leave," he whispered.

As they left the manor house, she stayed ahead of him. "Abraham," Yvette said, then paused and spun to face him. "I'm aware you love me. I noticed that recently you're attracted to Anne. You've mentioned her often and your eyes watch her every move. Is there something you should tell me?" Nothing had slipped past her.

Abraham trudged in silence up the hill until his guilt flowed out. "In honesty, I must admit finding myself bothered by Anne since summer." Then Abraham related to Yvette the story of their previous conversations and how it had seeded lustful desires for Anne.

"And now?" Yvette asked, becoming angry and looking straight ahead as they climbed.

"Do you mean to ask if I still desire Anne?"

She still did not face him. "Do you want her now that I know?"

"I don't believe so! It's angered you, I want nothing more to do with Anne," Abraham's adamant reply attested to the resolve.

Yvette turned to him and scowled, "That's the wrong answer!" Disgust filled her words.

It took Abraham a second of thought to realize his passions for Anne, if he willingly stopped, were superficial and selfish, he only had wanted her for sex. Although he intended his answer meant he loved Yvette, it also meant he'd still be desiring Anne if Yvette hadn't discovered it. The answer uncovered a shallowness in Abraham's character. No answer could have justified his lust or have been correct.

Neither spoke after reaching the cottage. Yvette went to bed, taking Michelle with her; Abraham curled up in a chair for the night.

At work the next day, Washington behaved as usual while Abraham acted more reticent and withdrawn. Washington assumed their argument over the war had caused it and tried to joke to mend their friendship. Abraham chastised himself repeatedly over his lechery and betraying the earl, a friend and employer. When Anne walked past later that morning, she exchanged a glance as though nothing had happened.

After he returned home that night, Yvette cooked supper and said little. Michelle wanted to be entertained, so Abraham told her Aesop's fables while they waited to eat.

"The food is ready," She snorted, banging the dishes onto the table.

"How did your day go?" He asked without looking at her, depressed over the incident in the nursery.

"I'd think you needn't ask," Yvette spit out in French.

"No, I can imagine. I'm so sorry," Abraham replied in English.

"I have more questions to ask, later," she said in French again, glancing at Michelle, who laughed at the exchange in two languages.

They ate without talking during the meal except for Michelle's infrequent comments and questions. Afterward, everyone sat before the lit fireplace. Abraham read one of the earl's books while Yvette crocheted and Michelle played.

When Michelle's bedtime came, both returned to the fireplace and Yvette grilled Abraham with questions she'd recorded in her mind the entire day. Abraham answered her with careful and honest replies.

After her interrogation, Yvette stood before him. "I don't comprehend your motives, Abraham. You've never done anything so witless before like this. Now that it's come to light, we must deal with the consequences. You're drawn to Anne, and she, as you've told me, to you. You both knew the possible results of your flirtations, but you pursued them regardless, risking everything." The words stung like a whipping.

Her arms crossed, she closed her eyes and frowned. "Since I cannot have half a man and will not stand by to wait to see whom you choose, I've decided to take Michelle and leave for France again. If you come with me, as I hope, we'll continue our marriage in France. Yet, if you remain here, you must decide where your heart lies before long or our marriage will end. If so, you can stay in England forever for all I care."

Abraham sat aghast at the sentence for his crime. "Don't leave me, Yvette! I can't unravel what's happening in my head right now. You know I love you!" he begged in anguish.

"I must have all of you or nothing, Abraham," Yvette demanded, then swiftly returned to her crocheting, torn between her love and distrust of him.

He had, in one night to her, become the reflection of René, whose fidelity she'd sought in vain. Those long-ago feelings had reemerged to inflict more wounds. In reliving it, she retaliated by punishing Abraham, in part, for René's transgressions.

Abraham said no more. Yvette's decision was irrevocable. Still, despite the threat of losing his wife and child, he had the overpowering urge to still carry on a relationship with Anne. Insanity, he thought, beyond control, yet the idea implanted itself in his brain. Before bed, Abraham told Yvette he'd stay to earn more money before going to Brest, although this plan had a dual purpose, and Yvette suspected it.

The next day, Abraham informed Washington that Yvette and Michelle were returning to France for Christmas and New Year, and he'd need time off work again to escort them to Dover. He gave Yvette most of the money he'd saved, covering three months of expenses in Brest, saying he'd come after earning enough to last a year in case French shipyard jobs remained scarce.

The day before they left for Dover, Abraham was working when Anne came to talk.

"Yvette is leaving until the new year? So soon after just returning. What shall I do without her company?" More months without a female friend vexed her.

He inferred she hinted at what *they* could do without her nearby. "The bonds to her family in France remain very strong," Abraham replied. "I'll accompany them to Dover and sleep overnight in London before returning."

"London? I'm going to our house there while you're on your trip. Instead of staying at an inn, use one of our rooms." She'd bend propriety's rules for her husband's friend to save him the inn costs.

"That's so kind. As soon as I arrive, I'll go there." Abraham determined this invitation as more than hospitality and it sealed his beliefs.

Anne approached Washington at his desk the day Abraham and Yvette left and suggested a visit to London.

"Washington, the construction dust and noise grows unbearable, and with Yvette and Michelle gone, I will go insane. I must get away and shop for a few days in London. Please come along."

"Well, I've wondered how you put up with the din. To go shopping is a superb idea. Yet with Abraham gone for a week or more, I must stay to supervise problems that might arise."

"I feared you'd have to remain." Anne pouted.

"My dear, I've neglected you for some months, although it's for a different reason this time. I must work." Washington looked down, frowning.

Anne dropped her gaze and sat on the edge of the desk. "Something has been on your mind and you won't say. What is distracting you from being with me?"

His hand slid to his knee, rubbing it. "It comes with the title."

"Not the madness of your uncle or brother, or a mistress, I pray?" Her eyes popped open wide.

"No, no. The richness of an earl's lifestyle has been afflicting me in a way I find embarrassing. All of my life I condemned Laurence's decadent habits. Now the siren's call of self-indulgence has lured me, too. I have gout."

Anne's face showed concern. "Gout in your foot?"

"The knees." He smirked. "That's why I've been visiting you less in your chamber. The pain is so intense when any pressure is put on them, I'd rather take a musket ball wound. I always took pride to live healthily and be fit to return to sea if the Admiralty asked it. Now age and excesses have plagued me with a wealthy man's curse."

Anne laughed loud and heartily, putting her hands to her mouth and eyes.

His head snapped back. "I find no humor in this. The surgeon says I must cut back on rich foods and meat to have any hope in curing the ailment." Washington's furrowed his forehead, not understanding how she derived comedy from his pain.

"Oh, dear. I've made a fool of myself." Anne turned red with embarrassment.

"How so?"

"I thought you had interests in someone else or found me undesirable. The fear concerned me to such a degree, to find out, I asked Abraham if he knew whether you favored another."

Washington began to chuckle, and then both laughed aloud together.

"I never have nor could find anyone as desirable as you," he said still chortling. "No doubt Abraham found the question interesting, though."

Anne left the next day for London, taking a servant and cook. After arriving, she sent them away on a one-day holiday after putting the house in order.

Later that morning upon hearing a knock on her door, Anne found Abraham on the doorstep, smiling and wide-eyed with his leather bag and clothing pack.

"Here I am as promised, my lady."

"Come in, let's settle you in a room and then go to the parlor for a refreshment. But we must do without servants. They won't be back until tonight." Anne greeted him with a broad smile.

After she showed him to the bedroom, he washed and changed into clean clothes and then sped to her as she'd requested.

"Yvette embarked on her way to Brest and should be there in a couple of days if the winds hold." Abraham had let no one know why she left.

"This has been so sudden." Anne's face drooped. "Again, I shall dearly miss her and Michelle."

"As I. Yet, perhaps we can get some satisfaction from it." Abraham slipped to her side and pulled her to him, putting his hands on her waist and kissed her neck.

"God, Abraham! What are you doing!" Anne shouted and pushed him.

He stood back, mouth dropping open. "Oh, forgive me! I thought…"

"I'm not sure what you thought, but you were wrong!" She glared at him.

"My lady, I assumed you needed me for intimacy. If I made a mistake, I am deeply sorry." He turned ashen.

"Abraham, how could you imagine that I might ever be unfaithful to the earl? If I've exhibited any coquettishness, it's not what I intended." Her face turned flush, accenting her red hair.

"When you said that you wanted a man, I assumed you meant in a physical sense. And you invited me to stay here and dismissed your servants."

Her eyes pierced his and her face now glowed hot. "The need for a man regarded the earl, not you. And I tried to be considerate when proposing you stay in the house to save inn costs. You've misunderstood and your impulses expose you as no gentleman!"

Abraham's hand inched to his brow and his entire body sagged. "Self-delusions have doomed me. Oh, God. Can you ever forgive me?"

"You've broken my trust in you. Please leave!"

"I am sorry. I'll get my things." Abraham sulked his way to the bedroom.

Moments later Anne heard a key turning the lock at the front entrance. She ran to it and called, "Who's there?" She now regretted sending the servants away.

"It's Robert. I was checking the house as Washington requested. I didn't know you were coming to town. Where's your maid?" Robert spoke through the door.

"I let them go for the day. Let me unlock it. They so seldom can enjoy being in London."

Robert entered and Anne poured out the story of Abraham's seemingly irrational assault. His eyes squinted at the liberties she had taken in offering a commoner a room and in Abraham's crude behavior. "He must go." Robert frowned, concerned for Anne's safety.

"He will. He's gathering his things."

Abraham finished putting clothing back into his travel pack and leather bag. As he did, he tried to recall all the false leads he'd judged flirtatious. He shook his head at his foolishness and went down to the parlor.

Robert was standing akimbo, scowling, and Abraham assumed Anne had told him.

"I'm speechless and thought you a better man," Robert growled.

"I've embarrassed myself and can only beg forgiveness of you both for my actions." His entire body drooped with humiliation.

"Pray my brother forgives you." Robert smoldered.

Abraham picked up his leather bag and clothes pack and departed without another word.

The coach to Leicester left the next morning. By the time he spotted Staunton Harold, the travel and worry over what Washington would say and do had exhausted him.

His remorse over losing his family and probably his position weighed on him. Anne and Robert returned to Staunton Harold two days later. After Robert departed, Washington approached Abraham that afternoon.

He glared at him. "Abraham, I have something to discuss with you."

"Of course, sir," He answered facing the door, with no doubt about the subject.

"My brother and Anne informed me of your attack on her. I'm dismissing you and demand you leave the grounds." Washington spat out and added, "Had you not been a friend, I'd do much more." His seething emotions abutted deep-felt guilt for not having gone with his wife to London.

"I understand. I can't depart without telling you my faulty reasoning has devastated my marriage and self-esteem. Not a minute passes I wish it had not occurred. I'm sorry for betraying your friendship in such an underhanded way. Perhaps someday you can open your heart to forgive me," he implored.

"Leave at once! Get out!" demanded Washington, furious.

Abraham, nearly cowering, held his head down. "Yes, sir."

He packed his few things in his leather bag and pack and returned the borrowed books to the library. As he walked the long road to Leicester carrying his toolbox, he glanced back at the manor, never to see his projects completed.

⌘

Nothing could have made Captain Mackenzie happier. Those few words scribbled upon a paper, *"to return to Portsmouth,"* stood out as if gilded. After four insufferable years, he was going home to Alana and Tommy.

The *Defiance* was now twenty years old and betrayed by her age. The navy decided to survey her for repairs or if too old, to break her up. Mackenzie wrote in a report that he considered her still a worthy ship for commissions. When he reached shore after a month-long sail to England, he rushed to the headquarters to turn in his paperwork.

"Say there, Captain Mackenzie!" A shout sounded when he left the last office. Maitland walked toward him, beaming.

Mackenzie smiled, considering him now to be a proper fellow officer after his valorous performance. "My word, Captain Maitland. It's good to see you've recovered from the tropics."

"Oh, the Caribbean doesn't bother me, I came to love the climate and people. I'm on my way back there again next week, still upon the *Renown*. And you? You look to have survived, and with praise, I hear, for nabbing two Spanish ships and a port near Havana."

"Yes, I suppose that's why they recalled me to Portsmouth, to recompense me for the prizes." He shrugged.

Maitland cocked his head. "It might have helped. However, I'd be thanking Captain Shirley for coming home."

"What do you mean? How is Shirley involved?" The mention of his name grated on Mackenzie.

"Didn't you know? It was Captain Shirley who arranged for them to return you to England." Maitland pointed his thumb behind him. "I ran into him in London not a month ago outside the Admiralty. He'd heard of your extended service in Jamaica and I confirmed that you wanted to come back. Besides the pull he had in the navy, he's an earl now. A quick note to the First Lord of the Admiralty Grenville and I'm sure they created the orders in days."

"Why on earth should Captain Shirley intervene on my behalf? Does he think I have no influence with the Admiralty?" Mackenzie bristled at the thought it was not his own brave feats that returned him, but Washington's status with the navy.

"I asked the same when I saw him." Maitland knew of Mackenzie's dislike of Washington, but the truth must come out. "He mentioned your association with Lord Fortrose. Before he died, Fortrose fell in bad graces with other members of Parliament. They never liked him much anyway. He had used your descriptions of the descents on Saint-Malo and Cherbourg and reports from the West Indies on many occasions to support Pitt. But when Pitt resigned, the whole of Parliament followed the king's lead. Your association with Fortrose and Pitt did you no benefit. When Captain Shirley learned of your plight, he hopped at the chance to help. He has high regard for you, sir."

Mackenzie stood for a second in silence. It had never occurred to him that Washington had respected him in any better light than how he felt about Washington. His mind tried vainly to construct an alternative reason for Washington's aid, one that was self-serving, but failed.

"Then I suppose I must write a letter of thanks." It was the only thing he could think of to say. He stood dumbfounded, realizing he had things so wrong.

When he returned to Scotland and Alana's arms and Tommy's hugs, he recalled the reason for the joyful homecoming, the kindheartedness of a captain he had always slighted. His experiences with Maitland, and now Washington, had dispelled his life-long feelings of inadequacy and bias against Lowland Scots and English nobles.

A week after he set foot in his house, he wrote a letter of thanks to Washington:

> *To His Honorable 5th Earl Ferrers, Distinguished Member of the House of Lords, and Royal Navy Captain Washington Shirley, Sir, I recently spoke to Captain Frederick Maitland who informed me you graciously interceded with the Admiralty on my behalf to return me to England from the Jamaica Station. I must confess that I was unperceptive you had such respect for me as to involve yourself so diligently in my welfare. Although I have, over the years, become more tolerant of life in the West Indies, the long assignment away from my home in Scotland distressed me greatly. The kindness you have shown in remedying this adversity will be long remembered by me. If any time in the future you find I may be of service in just repayment of your benevolent participation, please correspond your desires and I will attempt to service your request to the best of my abilities. Your Obedient and Grateful Servant, Captain George Mackenzie, November the 6th, 1762 at Inverness, Scotland*

In the letter, he had not contrived one word; such was the change in Mackenzie's nature over Washington's unsolicited intervention. His experiences and others' virtues had reformed his intolerance and rigid adherence to authority. In years to come, the navy would recognize the change to his command style, and it benefited him greatly.

"Yvette, you must stop this!" shouted Anton standing before her as she sat curled in a chair. "It's been three months already. Don't you notice how your melancholy is affecting Michelle?"

She sat wiping her nose. "Father, I can't help it. I miss him so and wonder if I'll ever see him again." The grieving had swollen her eyes.

"Well, you should have thought about that when you walked out on him," Anton scolded her, sitting beside her. "Even saints are sinners. Every person has moments of weakness or insanity and might cross that line, but a good spouse forgives. I'm sure Abraham's regretted it. Write and tell him to come home." Her sadness broke his heart.

She dabbed once more at her eyelids. "I don't know where he's living. Abraham last wrote from London, he'd lost the job at the manor after the earl learned of Abraham's attraction to his wife. That letter came months ago," Yvette blurted out between deep breaths.

"He'll be here soon," encouraged Anton. "Heed what I say, my child." He stroked her head and sighed.

"I'll light a candle for him, Yvette," added her mother, holding her crucifix, "and say a rosary, too."

"Thank you, Mama, though until Abraham is here, I'll worry. Why hasn't he written?" She sniffed and then put her hand on her head. "Maybe he's fallen out of love with us."

"Don't be foolish, Yvette. If you believe that, you'll be glum every second." Anton admonished. "Remember how he loved you. It will console you."

Louise encouraged her to pray for Abraham's soul. As often during difficult periods, Yvette's religious convictions re-awoke to offer hopeful comfort, but also, induce fears. Yvette contemplated that Abraham's adultery might be her punishment for choosing René over Abraham before their marriage. There was little difference, she believed, between the sin she committed in abandoning Abraham for René then, and the sin Abraham committed with Anne now. Abraham's infidelity chastised her—God's retribution for her own infidelity.

Yvette hadn't written to Abraham since returning to France, first out of anger and then out of ignorance of his whereabouts. By now, she assumed, Abraham was sure to be frantic over Michelle's wellbeing. Every few days when they first arrived in Brest, the girl asked when her father was coming, only to be told by Yvette, "Someday Papa will return. We must be patient."

Losing Abraham, she'd soon have to rely upon her parents for money. The costs and taxes for the country house amounted to more than Anton in retirement could afford. Within months, they would need to pay the increased taxes for the new year. They were desperate for income.

To make money, Yvette crocheted new designs for her needle lace. Time-consuming to make, it was becoming popular with dressmakers. The little she made from selling it didn't buy much.

One day, as she browsed the sellers' stalls on Rue de Mer near the dock for thread, a memory from long before moved her. Yvette stopped by the stall where she and Abraham had purchased her father a meerschaum pipe. The old Moorish vendor still haggled there with his toothy smile and fun-loving patter.

"Aha, you're still peddling the sultan's pipes, I see," Yvette said, and smiled at the old man.

"The meerschaums? They're the ones I love best. When I sell one, it's as if I've lost a wife," the vendor replied, but he didn't remember her.

"You must have the largest harem in France," she jested, pointing at the dozens of meerschaums.

The dark-skinned man laughed and raised his finger. "Or I'm the worst pipe seller."

"Many years ago, I bought one from you. My father still loves it and uses it daily. Your pipe has brought much joy to him. I wanted to thank you for it."

"It is my and the sultan's pleasure," he joked, nodding courteously. "I hope I sold it for a reasonable amount. Meerschaums are part of my family, and I price them so."

"The sum was fair, do you sell them often?"

"Not a lot. The long stem clay pipes are more popular, and cheaper. Meerschaum will last much longer and is a good stone for pipes. Not half an hour ago, I sold one to a navy officer." He paused and looked around. "There he is by the kerchief cart. That's Madam de Saint-Alouarn's son."

"Louis de Saint-Alouarn? François's boy? Why he was a child last I saw him." Yvette eyed the tall, good-looking man. "See what a handsome young gentleman he's become." Louis was around twenty-five years old and lanky, the same as his father. Although he looked nothing like François, then, neither did René.

"And on *le Royal Louis,* too," the vendor said, pointing to the huge ship. "There she is, the big one at anchor."

As Yvette stood there taking in the enormous vessel, Louis came back to the stall.

"Excuse me, sir, I forgot to ask you how to clean the pipe," Louis queried, smiling.

"Oh, kind officer, that's the beauty of meerschaum. You never need to clean it." The Moor's dark eyes glinted, his elbows leaning on the wooden cart. "After a year or two you'll see the white stone turning to a honey-yellow and after that to brown. Gently scrape out the bowl once in a while. Ask this lady, she bought one for her father," the old vendor told him.

Louis looked at Yvette, blinking.

"It's true," she said. "I bought one for my father long ago. He still uses it. Just as our friend says, now it's become a golden brown color."

Louis bowed slightly. "Thank you, madam."

"Sir, I was acquainted with your Uncle René and your father, and hearing of their passing saddened me." She waved a finger in front of her. "You don't remember me, but I met you when you were quite small."

"I'm at a loss to your name, madam." His brows rose.

"Yvette Robinson. I didn't go by that name then." She pointed to herself. "My name before I married was Yvette Façonneur."

Taken aback, he said excitedly, "Yvette Façonneur? Time has passed, but I do remember your face. Please, I must discuss a matter with you in private. I've something to tell you." Louis looked around, eyeing the street. "Is there somewhere nearby we can sit and talk?"

Yvette, curious, focused her gaze on him. "Not nearby. A café is located atop the hill." She pointed up the street.

Together they walked up the road to a familiar old café. Louis sat, sipping his coffee, and leaned across the table as she drank her cocoa.

"Madame Robinson, first I must tell you that I know much about you. René, my uncle, told me when the English held us prisoners in Leicester together. I recall he referred to you as his greatest love. In truth, he had a reputation for having many lovers." Louis set his cup down and grinned. "He talked, nevertheless, only with the utmost respect and deepest feelings concerning you. I thought you'd appreciate that." He sat, waiting for her reply, hoping he had redressed any hurt feelings she may have had.

Yvette chuckled at the memory. "That's kind of you to say. René held my devotion for years. He stole me away from my current husband. But soon after we were engaged, he broke my heart and I eventually married Abraham. Even so, whenever I hear his name I'm still flooded with warm memories of him. This all happened so long ago." She looked away and continued sipping her cocoa. "You mentioned you stayed in Leicester. I just returned from there. My husband worked for the Earl Ferrers at the manor, not far from the town."

"The Earl Ferrers?" he said, mouth opening. "I once befriended the countess, his wife. I did meet the earl one day, too."

"You knew Anne?" Yvette asked.

"No, her name was Mary. Perhaps a different…"

"Oh, you mean the old earl's wife," Yvette explained. "Countess Mary divorced him before they hanged him."

His eyes popped open. "Hanged? Why? For what crime?"

Yvette filled him in on the murder, trial, and execution of the earl, and the story took Louis aback. The crime had made the news throughout most of Europe. During that whole time, Louis was at sea.

"I suppose it was inevitable," he admitted and grinned.

"You'll be relieved to learn Countess Mary lives a far better life now. And the current Earl Ferrers, unlike his brother, embodies a real gentleman's morals. Yet, there's another curious twist I'll disclose. The new earl had captured *la Renommée* from your father and uncle, and commanded the *Temple* at Quiberon Bay. Strange, isn't it?"

"He commanded the *Temple?*" Louis exclaimed. "How extraordinary! But there's something additional that you must hear. Yet I can't tell you." Louis looked away.

"Sir?" She tilted her head. "What could you not tell me?"

"My mother has been searching for you for years and keeps a document for you from René." His voice was just a whisper. "We inquired at your parents' house, only to discover they no longer lived in Brest. People said you had moved to England. Where do you live now, if I may ask? My mother will pay you a visit."

"Your mother? Well, I'll tell you the directions to my cottage. My parents live with me outside Brest, up the river."

It puzzled her; she didn't expect René had needed to apologize for his actions of so long ago or try to explain the reasons for his philandering ways. She had forgiven him in her heart and mind.

Louis got up and excused himself, saying, "Madame Robinson, I must get a message off to my mother right away. You'll be hearing from her soon. It has been a pleasure and privilege to meet and talk with you. You remain as incredible as Uncle René described and the little I remember." Louis stood and bowed. "Until we meet again."

Yvette stood and curtsied as Louis parted, leaving her to finish her cup. She sat again, imagining René writing a letter for delivery after his death. For a romantic moment, she could see him penning it on *le Juste* just before the battle. Nothing he might devise, she thought, could erase the wounds he had caused her. Yet, Yvette hoped with fondness to read his final farewell.

A week hadn't passed before Yvette received a message from Madame de Saint-Alouarn requesting a date for a visit. Although not anxious, Yvette wondered why she didn't simply send the letter to her.

The carriage carrying Louis' mother arrived several days later. A servant walked to the cottage door and knocked. When Yvette answered, the man ran back to the carriage and opened it to help the grand old lady out.

The well-dressed and dignified woman glided along the path to the entrance, smiling. "So, we meet at last. Louis described you as a pretty woman. I find it true. May I enter?"

Her words flattered Yvette. Although she had never met the famous Madame de Saint-Alouarn, everyone spoke well of her. "Certainly, come in, please."

Madame de Saint-Alouarn had no pretenses and headed straight for a wooden chair near the kitchen table rather than a more comfortable upholstered seat in the front room. Like two neighbors preparing to chat, she sat and put two fingers on her chin, not knowing where to begin.

"Louis said you met him earlier." She began with a small smile. "I don't recall you at our manor."

Yvette shook her head. "No, I saw Louis as a child with René and François many years ago at my father's birthday party. You didn't travel to Brest on that trip."

Madame de Saint-Alouarn pinched her mouth and said, "Not unusual, I've always dreaded the naval gatherings and ships. So, now we come to why I requested to see you." She paused, exhaled, and continued.

"When my husband's brother courted you, I judged it unwise, not because of social ranking, but because he chanced to hurt you." She pulled her brows together. "I loathed René's infidelities and felt far more sympathy for your plight than ire over his despicable behavior. Of course, it's unkind to speak ill of him now."

"I agree," said Yvette, giggling. "Although René's memory probably makes it hard for many women not to speak ill."

"Exactly. But, I must tell you that of all those whom he wronged, you stood out as the singular exception. René adored you. Although he couldn't control those impulses that doomed him to bachelorhood, he regretted losing you more than any woman he cast aside." She reached over and patted Yvette's arm. "So at least in your case, please don't judge him too harshly when you remember him."

"I don't. Over time, those mean feelings no longer tempt me. I've resolved to live with as much love in my heart as possible, regardless of what men may do to hurt it." Yvette glanced down at her wedding ring.

"Men." The lady threw her head back a second. "They take what we offer and give back so little. Women, however, aren't their only temptations. The sea stealing them away hurts as much. As for René, he loved both women and the navy, but he loved you more than either. A year before he died, he put pen to this, a final proof of devotion to you." Madame de Saint-Alouarn pulled out from her cloak a parchment envelope sealed with two wax stamps.

Yvette eyed it curiously. "Madame, are you aware of what he wrote in this?"

"René told me. That's why I wanted to bring it to you myself, so you'd understand the context of his thoughts before reading it." She handed the envelope to Yvette.

Yvette took it and pulled at the flap, breaking the seals. She pulled out the folded paper and looked confused. "Pardon me, Madame de Saint-Alouarn, this isn't a letter, it's a legal document."

"Yes, Yvette." Madame de Saint-Alouarn paused with a slight sadness in her voice. "René bequeathed to you half of all that he owned."

When the supervisor called out the names, he wasn't on the list. Abraham walked away disappointed from the group of shipbuilders at the London dock who had waited around for day jobs. After arriving four months earlier, he'd found only a few weeks of work. Even rooming with four others in the cheap inn near the docks turned out too expensive for the little he earned. He had fare money to cross the Channel to Calais, but not enough to sail the entire way to Brest.

Since he had moved twice to cheaper inns, if Yvette wrote, it'd never reach him. Swarms of unemployed workers now competed with the discharged navy and army carpenters for the few available jobs. The wages dropped to the lowest he had ever seen.

With the rest of the day free, he parted to search in Woolwich and crossed over London Bridge for the long dusty walk. The bright spring sun beat down on him and the wide leather bag strap across his shoulder made him sweat. Most of the way he recounted his projects at Staunton Harold and how wonderfully the earl and Anne had treated Yvette and Michelle. By the time he neared Woolwich, the happiness he felt over the good memories had crumbled into guilt for his lecherous behavior. The same scenario of thoughts was occurring frequently, almost daily.

After trekking three hours to the shipyard, they told him they had no openings. He found a tavern for an ale to rid his thirst before heading back upriver.

Abraham rested and watched the workmen and sailors, officers, and women milling around in the alehouse. While eyeing faces, one naval man stood out from the rest. He looked familiar and exchanged glances with him.

The officer tilted his head as if thinking, then rose and crossed the room. At the same time, Abraham recognized the gait of the fellow crossing toward him. The officer had been his close mate while in the navy on the *Lark*.

"Lieutenant Burston!" he shouted. "Why, I barely recognized you. You've become the proper navy officer."

"How fare you, Robinson? It took me a moment to recognize you, too. How are you, my friend?"

"Oh, sorry—Captain Burston!" he exclaimed, noticing the captain's uniform.

"Ha, ha, never mind that. Tell me how you've been," he demanded, taking a seat across the table and pounding Abraham's shoulder.

"I'm well. You've been on warmer seas than the Channel," he said, pointing to the captain's tanned skin.

"We just returned from the West Indies. The ship I'm on is being surveyed to be laid up or repaired. Either way, I'll still be active."

"West Indies in the winter and the Channel in the spring and summer, perfect. You're lucky. How was the war for you?"

"We saw little action during the war, although we took several merchantmen. Are you working here in Woolwich again?"

"No, I'm inquiring if they need shipwrights. Earlier I worked for the Earl Ferrers in the Midlands. I spent a few years helping him rebuild his manor."

Burston looked surprised and chuckled, "Really? I thought you'd have bought an estate house yourself with the prize money we got."

"Prize money?" asked Abraham, his head tilted.

"From the *Fort de Nantz,* that Spanish treasure ship we took back in '46. Since you served as a warrant officer, you'd have gotten as much as I."

Abraham, stunned, replied, "I read the navy planned to return the bullion since it belonged to a neutral country."

"That's what Spain claimed. They didn't give enough proof, though. A year later they awarded the prizes to us. Didn't you get yours?" Burston's mouth opened slightly.

Abraham stammered. "There... there occurred confusion over whether I deserted, so the navy wouldn't have distributed shares to me as a deserter."

Burston's head jerked back. "Abraham, you deserted?"

"No, someone made a mistake. My captain wrote a letter correcting it. I never received the prize money. How much money was it?" Abraham asked, his foot tapping uncontrolled.

"The total came to over 1,400 pounds. The ship carried cargo full of gold and silver and then the enemy head-count and the ship's sale shares added up to more. Check into it right away. I don't know if they can award prizes after so long, though." Burston's knitted brows showed his concern. "I'm shocked you didn't hear of it."

"By then I lived back in France. My God, if that's true...." Abraham responded, his mouth opened and nothing more came out as he then realized he may become rich and would never have to worry about finding work again. He recovered moments later and they related their tales since they last saw each other. Ashamed, he left out the recent separation from his wife.

After an hour of catching up on the news, Captain Burston had to leave and wished him good luck in getting his award. Abraham's heart raced over the prospects of becoming wealthier than he had ever imagined. He felt as if he could run the ten miles back to London, but instead, he hired a boat. His only thoughts were how he'd return to

Yvette wealthy, and give it her as proof of his affection.

Abraham hurried to the inn to change into his best clothes and get the letter proving he hadn't deserted. He decided to leave his leather bag in the room and rushed to Broad Street to the navy treasurer's office to inquire about his prize money. Clerks sent him from office to office until he landed at the disbursement office for prizes.

"Sadly, claims carry a four-year time limit after the prize verification," explained the sympathizing clerk. "You forfeited the payment because the capture occurred in 1746 and they verified it in '48. I'm afraid you waited much too long to claim the prize money—twelve years too long." He shook his head and shrugged.

"Can I appeal since the navy's error caused the delayed claim?" Abraham pressed. "The desertion charge and why I'm claiming the shares late wasn't my fault, it was the navy's. They should have deposited my prize shares into my account."

"Who was the captain of the vessel who signed off on the error in the ship's crew roster?" asked the clerk, frustrated. "It began with his error for approving what he didn't read well."

"Captain Washington Shirley, who's now the Earl Ferrers."

"Unless the Earl Ferrers might straighten out the mess for you, I doubt we can do anything now. It happened too long ago. I'm sorry." The man's frustrated face did little to lighten Abraham's anguish.

He left the office fighting back tears of anger as he wandered back to the inn. The error Washington and the purser had made cheated him of more money than he'd probably ever own, and when he needed it most. His attack on Anne wrecked the chance her husband righting the wrong. How ironic, he thought, that Washington so long ago had unknowingly prepared his final and great revenge. Abraham slumped along the streets. His mind replayed the conversations with Anne that led him to believe she was flirting. It embarrassed him even now.

When he analyzed what she had said, he saw how his emotions had led him to infer far more than what she implied. It grew into a horrible spiral of taking anything she said or did as provocative. Together with his newly discovered shallowness, he questioned what other areas of his life were based on false beliefs. Gloom enveloped Abraham as he reevaluated his actions.

When he got back to the inn, he climbed the steps to his shared room. Each riser was a different height and each tread a different depth in the old, dilapidated inn. It made climbing the stairs tricky not to stumble. When he went to put away his letter of discharge, he saw his leather bag, clothes pack, and tool case missing from beneath the bed.

Abraham rushed down, disregarding the varying steps, he jumped the last few and ran to the innkeeper's door. After Abraham pounded, the innkeeper opened it a few inches.

"Yes?" He frowned at the racket.

Abraham blurted it out. "Who in my room checked out?"

"No one left. Everyone paid through the week."

"My possessions are gone. Someone stole them." His clenched fists made the innkeeper uncomfortable.

"Well, did you check around the area?" He said to pacify Abraham. "Maybe a roommate moved them,"

"I didn't see them anywhere. One of the other men took them." He jabbed the air upward with his finger, his face aflame.

"Sorry, we're not liable for goods stolen from the rooms. Ask your roommates when they return." Hoping his irate tenant would leave, the innkeeper shut the door, locking it.

Abraham's teeth clenched tight. The unspoken rule dictated not touching other's personal things when sharing a room at inns. Whoever did it not only stole but broke a long-standing tradition, he thought, violating the faith guests have in one another. How can people feel safe sharing rooms if they break that trust?

Then, leaning against the wall in the hallway, he laughed out loud at the absurd assumption. Placing confidence in a total stranger seemed far riskier than a wife trusting her husband. Yet he had destroyed Yvette's belief in him, a far greater crime. Abraham realized he had less right to be angry with the thief than Yvette had to be angry with him. The random act pointed out to him that trust is a belief, an expectation of behavior with unforeseeable results.

Abraham sat on the stairs and tallied what he had lost. The case with his tools was gone. The thief took his leather bag, clothes pack, a book, a shaving kit, and personal papers. His cloak still hung on the hook. So in total, it'd cost him two pounds to replace the personal effects, although nearly half a year's wages, to replace his tools. Abraham stood and left, disgusted.

If the crook wanted to sell off the loot fast, he reasoned, the crook would have taken it to a pawnshop. He might be able to buy back some of his belongings, so he searched for the nearest pawnshop. In the first one he found, his leather bag lay inside on a table. The book wasn't with the other books on display, nor were his tools or clothes anywhere.

"Excuse me, sir," Abraham said calmly to the shopkeeper. "Someone stole my belongings today at an inn. I spotted one in your shop."

"Sorry, without proof of what they stole or who stole it, we can't help you," the gruff man snapped, interrupting what Abraham began to say.

"No, I know the rules. I wondered if the thief sold you my razor and strop, soap brush, and cup from the leather bag. I also had a heavy chest of carpenter's tools and clothes and a book in the leather bag."

"We don't buy or sell clothes or tools. Try the ragpickers or ironmongers. I only bought the leather bag from a man earlier."

"Let me have the leather bag, and I'll need soap and a razor," Abraham said picking up the leather bag. "Can you remember or describe the customer who sold it?" He foresaw the shopkeeper's answer.

"The seller?" He shrugged and snorted, "No, I can't remember a thing about him."

After Abraham bought the shaving implements and his leather bag, he left and looked for other pawnshops where he might find his things. He'd lost his expensive tools and treasured adze forever.

That night at the inn, he placed the leather bag between his legs as he went to bed. The other renters acted innocent of any crime, although Abraham was sure at least one of them had robbed him. As he drifted off to sleep, he thought to himself, no job, no prize shares, and no tools, I only want to go home. He sighed, thinking—no home.

In the morning Abraham awoke defeated. No longer could he stay in London hoping for work without tools. So he elected to walk to Dover. Once there, he planned to work his way to France on a ship.

The little money he had in his purse under his belt might be enough for a coach ride to Brest.

Many carriages passed Abraham along the well-traveled route to Dover. The first day, he walked thirty miles, not quite half the way, and stopped once to eat. That night he slept in a haystack and dreamt of being back at the cottage in Brest with Yvette. When he woke, he sat for an hour before he rallied his spirit to continue onward.

Two days later, he arrived at the busy Dover harbor with ships lying at anchor or berthed at the dock. Abraham inquired at each for a carpentry job in exchange for passage. Most sailed for Calais, Le Havre, or Dunkirk, a few to Holland, but none as far as Brest. A sailor told him his captain, at the nearby tavern, might let Abraham work his way across the Channel.

Abraham headed for the tavern, and peeked inside from the door, spotting an old, grizzled captain at a bench.

"A fine day to you, sir," he said to the captain drinking an ale. "My name is Abraham Robinson. I'm a ship's carpenter heading for France. Do you trade passage for services?"

The captain turned his head toward Abraham and peered at him with one eye. At first, Abraham thought the captain had closed his other eye until he noticed it was a sunken empty socket beneath the eyelid.

"Ja, if you do goed verk," replied the old Dutch captain, eager to strike a good deal. "I go to Le Havre. Do you vant to verk fer me? I take you if you verk fer von full veek. Wit free food. Ja?"

"That would be most appreciated," he said. At least Le Havre wasn't as far from Brest as Calais, he considered. He sat with the older seaman and they traded tales.

The old man narrated how in 1756, an English privateer ship captured his vessel. Although his merchantman, the *Patience,* shipped from a neutral country, the captain of the privateer searched her for French goods, claiming he'd confiscate whatever was French. When the Dutchman showed him the papers for the English goods, the privateer captain tore them up and beat several crewmen to admit the cargo was French. The beatings soon turned to torture. When the Dutch captain attempted to intercede, one of the Englishmen struck him in the head with a pike, crushing his eye.

The old captain, curiously, held no ill feelings toward the English, saying, "Von man does not make a nation, ja?"

The crossing took two days and Abraham worked five more in Le Havre as agreed to put the ship in order.

After leaving, he discovered the prices of coach rides to Brest had risen with the post-war inflation. Abraham could only pay for fare to get to Saint-Malo, a little more than halfway and still 150 miles from Brest.

The coach wended along a hot and dusty road to the seaport. Abraham had just money left for food. He calculated a four- or five-day walk to Brest from Saint-Malo, perhaps less if he could get a free wagon or cart ride from someone.

After starting out on the coastal road southward, he walked through the remains of Saint-Servan, burned during the British descents, and many small villages and across streams that fed the River Rance bordering Saint-Malo. He planned to walk a full day to the larger town of Dinan, but the coach trip and having eaten little had exhausted him.

As Abraham slogged along, he contemplated how Yvette might greet him. If she understood how he'd suffered to get home, she'd realize his overwhelming love and need of her. Perhaps she'd forgive him and welcome him, or, he feared, she might refuse to speak to him again.

If rejected, he imagined joining a merchant ship's crew never to have a port to call home. Like a Chinese sailor he'd once met, who longed to return to his family, yet seemed doomed by fate to sail the seas forever. It was a depressing memory.

As the sun touched distant treetops before plunging the landscape into darkness, he spotted Dinan atop the hill overlooking the river. The village was still half an hour away. He'd make it there by nightfall.

An abandoned shed outside town caught his attention. Inside, he stretched himself on two boards he laid across barrel ends. It would be an uncomfortable night on the hard wood, but safe from vermin, filth, or dew. Abraham ate one of the bread rolls he'd bought in Saint-Malo and crawled onto the boards to sleep.

For days he hiked westward, climbing the hilly roads beside the river to catch the road from Rennes leading to Brest. Abraham was feeling the effects of his forced march and empty stomach, and with each stride, he weakened.

One morning he awoke under a sheltering tree to find himself soaked from the night's misty rain. Chilled and filthy, Abraham made his way down to the river to wash his clothing and bathe. The cold water numbed his limbs as he waded out up to his waist. As he splashed trying to clean himself using a kerchief and shaving soap, he heard voices nearby and hid by sinking to his neck in the water.

When the voices stopped, he stood again and finished his freezing bath and waded ashore. He laid out his wet clothing on bushes in the sunlight, and sat naked upon a rock drying himself in the rays.

Sounds of feet and voices came again. Abraham hid behind the bushes trying to spy who approached on the road above the bank. Then sounds of cracking twigs came nearby. Before he had time to react, a stranger stood behind him swinging a limb at him from his right. It caught him on the side of his head and sent him headlong into the brambles.

Dazed, he turned in time to glimpse the ruffian pounding the limb again onto his body. The limb broke in two as it smashed against his ribs, taking the breath out of Abraham's lungs. The man continued striking with the half limb in his hands.

"Please, I have nothing! Don't!" Abraham screamed. Another man then appeared and both of them beat upon Abraham's head and body with their fists.

To Abraham, the attack lasted an eternity. From the pain with each breath, they'd broken ribs, and now his face dripped blood from the pummeling. He held up his arms in defense against the two assailants, but it offered little protection. One of his eyes closed up and his tongue pushed a broken tooth around in his mouth. Yet, the cruel bludgeoning continued until one said, "He'll give us no trouble."

The muggers grabbed what they wanted from the bushes but missed seeing Abraham's brown leather bag hidden under another bush. One fiend grabbed his breeches, much too small for either and tossed them into the river.

The thug laughed at Abraham. "Go get them."

Abraham said nothing as parts of his body now ached from the damage. Blood flowed from his nose and mouth, and a large cut on his eyelid covered his face in warm fluid. Abraham brought his hand to his side, two broken ribs smarted to the touch. Just one eye saw. With an aching jaw, he asked, "Why?" as he stared at the huge brutes looming over him.

The bigger lout smiled and said, "Try to stop us." Abraham's question seemed to provoke the shorter robber who came over and kicked Abraham viciously in his rear and legs. The other enjoyed the sight and joined in again with his fists. The renewed beating lasted until Abraham passed out.

When Abraham awoke, it was early afternoon. He couldn't move, every part of his body ached, sore and swollen. Dried blood caked his face and chest. His tongue pushed against a few more teeth that were loose. Abraham's nose, now broken, bothered him most because he couldn't breathe through it, using his dry, opened mouth for air. Each inhale sent sharp pains through his side and into his belly where the highwaymen had kicked him.

Abraham realized he had to move or lie there and die, so with great effort, he sat up and looked around with his one good eye. He found nothing except his leather bag. The ruffians had ripped off the brass buckles and emptied it, taking the few coins he had left and his shoes and clothing.

With nothing but his empty leather bag and the hopes his breeches might have drifted to the bank, he rose on one leg to stand. Again Abraham waded back into the water and washed the blood off of his body and head. The coldness should help the swelling, he thought, and drank water to relieve his sore parched mouth.

After he limped to shore and picked up his torn, empty leather bag, Abraham hobbled naked along the riverbank searching for his breeches. Twenty minutes later, he saw them, snagged on a fallen branch and put them on still wet.

As he climbed up the riverbank to the road, Abraham wondered how he'd make it the entire way to Brest. His knee and left leg were burning. He limped barefoot, painful on the sharp rocks embedded in the road. With throbbing effort, he continued westward, drops of blood spotting the road behind him.

With each agonizing step, his tortured body sent pain to his brain from the many wounds. He tried to ignore them by concentrating on memories. Abraham reviewed the goals he'd made for himself during his life and how they turned out much different than he had dreamed. The shipwright career, travels, fears and desires, even his self-image had taken unexpected paths. The love of his family remained the only constant: Yvette, Michelle, Anton, and even Louise; loves he had placed in danger by unwise desires.

He had been selfish. His foolish lust for Anne had destroyed the tranquility of his marriage and his family's joy. In the future, he'd seek beyond desire to the soul for direction. Wisdom, he realized, was not an option, but a responsibility, and the results benefited everyone, not just himself. If he could make it to Brest, he'd live accordingly and throw himself down before Yvette for forgiveness.

His ribs hurt the most. While recalling his beating, he remembered the adage that to change a brute's ways, first take away his stick. The limb that cracked his ribs was no different than the warships he had built for the kings. He had enabled violence by crafting weapons that killed. It crystallized in his mind that he had to take responsibility even for distant outcomes of his actions, regardless of his original intent. He could no longer be a shipwright. After a long tormented mental debate along the road, Abraham decided that he'd build furniture, not ships, for the rest of his days.

Although Abraham had resisted claiming loyalty to either France or England, he chose Brest as home, the roots of his only living relatives. Now he only wanted to return, to live in his cottage with his family. In this pathetic and yet enlightened state, he staggered half-naked along the road. As evening neared, a horse approached from behind. Having nothing left to steal but torn breeches and an old leather bag, Abraham felt no danger of being robbed again. Not bothering to turn around when he heard the horse and rider close to him, Abraham struggled onward.

The horse slowed, and the rider spoke. "Are you all right?"

Abraham didn't understand how terrible he appeared with little clothing, bruised and scraped, cut and bleeding, and limping along the dusty lane. As he hobbled on without looking up, his swollen lips mumbled, "I got robbed."

"Sir, I need to bandage you. Come here and rest while I help you," said the young man in a uniform. The soldier climbed from his horse and led Abraham to the side of the road near a fallen tree trunk.

"Thank you," Abraham replied as he shuffled over and sat on the log. Next to it grew a single flower, a small rockrose.

"Where are you from?" said the cavalryman as he inspected the wounds.

"Brest." Abraham leaned over and stared at the blossom. The delicate plant's simple beauty and fresh growth defied nature's wildness as it struggled to live among weeds.

"I have medicine in my saddlebag. I'll get it for you," he said and in a minute returned with a handful of items.

"Put your arms up, exhale, and hold still," he said as he unrolled a length of bandage. The stranger wrapped it around Abraham's chest where the broken ribs showed dark bruises. Then he put one around his head covering Abraham's swollen and cut eye.

Abraham had scratches everywhere on his body from the beating and from falling into the bushes. Wherever the cuts were deep enough, the soldier put on a greasy jelly that he scooped out of a small tin. While the soldier attended to his wounds, Abraham explained what had happened.

"It's a good thing you keep these supplies in your bag," said Abraham, thankful for the soldier's aid.

"In the field, we learned to be our own doctors," he replied, searching for other injuries he could tend. "While I served in the army, I picked up a few tricks. Here, put this salve in your leather bag; it will heal you. I have more."

"Are you heading home now that peace has come?" Abraham grimaced from the sore jaw.

"It's been a long time since I've seen my family. Between wars I visited, but I haven't returned since then, almost eight years ago. In the first war I fought in the Rhineland with Marshal Noailles' infantry and during the last war in the cavalry under General Le Tellier in Hanover until we retreated. I received only one wound the whole time," he said, pulling back his coat and tunic to show a deep saber scar where his neck met the shoulder.

"Where does your family live?" Abraham asked, keeping his questions short from the stabbing pain in his mouth.

"Near Guengat. It's a very small village south of Brest. They work on the de Saint-Alouarn manor. My father, Vincent, passed last year, so it's important for me to return as soon as I can," he explained.

"Ah, de Saint-Alouarns," said Abraham, nodding at fate's consistency, amused. "I'm familiar with them."

"They've been very good to my mother and sisters. My older brother died in the army years ago. So it'd have been up to me to support the family. When my father died, Madame de Saint-Alouarn allowed Mother to stay in an estate cottage without rent and gives her an annual allowance. She's a *saint,* indeed," he said, making a pun. The young cavalryman stood and went back to his horse and rummaged through his bags.

When he returned, he gave Abraham a pair of old shoes and a loose tunic to wear. "Here. These are old, though better than traveling around getting sunburnt or cut by rocks. I hope the shoes fit."

"Thanks, that's kind of you," replied Abraham gratefully. He tried on the shoes and stuffed dried grass in the heels and toes until they fit well enough. The worn shirt was almost his size and hid the bandages and cuts everywhere on his body.

"Well," added the cavalryman, "my name is Vincent-Louis, after my father. If you're able, you can ride up on the horse. You shouldn't be walking with a knee so swollen."

"That's most appreciated. At the speed I'm shambling it'd take me a month to get to Brest. I'm Abraham."

"We'll be there tomorrow, or the next day if there's rain." The soldier helped him stand and onto the horse. Soon they were on their way and the day stayed fair.

∽

"Papa!" cried Yvette as she burst through the cottage door, frightening her parents. "This is incredible. Guess how much René left me!"

Anton, who'd been sleeping in the chair, startled awake. "Wha... oh, how much?"

"Mama, Papa, stay seated or else you'll faint. René's legal counselor said I've inherited a fortune," she said with eyes widened. "I'm an heiress!"

"No. I don't believe it!" shouted Louise, unable to control herself she waved her hands in front of her face. "No."

Anton calmly smiled and then began to clap his hands fanatically. Michelle, sitting and playing by the fireplace, looked up in wonder at the sudden pandemonium.

"Yes," Yvette held up a document for them to read. "It's 23,472 livres! We need never worry again over money."

"Oh, we can pay the new taxes," said Louise, crossing herself with eyes closed.

"Mother, we can pay them tenfold and still buy two houses in town if we desired," Yvette told her, "and a gilded carriage or even," she grinned, "a bookshop!"

Anton sat again, his chin in his hands, and reflected on the trials René had put them through: his daughter's languish and hurt, and his own bitterness and frustrations. He concluded, although he behaved like a rascal, René must have loved Yvette deeply to endow so much to her. Just as he and Louise had come to love Michelle, regardless of her mother's history, so too, did Anton decide to accept René's faults.

They decided to celebrate the occasion by going to town, arriving by late afternoon at the hotel for drinks and dessert. Yvette, sitting with her parents, grinned over her new financial position, conceding she'd never lack wealth and was now twice richer than most wealthy patrons in the hotel.

While Anton and Louise discussed good investments, Yvette's eyes drifted around the room. In this very dining room, the end of her engagement with René began when she had confirmed his disloyalty.

Yvette, grateful she hadn't married him, concluded although he had been untrue, his resolve to amend his deeds was final. René, at last, made restitution, not with the faithful love she desired from him all those years ago but by compensating her heartaches with a gift. It seemed his ghost hovered near, trying to repay for his deceitfulness.

Her emotions of fondness then moved to sorrow when realizing Abraham might enjoy none of her fortunes. Somewhere, Yvette envisioned, he lay with another woman, or alone, with no concern for her or Michelle. He might be working if he found a job. Or he might be trudging back to London from Woolwich or Deptford. Like René, Abraham may have been unfaithful. Even so, she realized how he did his best to please her and provide for her. Work, love, and compassion were his hallmark qualities. She missed him beyond words.

Anton glanced at his daughter and suspected what dwelt in her mind as her mood had changed from exuberance to sadness in minutes. "Yvette," he said. "He will come. I know Abraham. He will come."

"But will he forgive me?" The words were flat, rising from deep thought.

"Forgive you? Wasn't it he who betrayed your love?" Anton cocked his head.

"Betrayal after so many years of marriage is not a surprise. Things grow old and stale. He made poor decisions he hoped would save his sanity but not to destroy our family. You know, he never once criticized me for returning to René and hurting him so long ago." She bowed her head. "His act is understandable, but my betrayal happened when our love was fresh and still in the forge of a new passion. My sin was far greater, as must be my guilt."

Anton and Louise looked away, unable to comfort Yvette as their little party became quiet and insightful. The inheritance they welcomed, but money couldn't mend the hole in their family.

Yvette's crushed spirits persisted until she picked up on a feeling. It started as a shimmering sparkle of hope growing in intensity. The fearful gloom withered as joy replaced hope and soon ecstasy replaced joy. As with earlier premonitions, the intense emotion centered upon one person and demanded action. Yvette didn't understand what she needed to do, yet she sensed an overpowering urgency to go somewhere. Exactly where she couldn't pinpoint, still it was paramount she hurry there and hurry there immediately.

"We have to leave here *now!*" Yvette's urgent voice ordered.

"Yvette, we've just arrived," said Louise, pouting.

"I can't explain it. We must go. It's... it's wonderful!" Yvette exclaimed. "Come on, quickly!"

Bewildered, Anton and Louise grabbed Michelle's hands and followed Yvette from the hotel. They dashed through the tangle of streets, following Yvette's lead toward the eastern town gate of the massive wall surrounding Brest.

"Soon! Soon!" Yvette exclaimed as she led them on. "Somewhere this way and soon."

As they passed through the gate, Yvette spied a young cavalryman riding a horse into the city with another rider behind him on the rump. The second man's face was covered in bandages. At first, she ignored the men, but something familiar in the second rider caught her eye—the leather bag. She stopped and pointed, wide-eyed, "There! It's Abraham!" she cried.

"Oh, my God!" Anton cried as he raced ahead.

When he got to the distant riders, he pulled Abraham from the horse and hugged him as Abraham winced from the pain.

"You look terrible!" Anton laughed and joked, "How many times did you fall off this horse?"

Abraham grunted out, "I'm on the mend."

Vincent-Louis turned his mount. "I hope you heal well. Good fortune to you," he bade and rode off.

Yvette and Louise rushed to join them as little Michelle grabbed onto his leg. Tears streamed down Yvette's face.

Abraham, downcast, turned to Yvette as she reached him. "Dear, I love you. Can you forgive me?"

Yvette put her hands on his shoulders. "Forgiveness is part of love. You're home!" she said to Abraham, gleaming.

"Yes," Abraham replied with teary eyes before he kissed her. "Home forever."

EPILOGUE

History reveals that Captain George Mackenzie did not remain long in Scotland or England. He returned once again to Jamaica, not to cruise on patrols against smugglers after the war, but as the Commander-in-Chief of the Port Royal Station. Long after, Thomas, his son, joined him there as a captain. And many years later, after a successful career in the Royal Navy, Mackenzie retired as Vice-Admiral of the Blue. He died in 1800 and Alana received from the navy a substantial pension of £200 per year. Their son went on serving the navy, also to become an admiral.

Louis de Saint-Alouarn continued in the French navy until shortly after the death of his wife, Marie, at the young age of only twenty-eight years. She left him with a daughter and three sons. He resigned his commission in the navy and with the backing and permission of Versailles, he and his childhood friend, Yves de Kerguelen, set off on a voyage of discovery in the South Pacific.

After a challenging trip across the Indian Ocean, his ship, the *Gros-*

Ventre, came upon the enormous western coast of Australia. There, Louis claimed the land in the name of the King of France and buried a bottle holding a document of claim and a coin. He then set sail eventually to arrive in Île-de-France (present-day Mauritius) in 1772, where at thirty-four years of age, he tragically succumbed to tropical diseases. In Turtle Bay, Australia in 1998, amateur archaeologists searched for and found the bottle Louis left 226 years earlier, filled with sand and the coin.

The West Indies saw Captain Frederick Maitland return often throughout his long service to the king. He, like many officers in both the navy and army occupying the islands, had purchased land, owned slaves, and fathered children there. He also married later and had offspring in Scotland. In 1786, Maitland rose from his seat, walked to a window, opened it, and fell back into the chair, dead at fifty-six years old. The navy had promoted him to rear admiral, but he died at Rankeillor, in the County of Fife, Scotland, before hearing the news.

The Fifth Earl Ferrers, Washington Shirley, continued to rebuild his manor, Staunton Harold, for the rest of his life. To finance the project, the earl sold off much of the family's traditional estates, lands, and commercial properties. The hall, now privately owned, has been lauded as one of the finest examples of Palladian style architecture. Interest in the sciences continued to occupy his attention for the rest of his life. The naturalist, George Edwards, who received the stuffed Guyana birds captured in the taking of the *Nannon* named one of the exotic birds for him, the Shirley. Then as a final notable achievement, the Royal Navy promoted him to Vice-Admiral of the White. He died in 1778 without producing an heir and the title transferred to Robert Shirley, Washington's younger brother. To this day, a descendant still holds the title.

The fictional characters' futures held great things. Abraham and Yvette never again left France and continued to live in their country home. Little Michelle grew up to become a major hat designer and moved to Paris, achieving great acclaim both on the continent and in Great Britain.

With a new outlook on life after his near-death beating, Abraham turned away from shipbuilding. He took up making furniture made of cherry from his woods, and attained notoriety in Brittany for his fine carpentry, unique designs, and "Robinson" chairs.

In 1771, a large crate arrived at the cottage from England containing the figurehead, the Goddess of Fame, taken from the *Renown*. The navy had broken up the frigate at the Woolwich shipyard after serving twenty-seven years under two flags and sold off the timbers. Abraham realized the figurehead was a gift of forgiveness from his old commander and friend, Captain Shirley, although they never saw or communicated with one another again. The sculpture graced his garden for many decades until weather and time carried her away.

In Brest, near the old café, Yvette opened a prosperous bookshop named *Livres de Chevalier*—The Knight's Books—that she managed until her eighties. She and Abraham had no child other than Michelle, who filled their hearts with grateful love their entire lives.

About the Author

D. E. Stockman is an illustrator and award winning writer who was reared in a small town in the Midwest and now lives outside Chicago. After graduating college, he worked in various aspects of the graphic arts for imprints of Simon and Schuster, Harcourt Brace, and Pearson Education, and wrote articles for an e- zine and trade journals. In his spare time, he researched the history of a French frigate for over a decade. The ship's story is recounted along with fascinating fictional and historical characters in his tall-ship *Tween Sea & Shore Series*. His debut novel, *The Ship's Carpenter*, won two Page Turner Finalist 2020 Awards in international competition for both writing and ebooks. Visit his author's website for free downloads and updates at: www. stockmanbooks.com

For the Finest in Nautical and Historical Fiction and Non-Fiction
www.FireshipPress.com

Interesting • Informative • Authoritative

All Fireship Press books are available through leading bookstores and wholesalers worldwide.

CPSIA information can be obtained
at www.ICGtesting.com
Printed in the USA
LVHW092105080421
683894LV00012B/372